Hig
SECRET RULES T
by Jessamyn Violet

M000044774

JESSAMYN VIOLET'S RIVETING debut novel, *Secret Rules to Being a Rockstar*, gives us Kyla Bell, an endearing character who strives to balance the life of a rockstar with that of the honest and loyal daughter and friend she has always been. For this, Kyla needs a complicated set of rules, and the journey that follows—vivid and wise—is both poignant and exhilarating.

JILL McCORKLE, *New York Times* Bestselling Author, *Life after Life*

A SPARKLING DEBUT that will become a favourite and comfort read. Violet's stellar wit and pacing never allow for a dull moment, sweeping the reader up into a world of glamour, uncertain romance and rock stardom.

THE NATIONAL (SCOTLAND)

JACK KEROUAC COLLIDES with Lester Bangs, cynicism with hope, and the result is a book that is as sweetly pop as it's starkly punk. Violet's work will seem familiar, for better or worse, to most that have sought to make music their life. It's that authenticity that makes it such a valuable read.

BRETT CALLWOOD, *LA Weekly*

JESSAMYN VIOLET IS a real rocker and a real writer. You will love her as much as I do.

ALICE HOFFMAN, *New York Times* bestselling author of *Practical Magic*

SECRET RULES TO BEING A ROCKSTAR crackles with the incandescent, electric thrill of being young and letting the pure act of creating art fill your soul. Your heart will beat like you're falling in love for the first time on a Los Angeles summer night when you read this book.

JEFF ZENTNER award-winning author, *The Serpent King* and *In the Wild Light*

THIS IS A sparkling, exhilarating, and moving debut about a young woman on the cusp of everything—but it's an even greater meditation on the ways in which, to paraphrase Kyla, we rough ourselves up in the name of art. I loved it!

JESSIE ANN FOLEY, author, *The Carnival at Bray* and *You Know I'm No Good*

SECRET RULES TO BEING A ROCKSTAR breaks open the experience of being a new-to-the-scene musician to reveal the glittery tangle of excitement, inspiration, and danger that comes with sudden success. Jessamyn Violet's queer protagonist, Kyla Bell, might be green, but she is the only person we can trust to teach us the rules to surviving—and maybe even thriving—in the 1990s Hollywood music industry. An impressive, introspective debut!

KELLY ANN JACOBSON, author, *Tink and Wendy* and *Robin and Her Misfits*

AS HOT AS North Hollywood in July, *Secret Rules to Being a Rockstar* sears with a youthful sincerity and heat. Jessamyn Violet effortlessly captures the seedy world of music in '90s Los Angeles and the scary, sensitive, sticky feeling of being a teenager in an adult world.

TEGAN QUIN, musician, Tegan & Sara

SECRET RULES TO BEING A ROCKSTAR is a magical story that reminds me of when we were first getting started with Skating Polly. I could not put this book down and definitely cried at parts. I'm proud to support such a cool, fun and feminist tale. It's the book I dreamed of reading as a teenager!

PEYTON BIGHORSE, musician, Skating Polly

JESSAMYN VIOLET presents readers with the sights, sounds, smells, and, above all, the tumultuous thoughts and feelings of a young life in music. This story rings true from its overture to its coda.

SUSAN ROGERS, Director of Berklee Music Perception & Cognition Lab; author, *This Is What It Sounds Like: What The Music You Love Says About You*

SECRET RULES TO BEING A ROCKSTAR is a colorful story full of hope and wonder, immersing the reader in the near-dystopian dreamscape of the music industry in 1990s Los Angeles—and I know because I lived it.

EVA GARDNER, musician, P!NK and Cher

A ROCKSTAR TALE of a young queer woman navigating coming out while also diving pink hair first into a caffeine-fueled Boogie Nights-esque Los Angeles night life. I definitely would have dog-eared soo many pages if I'd gotten to read this kind of book when I was a teen.

MAYA MILLER, musician, The Pack A.D.

SECRET RULES
TO BEING A
ROCKSTAR

SECRET RULES
TO BEING A
ROCKSTAR

a novel

JESSAMYN VIOLET

THREE ROOMS PRESS
New York, NY

Secret Rules to Being a Rockstar
A NOVEL BY Jessamyn Violet

ISBN 978-1-953103-29-1 (trade paperback)
ISBN 978-1-953103-30-7 (Epub)
Library of Congress Control Number: 2022945950

TRP-101

Publication Date: April 18, 2023
First Edition

Young Adult Fiction: Ages 14+

BISAC Coding:
YAF031000 Young Adult Fiction / LGBTQ+
YAF047030 Young Adult Fiction / Performing Arts / Music
YAF011000 Young Adult Fiction / Coming of Age
YAF024170 Young Adult Fiction / Historical / United States / 20th Century
YAF022000 Young Adult Fiction / Girls & Women

COVER DESIGN AND ILLUSTRATION:
Corina Lupp: www.corinalupp.com

BOOK DESIGN:
KG Design International: www.katgeorges.com

DISTRIBUTED IN THE U.S. AND INTERNATIONALLY BY:
Publishers Group West: www.pgw.com

Three Rooms Press | New York, NY
www.threeroomspress.com | info@threeroomspress.com

To all those who write their own rules.

"I just want to feel everything."

—FIONA APPLE—

SECRET RULES
TO BEING A
ROCKSTAR

THE GROUND RULE

I FELL IN LOVE WITH MUSIC like it was a person. From a very early age, I ate up anything a stereo speaker had to say and found something to appreciate in everything from pop hits to the most obscure genres and songs. The first thing I wanted to know about anyone I met was what kind of music they listened to, and the last thing I became hungry for before my life exploded was validation that the feeling was mutual— that music and I were in love *with each other*. Because I didn't just *listen* to music. While other kids my age flirted and fooled around with each other, I found my own version of making love: fingering the chipped ivory keys of our ancient piano in the basement while my voice entwined with the notes. I covered every song I loved and fantasized about being a professional musician. I cranked out original material like I might just die otherwise. Then I turned eighteen and decided to play before an audience to see if it was really meant to be. And while western Massachusetts wasn't exactly brimming with opportunities that matched my imagination's version of my onstage debut, it was my best and only option.

It was time to start the grind from the ground-up.

ROCK STARS ATTRACT ROCK STARS

My hometown of Northampton, Massachusetts had just enough spice to taste like a small city. It wasn't a billboard and skyscraper kind of place, but it had its own little pockets of cool. Main Street was lined with record stores, cafes, bars, hippie shops, and eclectic little themed restaurants like the one that happened to change my life, The Porch House.

The old-timey barbeque shack had sagging steps that led up to oversize double doors. Inside, the uneven wooden picnic tables were decorated with rolls of paper towels and bottles of barbeque sauce. The floors were covered in sawdust, and there was enough taxidermy on display to make any animal lover shiver. The bar was one gigantic, polished slab of tree trunk and the bartenders and servers wore ascots and hats, most likely against their preference. In the back corner was a dusty upright piano, much like the one in my basement except that it gave my songs a little twang like a pedal effect that wasn't entirely wrong for the mood.

Jenny and I were miraculously on time, even though she had made me change my outfit twice. Jenny always pushed me to take more fashion risks. Ugh. That word: *fashion*.

I hadn't wanted to perform in anything more than my usual T-shirt and jeans, but she pressed me to "take myself more seriously." Somehow that translated to "more sparkles" and I ended up in her mirror-studded peasant skirt and bejeweled tank top. The outfit was embarrassing, but even worse was the fact that I kind of liked it. It made the show feel like more of a staged performance and less of an open exposure directly into my soul.

The restaurant was warm, packed, and reeked of its familiar combination of wood smoke and beef. Except something felt different that night. There was a prickly pulse in the air, an electricity that hadn't been there before. I gave Jenny a look. After ten years of friendship, we could easily communicate without words.

"Right?" Jenny whispered. "That's called buzz. And you got it."

"What I got is nerves," I grumbled. "What am I doing in this bohemian sparkle Barbie outfit?"

"Pulling it off," she said, grinning. "You know you love it."

I shook my head and headed straight to the back of the dining floor while keeping my eyes fixed on the piano, my life raft. I didn't want to recognize anyone. It was way easier playing to a room full of hypothetical strangers. A gigantic moose head with Christmas lights draped around its antlers hung on the wall above the piano. I gave him a little nod before I sat down. It seemed the respectful thing to do since he was stuck in such an unfortunate afterlife.

The manager, Bob, a science teacher-looking type in a corduroy jacket and tweed pants, came over with a mug of hot chocolate, per my usual request. I sat down at the piano bench, cracked my knuckles, and gave him a nod.

"Attention," Bob said as the lights dimmed and people started to shush. "May I have the honor of presenting Northampton High's own up-and-coming talent, Kyla Bell!"

As applause warbled in my ears, I struggled to breathe. The time had come to crack myself open again, revealing my inner self to the crowd. Nothing to do but plunge in headfirst, lose my surroundings by disappearing deep into the songs. Playing was a form of time and space travel for me. The piano was my ship, transporting me to far away soundscapes with the press of the keys. My voice loved to weave with the sound of thick strings being hammered into melodies. I burrowed deep into my songs to create cocoons of sound that kept me spinning in an orbit between light and darkness, hope and sadness.

Performing was a particular kind of fix and I was definitely hooked.

After I finished, the clapping seemed to go on forever. I smiled so hard it started to hurt and quickly sought refuge at the table Jenny had claimed in the corner.

Bob sped over to us. "Your best set yet," he raved. "Dinner's on the house." He handed me a twenty dollar bill and smiled shyly before rushing back into the kitchen.

"Oh, yay," Jenny joked when he was gone. "Free terrible dinner. You definitely burned up the place. Everyone's staring at us. Try not to look stupid."

I laughed, grateful for her humor, even though the truth was I did feel I looked stupid. I always had the problem of not knowing how to "look." I wasn't one of those people who practiced expressions in front of the mirror or anything. But for both our sakes, I tried to make my expression as blank and aloof as possible while savoring the sliver of pride I felt at how I had played.

There was something burning into the back of my neck, though. I turned to notice a guy with long, dark hair emitting a microwave-magnetic stare at me from the table he shared with two other scruffy musician types. I looked away but could still feel him approaching.

"Hey."

I forced myself to look into his laser beam eyes. Jenny did a bad job stifling a giggle and I cringed as he cleared his throat.

"Really dig your stuff," he continued, ignoring my paralysis. I stared at his stubble. Why did he look so familiar? He was definitely too old to be in school. "You had me hearing some cool guitar parts in my head. Your voice is so deep, and I'd call you punk if your songs weren't so smooth at the same time. Congratulations on creating your own sound. How long have you been playing?"

"Ten years," I said, hoping that was the end of it.

"Wow. Since what age?"

So he was forcing it out of me. "I just turned eighteen."

He laughed. "That's what they all say! Kidding. Oh, you're probably wondering who the creepy compliment guy is. I'm Brian Brighton, singer for—"

"Oh, totally—from Eyes Wander!" I interrupted, dropping any little bit of cool I'd maybe had. "Um, yeah, we've heard of you guys . . ."

"Ha, she's kidding," Jenny blurted out. "We listen to *Thieving Dreams* all the time!" Her dimpled smile made her look more like a freshman than a senior. She could turn on the charm when she wanted to, though. Unlike me.

"Awesome. So . . ." Brian seemed to be making up his mind about something. Whatever it was, I hoped he'd figure it out before a large plate of smelly food was set in front of me. Jenny and I hated to eat in front of strangers. It was what we called *totally un-slick*.

"Well, thanks for saying hi," I said with a note of finality.

He looked across the room toward the other two guys sitting at his table. They were watching us in amusement. I wondered what kind of joke we were to them. Or maybe they had some other plans for us, inviting us somewhere and putting the moves on us. The thought made me uneasy and I suddenly wanted to get out of there. This scene wasn't normal for The Porch House. We were usually forced to talk to a few gushy grownups before slipping out the side door and running down to the coffee shop to make fun of people and listen to whatever hip hop DJ was spinning vinyl that night.

Instead, here we were, stuck in this clumsy exchange.

"That's the rest of the band," he said, gesturing at the other guys.

"Of course," Jenny said smoothly, waving at them. I winced. They looked intimidating, their coolness contrasted by the hokey restaurant backdrop. Why were they even *at* The Porch House?

Brian seemed to read my thoughts. "We always come here when we pass through. The drummer's got a taxidermy fetish. Been trying to buy that piece off the owner for years."

He pointed and I looked over at the stuffed mongoose above the bar, fastened to a log, cold, marble eyes wide and teeth exposed. "Creepy fetish," I mumbled.

"You should see the grizzly bear he has in his living room back in LA," Brian responded.

I laughed uneasily. "No . . . thanks?"

"So, will you two come join us?"

I shook my head immediately and Brian looked offended.

"We gotta get going," I said with zero finesse.

"Well at least come say goodbye before you leave, all right?"

I shrugged and nodded in a non-committal way, and we watched him walk back over to his table.

"What the hell was that?" Jenny hissed at me as soon as he was out of earshot.

"What, we're supposed to go over there and hang out with Eyes Wander? I don't have anything interesting to say to them."

"So what? Make stuff up. Brian seems sweet, he's a dreamy singer, and he's obviously into you! What more can you ask for?"

I couldn't exactly argue with Jenny, but she didn't know how little I was into *him*. I had been faking enthusiasm about guys for years. I would pretend I adored famous front men and claim high school guys didn't interest me at all. That left me with absolutely no reason not to hang with the famous, older, hot musicians in front of us.

The reason presented itself as slabs of brisket and onions were set in front of us, a stinky, un-cool nightmare. I wasn't hungry, nor would I even want to eat with a well-known band sitting behind us. I couldn't just bail, though—that might be considered rude enough to ruin my only gig in town. But Jenny always knew what to do. She asked the waiter to wrap it up to-go immediately. He glared toward Brian.

"Was that guy harassing you?"

"No, not at all," Jenny said. I nodded in agreement.

He looked unconvinced but took our plates away. When he returned with the takeout bag we headed over to their table as casually as possible, which meant I bumped into at least three chairs.

"Hey, ladies," said one of Brian's bandmates, a surfer guy with bedhead hair and laughing eyes. "Sit down and join us!"

"We can't," I said quickly. "We have to be somewhere." My every move screamed *amateur* hour to me. This night that had felt more special than any other had suddenly morphed into a bad sitcom: "The girl who didn't know how to talk to guys so her best friend ditched her" episode. As if reading my mind, Jenny dug her fingers into my side. I stepped as far away from her as possible and shot her a *help-me-out-here* look.

"You've got a cool vibe," the surfer guy said. I suddenly pinned him as the bassist for Eyes Wander, Calvin. "You yowl like a girl from the past stuck in modern times, trying to make sense of everything."

"Oh! Thanks?" I said.

"Don't mention it," he said, pushing his hair around his face. I could tell he thought he was adorable. Jenny could tell I needed a hand.

"Where you guys off to next?" my heroic partner-in-crime asked.

"We're actually playing the Paradise tomorrow," Brian said. "We've got Knives opening for us. Sold-out show."

"Wow!" Jenny and I said at the same time. I knew she didn't know who they were any more than I did, but she hid it a lot better. Tommy, the taxidermy nut—who had clearly been in a lot of bar fights—started drumming on the table with two dinner knives.

"We booked this Berklee band to kick it off, but we just found out the lead singer has mono, so they're out."

"That's too bad," I said.

"What do you think about filling the slot?"

So Brian wanted band suggestions.

"I don't know many Boston bands," I said. "I'm not really in on that scene."

The guys laughed. A heatwave of shame flooded through me. Jenny looked at me sympathetically—the worst of all looks you could get from Jenny.

"We want Kyla Bell to open the show," Brian said. "Do you think she can?"

Tommy stopped drumming with the knives and raised his eyebrows, challenging me. Shock hummed and thrummed through my veins—a whitewash of white noise—as what was happening slowly registered.

Eyes Wander wanted me to open for them?

They were in music magazines, toured internationally, sold out shows. I was a teenage piano player with a little backpack of unreleased songs. I'm not sure which face I was making, but judging by the way the guys were looking at me, my reaction was amusing. Well, I wasn't here for their amusement. I wasn't going to be the naïve girl from the smokehouse who they'd both tricked and heart-broken in the span of five minutes.

"You guys are kidding, right? It's not very funny."

"She's the one joking." Jenny said quickly. "Right, Kyla?"

"No joke. Promise!" Brian said. I stared at him, incredulous. "So are you in?"

I remained skeptical. It really felt like a trick.

"You can stay at my sister's place," Jenny whispered in my ear. "Just say yes, Ky. You deserve this."

I cleared my throat. "Um . . . I don't know . . . I guess so?"

Brian clearly wanted to laugh but knew better. "Alright! The pay situation is embarrassing, but you'll have twenty minutes to light 'em all up with your magic."

"Thank you," I whispered, a ghost of my former self already. I didn't know what else to say. A real show? In Boston? With a known band? Was I really fast forwarding from The Porch House to the Paradise Rock Club?

"Oh, look at the time! We really have to go now, unfortunately," Jenny said, throwing her arm around me and cross-shoulder carrying me away from the riptide of my social inadequacies.

I don't remember actually leaving The Porch House. Pretty sure I was drifting into another dimension. I do recall giving my doggie bag to the homeless woman outside Store 24, who didn't seem very grateful after she looked inside.

DON'T ASK PERMISSION

I WAS USED TO PRESSURE. Not so much from peers, but definitely from my father. *Father pressure.* Kids in my class were easy to dismiss, but my dad's demands had always been tough to brush off. He pushed me to stick to school, keep my head in the books instead of the clouds where I couldn't see the ground.

I did well at school. *Really* well. But I also played piano every day, straight through the endless refrain of his discouragement from taking myself seriously as a musician.

I was more practical than I wanted to be—maybe a byproduct of having such a no-nonsense father—so I tried to beat down the desire to live only for music, but it proved to be a weed that grew relentlessly despite how many times I tried to rip it away. It persisted no matter how often I was told to keep my head down, stick to the books, choose a set career path.

My family's house, a small split-level built by my great-grandfather, looked even smaller at night. I smelled waffles as soon as I walked through the front door, my father's go-to meal at any time of day, but at night the scent usually meant he'd been drinking. I knew it was probably a bad time to tell him I was asked to play a show in Boston at the Paradise. He wasn't exactly easygoing when he'd had a bit. I took my boots off with a sigh and walked down the creaky hallway toward the kitchen.

He sat at the table in front of a tower of waffles with his reading glasses on. They made him look fragile despite his sturdy carpenter's build. He seemed absorbed in the newspaper but put it down when I opened the fridge.

"Hey, Pops."

"How was the show?" he asked, looking me over with disapproval. I knew he especially hated my street-bum-chic thrift store corduroy jacket, and absolutely anything with sparkles on it. That was my pops. No frills. No fairy tales. I knew my deep, dark songs made him uncomfortable. It was probably for the best that he didn't attend shows.

"It was fine. Where's your car?"

"Damn thing died on me coming home from the store this afternoon. I had Tyler tow it."

"You need a new car."

"We need a lot of things, Kyla. Why don't you worry about getting into college and get a job in the meantime to help pitch in around here."

Eyes Wander had mentioned there was pay. Little pay, but still . . . it had to be more than The Porch House paid me. It was an angle I hadn't considered before. "Well . . . what if my job was performing? Maybe getting regular gigs in Boston and stuff?"

"Yeah, and maybe I'll get a job skating with *Disney on Ice*."

I held my tongue and walked out of the kitchen, blinking back tears. It was bad enough my father wouldn't come to my shows, but he didn't have to flat-out dismiss my ideas like that. His words stung like a sunburn. Well, forget asking him anything, then. I hated having to lie, but he wasn't showing me any respect, either. I'd say I was sleeping at Jenny's after the game—which was why she couldn't actually come with me to Boston. Against all odds, Jenny was a talented and committed cheerleader.

Upstairs, I saw a light shining from under my parents' door—unusual for this time of night. I opened the door slowly. Mom was sitting up in bed wearing a faded flannel nightgown, the goose-shaped nightstand lamp switched on next to her. The combination of radio jazz and the air perfumed by her favorite almond-scented lotion made the room feel cozy. In these first quiet moments I almost forgot what I'd done to her. Who she was, now.

"Ky-ky," she said softly.

"Hi, Mama. How are you?"

"Sleepy," she said. "When I close my eyes, I see little puffy clouds with bears dancing on them. One of them told me to tell you something."

She was such a wild card. I took a deep breath. "What's the word?"

Mom frowned. "He said he would be watching out for you when the wolves from the west come sniffing around."

"I'll keep that in mind," I said, perching on the edge of the bed. That was a new one. Was Eyes Wander from California? It seemed likely . . . And made her comment even weirder.

My mother grew more agitated, small wrinkles piling up on her delicate forehead. "You don't understand, you have to get out of here."

I fell back on her comforter and sighed. "I know, Mom. I'm trying."

"I don't want you to see what I'm going to turn into . . ." She grabbed my hand and gave me a startled, haunting look. "I can see it, practically feel it, and it's not good. I can't let it happen. You have to get out of here. Promise me."

The familiar claws of anxiety were churning inside. I'd thought it was okay to come say hi this late, but I should have known better. She'd been having more flashbacks lately, even though the accident that I caused had happened over two years ago. The hardest part was that she was confusing the flashbacks with premonitions. She was somehow convinced she kept seeing what was going to happen to her, to us. But for all the times I'd promised her I was leaving so that it wouldn't happen to me, to *us*, it was that much more heartbreaking because I would do anything to go back and avoid that night, too. But I knew we would never be able to dodge that chapter of our past. It had already been written in permanent ink, though it seemed she'd never grasp that.

The best move was to distract her with a diversion. Otherwise, it was a matter of seconds before she propelled me out of the room to go pack my bags and pretend to move out. *Again.* Sometimes it was the only way to get her to calm down. I'd sit out in the garage until my dad got her to take some pills and fall asleep.

"Mama, guess what?! I was offered a really cool gig tonight. The biggest one yet! I'm a little nervous about it."

You could see the slow shift in her face as the tragedy of that night was replaced by the image of me playing piano to a large audience. I watched as her tiny frown wrinkles disappeared.

"It's great you're playing out so much these days," she finally said. "Maybe I'll be able to make a show soon. I love to hear you play."

"It's okay, Mom. I know."

She reached over and stroked my hair for a little while. The familiar tug of grief pulled at my mind, dragging it back to that day when everything changed.

It was a blizzard and I'd convinced her to let me drive. I'd said I needed to learn how to handle bad weather. The irony is sickening now. I hit a patch of black ice and slid off the road. I wasn't hurt, but Mom nearly died.

She was laid up for months with a broken arm, eight fractured ribs and a shattered collarbone, eating painkillers and watching bad TV. When she was able to move around all right again she tried to go back to work at the bakery but ended up getting fired for sassing back to rude customers, something I personally found heroic.

Left to her own devices at home, she bought a mower at a yard sale and began to mow people's lawns without asking. More than a dozen times, neighbors dropped by and asked her to stop. People even started calling her "the crazy lawnmower lady" behind her back and harassing my dad at work to get him to do something. We were so ashamed by it all that finally my dad sold the lawnmower and brought her to a psychiatrist.

Dr. Reece hadn't been able to figure out exactly how to diagnose or handle her. It was a form of PTSD he hadn't seen before, he said. She baked a lot when she was in a certain calm state and almost seemed normal. Other times she would have terrible waking nightmares and flashbacks, talk nonsense, and if you tried to talk her down, she would become so agitated she'd become another person entirely. Dr. Reece had made a joke about her being a "psychological adventurer" who "dabbled in all types of emotional disorders but couldn't commit to one." The situation turned my father's hair from black to gray in the span of two years.

My mom would always be my first and biggest supporter, though. That made the guilt all the more crushing. I had to get out of there.

My room was the usual amount of messy. I grabbed sweatpants off the floor and a ratty sweater I'd been using for a pillow. After washing my makeup off in the bathroom I plucked my eyebrows for a little while, relishing the tiny pricks of pain with each tweeze. It helped blot out the ever-stinging sarcasm of my father.

I knew my sad little family relied on me being around in the future to help out with the bills, but I really wanted to get out of there for good. I couldn't wait to go to college, if only to get away from my miserable parents. Not having to witness their misery every day was my *real* first priority in life. Of course, I'd only been allowed to apply to schools within a 50-mile radius, so I could come home to witness their misery a.k.a "help out" on the weekends—unless I got a job, thereby sacrificing all freedom. But now, another option began to form, an escape plan in the event that I didn't get a scholarship. I could get a job—*any* job—in Boston. Move into my own place. Play gigs on nights and weekends. Force my dad to deal with it.

My freedom could be closer than I thought.

ALWAYS DO WHAT SCARES YOU

When I stepped onstage at The Paradise, the jolt of adrenaline hit me like high-frequency feedback. My whole body felt electric-scratchy as invisible lightning licked beneath my skin. The place was jammed up to the rafters. They'd told me that people sometimes show up early because of the weather, but I definitely hadn't expected to play for a full room as the opener for the opener during a snowstorm in Boston. It was at least twenty times the amount of people I had ever played for in my life, and my first time performing at a real venue. My first time performing on a grand piano, for that matter. My mouth became the desert, my tongue a cactus that couldn't rest comfortably anywhere. Why did I want to be a musician, again?

Stop. I was here to prove I belonged here. That I could make it. Make it worth lying to my parents. Make it worth forcing myself under the alarmingly hot beam of a spotlight.

The dim sea of silhouettes stood waiting, eyes full of reflected light trained on me. Fear thundered into my ears, temporarily deafening me. I forced a thin smile, took a few tiny, weak breaths, and focused on the word Steinway written over the keys in gold lettering. I closed my eyes and was at home in the basement, just me, playing to the old photos and posters on the walls. I finally felt my mind slip back into my body and reattach itself all the way through to my fingertips. I pressed a key by accident and my hands jumped back, the overreaction causing some laughter. I shook my head and produced an unnaturally-high laugh at myself. No way I was going to speak into that microphone to babble an apology and tell them this was my first "real" show. Nope. That was not cool. There was nothing to do but launch headfirst into the opening song, begging my melodies to transport me and everyone in the crowd. Exposing my private poetry over piano chords was terrifying, and if any other performers thought different, they probably weren't writing the kind of songs I write.

I didn't pause to explain anything before starting the next song, just took a few breaths when I could. I led them through my lonely ballads and angsty bangers, being my own weird, plain-looking small-town girl in jeans and a T-shirt (because Jenny wasn't there to stop me). I sang my threadbare heart out like my life depended on it. Everything had a level of urgency behind it. This was the only way I felt like me. Performing was my mirror.

The audience was kind. The piano sounded like a dream and the microphone was hands-down the best I'd ever used. The sound of my singing was so beautifully amplified that I hardly recognized my own voice. I grew more confident, hitting notes I didn't usually try for. I felt the attention press around me so powerfully that I burrowed deeper than usual into my songs. I basically blacked out onstage, which might be a good thing sometimes.

The last piece was a newer song, so fresh in my mind that it was bursting with energy and begging to be played. "This last one's called 'Take Me Away,'" I said into the mic with a little bit more confidence. The crowd cheered encouragingly.

The song was a dark, pleading ode to being stuck in an existence that didn't feel right and begging to be rescued by a miracle of fate. I threw in heated keystrokes, pushing the limits of the unfamiliar, pretending there was a whole five-piece band onstage, backing me up. Maybe it was sloppy, but I didn't care. This last one was for me.

The applause was overwhelming. I sat there for a minute, eyes closed and smiling, hair sticky around my face. I let the sound of their enthusiasm lift my heart back into its proper resting place. I had done it. I had exposed myself without bombing.

The biggest thrill was realizing that this thing I'd built was a vessel with the power to take me far away from reality— if only for the length of a set.

NO DISCLAIMERS

THE NIGHT WAS AS CLOSE TO a perfect dream as I'd ever had. Eyes Wander was halfway through an incredible show and I was tipsy and loving it. It wasn't like it was my first time drinking or anything, but it was certainly my first time drinking in public, surrounded by strangers who were all at least several years older than me. That was a separate thrill of its own. Brian had snagged me a wristband and people kept offering me drinks and compliments. Jenny and I had done some drinking with her older sister's friends so I thought I could handle it, but I felt adrift without my co-pilot by my side. I was also thoroughly amped up by the all the newness of the night, which kind of zeroed me out to an even keel. I wasn't just some teenager-in-headlights. I was holding my own at one of the coolest venues in the Boston area.

"They don't call it the Paradise for nothing," said a voice as if inside my head. The bartender, a short girl with ivy tattooed up her arm, put down a shot in front of me and grinned. The liquid was a bright red five-star alarm. "From an admirer," she added.

I looked confused so she pointed down the bar and there she was: Ruby Sky. The Ruby Sky I'd stared at in so many pictures, the lead singer of Glitter Tears, the rockstar chick with violet hair and a single sparkly tear under her eye—and definitely the biggest celebrity I'd seen in person. She appeared to be smiling at me. Me? Kyla Bell, unknown nobody from the middle of nowhere, Massachusetts? Not a chance. I looked over my shoulder to be certain I wasn't about to make a fool out of myself before smiling back. She laughed and disappeared into the crowd.

And just as soon as my heart got sent aflutter, it was deflated. I took the shot in my hands and rotated it on the bar, watching the multi-colored lights dance in the fiery liquid, feeling the familiar burn of disappointment.

"Are you gonna drink that or stare at it?"

I turned and there she was in all her wondrous, alternative glory: silver miniskirt, shiny boots, a fishnet long-sleeved shirt under a T-shirt of a cupcake making an evil face, "SWEET?" written under it. Her purple hair looked almost black in the dim lights of the club. Her iconic rainbow glitter tear twinkled in the lights.

I was too swallowed up by her presence to speak.

"Well?" she asked. "Do I need to do one, too?"

I nodded. My tongue had apparently fallen into a coma, so I bit it to wake it up, wincing with pain.

Ruby Sky laughed like this happened to her all the time, and maybe it did, because somehow the bartender knew to bring her another neon red shot. She picked it up and motioned for me to do the same. We clinked glasses and tossed them back together. I tried to respond as if it was something I did all the time, but it burned something awful so I snorted and then coughed from the overwhelming cinnamon taste. Totally un-slick. She was still laughing at me when I recovered.

"I think I just swallowed mouthwash," I croaked, feeling my stomach clench. Those were my first words to one of my idols? *Ouch.*

"Cinnamon bombs," she said. "I loved your set!"

Again, I almost looked around me to see if she was talking to someone else. Had Ruby Sky given me a compliment? Given *me* a compliment, on *my* music? This was surely a dream, if not for the slosh of gross cinnamon in my stomach.

"Wow, thanks! I'm totally a fan," I said. Uh oh, the flood gates were opening. "I have all your albums! You're one of my favorite—" I halted there and cringed, struggling to stop the giddy little fan girl that was getting out. "I'm sorry," I rocketed on, "I'm so, I'm such a—you know. You've been a real inspiration to me. I've written piano parts to a ton of your songs." I hadn't expected that to come out, but it at least seemed cooler than revealing my love for screaming her lyrics into my hairbrush.

"Oh yeah?" she asked, way more interested than I'd expected.

"Um . . . Yeah!"

"Well, you have to play them for me," she said.

"Wow. Okay. Wait. Now?"

"Is there ever a better time?"

She winked as she took my hand and held it tight. The thrill of her fingers clutching mine tickled every nerve in my body, even in places I'd never felt before. Forget music. Was *this* what being on drugs felt like? I floated behind her as she cut fearlessly through the crowd and opened the door backstage.

All at once, the music stopped and we were away from everyone, just Ruby Sky and me in an empty hallway. The cheering crowd sounded so far away as my heart became a heavy kick drum thudding in my ears. Ruby led me behind the stage to the area the grand piano had been stored. I immediately went to the bench and sat down. I was so nervous that standing felt awkward. Why could she possibly want to do this now? How was she possibly that interested in my interpretations of Glitter Tears' hits?

"Why are you here?" was what I ended up blurting out. "I mean, I'm just surprised . . ."

"Brian's a really good friend," she said. "I've known these guys for years. I'm in town for a record release event, and I love these dive-y venues."

"Yeah," I said, even though to me, Paradise Rock Club was a palace.

I thought she was brave for coming to this place, being part of the average crowd. People were probably too intimidated to approach her. Her eyes were so frosty I felt deliciously chilled looking into them. She had high cheekbones and her face was thin but not pointy, just delicate. The sparkles applied to her tattooed tear flashed under the overhead lights. She was hypnotically beautiful. It was hard not to stare.

But Ruby Sky didn't seem to mind. She stared back, all confidence and clairvoyance, seeing right through me.

"You don't have much experience, do you, Kyla?"

"What do you mean?" I stiffened up immediately. Then I relaxed my shoulders, reminded myself to keep cool. It was as honest an assessment as any, if only I could drop my defenses and desperation to seem older.

"You're so self-conscious, as if no one's ever really seen you before."

"I guess . . ." I said at last. "Maybe not. I mean, maybe not many have."

"I noticed it even when you were onstage. I want to know your story," she said. "Where have you been? You don't fool me with your act of modest insignificance. I can tell you have a lot going on inside."

I felt my entire body blush like it had just been stroked by the hand of a goddess. Still, I could not speak.

"Play now," she commanded.

"Okay." I hesitated. Would I even remember my arrangements of her songs in this state? "I'm a little buzzed, just warning you—"

"No disclaimers," she interrupted. "Let's get that straight upfront. They're weak. Don't make excuses. Stand behind yourself and your work, always."

I sat up like I'd been slapped. "Right," I agreed. It was just that I'd never played for anyone while intoxicated before. "I'll start with the part I wrote for 'Rumble' if that's okay. . . ."

I struggled out of my shyness, tried to forget Ruby's presence, and shut my eyes for a second. Even though the room smelled of spilled drinks and sweat, not musty laundry like my basement; even though I could hear the audience's muffled screams for another encore instead of the scuffling of vacuuming above me, I recalled my version of Glitter Tears' most popular ballad. It was one of those times when the pressure's so high that you don't think you can be what you want to be, but something inexplicable comes and takes over your body for you. She started to sing along right there next to me and it shot chills down my back, almost making me mess up. Ruby Sky had a riveting rock voice, so sexy, raw and powerful that it gave me the strength to finish.

Someone started clapping as we wound our way out of the song.

"Wow," Brian said. "I see you two have met."

"Hey, babe." Ruby smiled and danced over to his side. "You guys were on fire tonight!" They embraced and she gave him a kiss on his mouth. He looked extremely happy. His shirt was wet with sweat and his eyes were flashing.

I wondered how much of the set Ruby had actually watched. Brian swelled with pleasure at her words. I noticed he'd somehow gotten cuter, as if his body itself was trying to impress Ruby. Even the way he was standing was different. He looked straight into her eyes. She stared back, no trace of embarrassment or awkwardness, just a confident hold on her power over him.

"So, Kyla—" he began.

"Oh, yeah, I've met Kyla."

"Isn't she great?" he said. "I knew you'd love her." I looked down at the ground, embarrassed to be referred to in the third person while in the room with them when they were clearly intimate, or had been, or were going to be very soon.

"I'm gonna take her on tour with me," Ruby said casually.

Laughter exploded out of me. The notion was too ridiculous. Then I stopped laughing as I realized they were studying me. Ruby whispered something to Brian and he nodded as if he was almost pained to admit something. I felt a flash of fear.

"Well, Brian says you're of legal age to do what you want," Ruby said to me. "So why not?"

LET IT GO

I LOVED VISITING CAMBRIDGE AND FELT at home among the colorful, scrappy street punks and quirky little shops in Harvard Square. Jenny's older sister had lived there for a few years so we stayed with her as often as we could and got to pretend to be city cats. When I walked around, I'd get nods from kids as if they knew me, and it was one of the only places my low-key (read: gutter-grunge) style felt right. I loved exploring the tobacco shops with their strange smells and funny pipes, the spiritual shops full of crystals, tapestries and tarot cards, the endless book and record stores. Harvard Square was an eclectic collection of cool stuff like nowhere else. If I'd been lucky enough to grow up in Cambridge, I was sure I'd make more sense to myself and everyone else.

The Greenhouse Coffee Shop & Restaurant was a diner with a tropical feel to it, ashtrays on the tables and plants everywhere. Jenny and I had gone in for French fries and sodas a few times before. I felt way underprepared to meet Ruby's manager, Kevin. I wasn't sure what he was going to be screening me for, nor had I any clue what I was supposed to be saying or doing to win his approval. I could scarcely wrap my head around the situation myself. The word "shabby" popped into mind as I looked down at my faded, torn jeans, dark green flannel I'd had since the first year of high school, and homemade scarf my mother knit years ago. But there was nothing I could do. I'd had no time to prepare for this life-changing interview that had dropped into my lap the night before. I didn't have the cash for a new outfit. The amount they'd paid me out the night before was barely enough for a bus ticket home. And Jenny's sister was just as grungy a dresser as I was, so it was pointless to borrow anything from her.

I was headed into the most important interview I'd ever had, and it was all I could do not to trip on my combat boots.

Ruby and her manager were seated in the corner. They didn't see me approaching. The manager was sharply dressed and had piercing eyes, short-cropped hair, and a close shave. His black collared shirt and crisp, dark jeans made him look straight out of a fashion ad.

Ruby looked as fresh and beautiful as ever. She gave me a bright and engaging look that unleashed excitement within my constricted chest, bubbling over my nervousness like hot springs to help ease the tension.

Her manager turned to study me.

"Hello," he finally said. We shook hands and I tried to put some firmness into it. "I'm Kevin Milton, with Cypress Management."

"Nice to meet you," I said. "I'm Kyla Bell."

"Sit down, Kyla!" Ruby patted next to her on the booth. I plopped down next to her in relief, breathing in her sweet honeysuckle vanilla scent and willing myself to be more confident. This was my golden ticket out of my sleepy hometown. I could not blow this.

Kevin studied me. He had a chiseled jawline and was definitely the most intense man I'd met before. Did all music managers look like fierce, starving models? My stomach was tumbling on high and I decided to only speak if spoken to first.

"Ruby's told me a lot about you," he began.

"But," she interjected, "There's obviously still a lot I don't know."

"Let's order before we get to that," Kevin said, waving his hand impatiently in the general direction of the staff. "I'm starving."

We looked over the menu as someone came to take our order. I wasn't hungry at all. Ruby ordered a house salad so I did the same. She smiled encouragingly at me. Definitely the right choice. All I had to do was follow her lead and I could probably be fine. Kevin ordered egg whites with a side of steamed broccoli. As soon as the waiter left, he checked his watch, pulled out his cell phone and excused himself to make an "urgent call." I was grateful to be alone with Ruby for a minute. She looked me over again.

"I'm sorry," I said again, after a moment. "These are the only clothes I have."

"Don't worry about it. I filled him in on the whole story, he knows you're as surprised as he is."

"What did he say?"

"He's worried, but I think it'll be fine."

Her confidence was almost contagious, but pressure still pressed down hard. She couldn't possibly understand how much this would mean to me. If I had to stay at home much longer, I would most certainly go insane. I bit the inside of my lip and tasted the iron-salt of blood. I needed this. I needed it more urgently than I could even fully admit to myself.

Kevin returned a moment later, annoyed.

"Just checked in with Tumble. They want you there an hour earlier, now. These record stores are so disorganized, I swear to Christ, I'm not sure how they even function at all. We'll have to be quick."

I took a small sip of my water. Kevin was certainly frightening. My heart was shrinking by the second. He was everything I expected LA people to be: impatient, annoyed, alarmingly good-looking, and bored stiff by people like me.

I watched him gather all the focus he could to ask me about myself.

"So, Kyla," he began. "Ruby wants you to join the band for the upcoming national *Perpetual Twilight* tour but you're still enrolled in high school as a senior, yes?"

"Um . . . yes," I said uncertainly, feeling like I was giving something away that already put me at a disadvantage. I glanced at Ruby but she just nodded encouragingly. "But that's not, like, a problem. I can just drop out and get my GED later."

"Any plans for college?"

"I haven't heard back yet," I said, sounding meek. "I don't care."

"What did you apply for?"

"Not sure," I said, wishing I had a better answer. "But I am sure that all I really want to do is to play music and travel."

"Have you done much traveling?"

He had me up against an invisible wall, firing questions too fast to fake answers.

"No. Not really."

"How do you know you'd enjoy it?"

"I'd imagine anything's better than staying in the same place your entire life."

He sat back. "What about your experience? Have you played with a band before?"

"No."

"Why not?"

"I haven't met the right people. I don't know, I'm from a small town. There aren't many options. I haven't really been looking, anyways. Most of the stuff I focus on is for the piano and me."

"Ruby says you've written parts to her songs already."

"Yeah, exactly," I said, flushing. It was difficult to look in his eyes. He made very criticizing eye contact. "I've been a fan of Glitter Tears from the start."

Ruby gave my leg a little squeeze under the table. "Kyla's who I've been searching for," Ruby said. "She's perfect."

My shrunken little heart swelled back up like a water balloon, hearing these words come from the lips of one of my heroes. Knowing she thought that was enough for a brief, glimmering moment.

"You've mentioned," Kevin muttered. "But of course she hasn't even heard the new album."

We shook our heads in unison. He opened his briefcase, slapped a promotional copy of the album down in front of me, and looked at the kitchen. "This place is so slow I feel slower just being here. I bet they haven't even started our order, yet." He announced it as a challenge and waved down the waiter.

"We need to be out of here in fifteen minutes. Do you think that's possible?"

The waiter looked doubtfully at the kitchen. "It, uh, could be."

I examined the CD cover for *Perpetual Twilight* in front of me. It had "Advance Copy" printed over Ruby's gorgeous face.

"Can't wait to hear it," I said.

Ruby smoothed my hair and I gave her a grateful smile. Kevin stood up abruptly.

"We don't have time for this. We have to go, Kyla," Kevin said. "We'll talk it over and let you know."

Let you know seemed as good as *let it go.*

GET BETTER AT BLUFFING

SNOWFALL HAD ALWAYS BEEN ENCHANTING TO ME—until the accident. Ever since, it signified doom and gloom in the worst ways: the nostalgic *before* and the unsettling *after*. The never-ending ache to feel life as it was before I had to stare into death's blank face amongst the flurries as our car ricocheted off the road. I lay burrowed deep inside my messy nest-bed, watching the snow spin off the treetops outside with a ball of dread sitting in my stomach. My mother came in wearing her flannel robe. She had a towel wrapped around her head and her skin was dewy from the shower. She almost seemed her old self as she stared thoughtfully out at the snow through the window while stroking my hair.

"Pity your dad cleaned out the shed," she said. "All this snow and no mower."

Once again, she was back to the somewhat-empty shell of a mother I'd become used to. Not making much sense, but trying to connect in her own way. I could smell breakfast, though, so I forced myself up and out of bed. Downstairs, there was a cup of cocoa ready for me on the table. My dad stood over the stove and tended to his waffles. If there was one food my father had mastered, it was waffles.

"Good morning!" he said, cheery as I'd ever seen him. He came over and kissed me on the cheek. I sat down and eyed his mug. Was there whiskey in it already? I took a sip. No booze yet. He turned around and plopped two hefty waffles onto a plate in front of me.

"Wow, Pops," I said. "I'll be lucky if I can finish one."

He smiled and handed me a thick envelope he had hidden next to the toaster.

"Well? Open it."

I saw the Holyoke stamp and noticed it had already been opened. My stomach clenched as I pulled out the cover letter and scanned it. I'd been awarded a full scholarship to attend the university full time in the fall.

I felt deflated.

"Can you believe it?" my father said. He pulled me into his arms and hugged me with his workman's grip. I stumbled back when he released me, blinded by the headlights of his approval. "My own daughter, offered a full scholarship to a top school!"

My mother didn't look as happy as I'd thought she would at the news. She seemed aware of my conflict even though I hadn't told her anything. Neither of them knew I'd per-formed in Boston but they seemed to sense something was up. My father eyed me closely.

"You're not happy?"

I was in no rush to crush his elation.

"Yeah, of course I'm happy," I said, forcing a big smile. "I can't believe it."

"Me neither," he said. He squeezed my shoulder again. "And you'll be so close to home. It's almost too good to be true."

I stood up with a start, squeaking the chair legs on the linoleum floor. I could see how attached he'd already gotten to the idea, and I didn't think it was right to let him continue on like this. Also, my mother kept looking at me and not saying anything. She was so strangely intuitive. It was baffling how that sensitivity had been preserved through the trauma.

"Dad."

He knew it was serious when he heard me call him that. His smile faltered.

"What?"

"I—"

The phone rang.

"That must be your aunt!" My father rushed over to answer. "Hello? Who? Ruby who?"

I practically knocked over my cocoa in my haste to take the phone. My father furrowed his brow and stayed next to me as I spoke into the receiver.

"Hello?" I reminded myself to steady my voice.

"Kyla!" Ruby's voice filled my ear, sweet as syrup. "How are you, pixie stick? Miss you already!"

I felt the warm rush of pleasure that only she seemed to know how to conjure so quickly. My cheeks flushed and my father hovered by my side. I took the phone into the bathroom and shut the door.

"Do you have your own line so I don't have to keep bothering your family?"

"No, unfortunately not."

"You poor thing. I can't imagine."

"It's pretty bad," I said.

"Hey—you know Jeremy, my drummer? He's got this issue with his back and had to go to the hospital last night at three in the morning. I'm on my way to see him right now."

"Oh, no! Is he okay?"

"Yeah, he'll be all right," she said. "Spasms. He's on a lot of meds. Anyway, that's not why I called. I wanted to let you know that Kevin has some . . . concerns."

I remained quiet, terrified of what was coming next.

"He's worried about you being the right fit, image-wise, for the band."

I stared at myself in the mirror of the bathroom. My dark brown hair was stringy and hanging in my face. There were circles under my eyes. My puff paint sweatshirt was at least five years old, and the once-bright kittens now looked like they'd been playing in the dirt. I was more of a greasy geek than a rock star, so who could blame him for thinking that?

My voice choked up inside my throat. All I could manage to get out was, "Huh."

"But listen up, girl. You know I'm a fan of you the way you are. Kevin's a businessman at heart, so he's worried about 'selling' you to the fans and all that crap. You know, Glitter Tears has a certain image, and he's wondering how you're going to fit into that."

As soon as I heard *fit in*, my hopes really hit the floor. I knew all about "fitting in." I'd never been good at it. For as long as my memory could recall I hadn't been a solid part of any group. I'd tried, at times, to shift myself in one direction or another, but I wasn't a natural faker and that always ended up being the problem. I'd never learned how to be a convincing cool kid. Hadn't Ruby noticed this before she'd invited me on tour? I'd nearly—

"Kyla? Hello? Did I lose you?"

"I—I don't know what to say."

"Oh, you silly thing, don't take it so hard. Please! You know how Kevin is. I insisted you only need a makeover. It'll be fun! Stuff like hair and wardrobe and all that. Maybe a little social breaking-in so you're not as green as you seem. We'll figure it out. There is, however, the problem of how you're going to get this all going on before the tour, especially with you being in school and all."

My mind raced. I didn't have any answers for Ruby. I didn't have any answers for my father. In the course of a week I'd been somehow selected for two grand opportunities, neither of which I felt particularly well-suited for.

"I told the band all about you, and they're dying to meet you."

My hope zoomed again. "I'd love to meet them, too."

"You will, silly! We came up with an idea."

"What!?"

"Okay. So here's the deal. There's this guy, my friend Robert Jeffs, he's a big, fancy Hollywood music producer. One of those guys everyone wants to work with. He did the first few albums by Back Alley Bandits *and* Interrobang, plus, like, a million more. Five Grammys on his shelf. He lives up in the hills of Laurel Canyon in this huge place. It's kind of his castle, really, with this killer view of Hollywood, especially at night. Anyway, he was considered one of those producers who can turn anything into gold, but he went through a rough divorce and lately he's sort of fallen off the hits. He's been asking Kevin to get him his next big project."

She paused and I wondered where this was going.

"So, I had this idea that you could come out here and live with him for a little while and let him fix you up for the tour. He can help develop your new image. He's great with that stuff. He's really a 360-degree producer. So we asked him if he's up for being drill sergeant for your rock star boot camp makeover—and he went for it! He says a little time with him and you'll be the most badass member of the band. How do you like that?"

It took a minute to digest the complete craziness of the plan. "Um . . . Wow. I don't know what to say." It sounded weird, *really* weird, but at that point I think I would have signed on to live in a leaky dungeon if it meant playing music with Ruby Sky.

"I know. Unreal! But you need to fly out here as soon as possible. As in, next week."

That certainly didn't sound like something that would sit well with my father, especially after getting the full ride to Holyoke. I was basically going to be throwing myself into scalding water with no life raft in sight. A quote floated to the front of my thoughts, from an interview with Glitter Tears' guitarist Slinky that I'd reread the night before. When asked what fueled his pro-skateboarding passion, he'd responded, *"Things that can crush you are ultimately worth doing."*

I didn't need more of a push off the ledge than that. Whether or not anyone approved of my chosen route, I had the eighteen-year-old privilege of taking the wheel of my own life.

So I took a deep breath and said, "Yeah, I'm in."

"YAY!"

My father was knocking on the door. "Kyla? What's going on in there? We're in the middle of breakfast."

I covered the receiver and called "Be right out!" Then, hushed, into the phone, "I have to go now."

"Okay! I'll call you as soon as I have more news," she said. "You won't regret this."

It was a bold thing to say, but I believed her. We hung up and I flushed the toilet and pretended to wash my hands, pushed my hair behind my ears and then turned off the light. I had a celebration breakfast to get back to. I had waffles.

When I reentered the kitchen, my father was sitting across from my mother at the table, not touching his syrup-drowned plate. He raised an eyebrow at me. I sunk into my chair, took a sip of lukewarm cocoa, and made another attempt to smile.

"Who was that?"

"Um, a friend," I said. "A girl I met."

"She didn't sound like a girl. She sounded like a woman."

"She's like twenty-five or something. I dunno. Whatever."

"'I dunno, whatever?' Why don't you tell me what's up, Kyla. You're as readable as a highway sign."

I forced a big bite into my mouth and chewed it slowly, taking my time. My dad watched me. I wasn't used to having so much to hide. It was a pretty uncomfortable feeling. I wondered how long I could go without saying anything. But my father was a stubborn man. He knew how to force things.

"So you're taking the scholarship?"

I shrugged, unable to meet his eyes.

"I can't believe this. I didn't think it would even be a question. Why do I get the feeling I'm going to be disappointed here?"

I shrugged again and kept my eyes fixed on the tiny squares of the waffles before me, barely able to move. I wished I had the skills to play it off better, but I just wasn't used to having much to hide.

"Kyla? Answer me! Where did this Ruby person come from?"

Then my mother decided to say something truly strange. "David, why don't you put on some more coffee?"

We looked at her.

"You don't drink coffee anymore," he said warily.

"I know," she said. "But if you're going to question our daughter like a criminal suspect, you might as well play the part and get yourself some more coffee."

We both stared at her in shock. Then my dad got up, threw on his puffy hunting jacket, and stormed out of the house.

"I wonder if we'll ever feel a real sense of family again," my mother said wistfully.

The cold waffles lay out before us, rubbery reminders of how unlikely that was.

ROADBLOCKS MEAN YOU'RE HEADED IN THE RIGHT DIRECTION

I COULDN'T LEAVE WITHOUT ANY NOTICE at all, although I did briefly consider it. Jenny, forever my wiser, older sister-by-choice (with the six months she had on me), had convinced me to talk to my father to try to gain his approval of this incredible opportunity that I'd earned through my music. But deep down, I knew it wouldn't change a thing because celebrity was a worthless currency to my father. He openly despised show business. I didn't want to shatter what little bond was left between me and my dad, but I was pretty sure he wouldn't leave me any choice.

We were sitting at the kitchen table, the envelope from Holyoke between us. I hadn't filled out the acceptance forms. In my jacket pocket, I had my high school drop-out forms.

"Something's happened, Pops."

He sat back in his chair and sipped his mug. "I was wondering when you were going to tell me what's been going on with you."

He fixed his stare on me. My tongue lay at the bottom of my mouth—heavy, stubborn, stuck. I stared at the cow embroidered on the old towel hanging on the oven. Everything was so worn out around the house, each worn object a glaring sign that we were missing our "woman of the house" touch. And it always felt like my fault.

I took a shaky breath and began again. "I've been trying to find a way to tell you. It's hard because I . . . I feel weird saying the words to you."

He didn't offer any encouragement, so I took a deep breath.

"Okay. I went to Boston a week ago when I said I was staying over at Jenny's because this amazing band asked me to open for them at a well-known club in Allston." I forced myself to look in his eyes. There wasn't as much anger as I expected to find, which I took as somewhat encouraging. "So I said yes, because the band is a pretty big deal, you know, and I was flattered. I mean, actually, I was really excited about it. It's a 21+ club, and I didn't think you'd let me play there. I'm sorry I lied about sleeping at Jenny's. It was a big deal, though. I mean, hundreds of people were there."

A slight raise of his eyebrow. Was he actually impressed?

"That's what you wanted to tell me? That—"

Nope. He was unimpressed. "Please, Pops. Hear me out." He frowned at the interruption. I rushed on before I lost my courage. "So I played, and I guess I did well because the singer of this other even bigger band, Glitter Tears, talked to me after. I told her I'd written some piano parts to her songs and she asked me to show her, right there on the spot."

I looked at him. He gave me a stiff nod to go on.

"And so that's Ruby Sky, who's been calling," I said with a giant sigh. I wanted to be happy about the story, but it was hard to feel anything good under his dead-eye stare. "So it turns out that they've been looking for a keyboardist to perform with them. And Ruby invited me to tour with her band this summer. I'm supposed to go out to LA to start rehearsing as soon as possible."

I paused, needing a moment to deliver the final punch line.

"So I told her that I would. As in, now. As in, my flight leaves tomorrow. I'm catching the Greyhound to Logan first thing in the morning."

It was a different kind of silence—a kind I'd only read about in books. I could almost see the mechanics of my future adjusting in his mind, a screw wobbling, things falling to the floor and breaking apart in slow motion. My father never spoke quickly, especially in difficult situations. He was the king of building tension. He released his words with great weight.

"Are you serious about this decision?"

"Absolutely."

He stared up at the ceiling and I felt his blood boiling through his veins. I was terrified so I rushed on, hoping to deactivate the impending explosion.

"Dad—I really need to do this, or I'll never be okay doing anything else. You know? I'll always wonder, otherwise. I can finish high school later. I can go to college later. This is something that I never saw coming and may never come around again. It's a chance to do music full time. As a *job*. And it's happening *right now*." I laid the official withdrawal form out in front of him and watched the veins begin to bulge around his forehead and neck as he looked it over. Hoping to take the edge off with humor, I mumbled, "It's my *Disney on Ice*, Pops."

My father stood up and slammed his hands down on the table. "You're going to drop out in the last months of high school to become a touring musician?" he roared.

Ruby's words echoed in my ears, *"You're the one, Kyla, I know it, so believe it . . ."* I nodded solemnly, writhing inside, struggling to keep a blank exterior.

"You've only just turned eighteen, Kyla," he shouted. His veins were bulging so painfully I prayed he didn't have an aneurism on the spot. "Do you have any idea what you're about to get yourself into? Musicians are, by *definition*, the most unstable people, and you want to throw away everything you've worked toward to—"

"—I've been working toward *this!*" The tears came fast, though I'd wanted to remain calm and rational, but it really ripped me open that he couldn't be even slightly under-standing or excited for me. "Haven't you ever noticed I spend more time in the basement than anywhere else? Music is the only thing I know about myself for sure, Dad. It has been since I started playing. There's nothing I'd rather be doing. You know it's true, but you ignore that. You've never come downstairs to listen to me play and I refuse to beg you. It really is the only thing that matters to me, though. I don't want to get some stupid job at a shop over the summer to go right back to school to learn about more things that mean nothing to me. . . ."

"Playing piano is a hobby, Kyla. Your *hobby*."

I sighed. My whole body was stinging with frustration as he attempted to crush me from above with his jaws-of-life stare. He would never understand, and I would have to live with that.

"You know what happens when people turn their hobbies into their jobs?" he sneered. "Ask anyone with a job. Look at the musicians making money right now. Do you think you're like them? Tell me what you're going to do when this doesn't work out. Tell me your plan after this falls through in a couple of months."

My mouth had gone dry. All the tears were right there, burning in my eyes, but I didn't want to give him the satisfaction of seeing them fall. I thought of my current two possible futures and reattached to my decision, forcing the hurt down deep for the moment.

"My plan is to try to—to be a musician, Dad. Ruby believes in me. I'm trying to believe in me."

I'd never heard him speak back so quickly and harshly. "I'm sure that you two have gotten really close with your five hours logged on the telephone in the last week, but have you considered *anything*? You read magazines, you've seen the lives these people lead. Now what, you think you're going to get rich and famous overnight? What is this woman telling you? You really think that some seasoned rocker is going to be honest with a teenager from western Massachusetts? If this is how you respond to the first piece of fake bait dangled in front of you, then I'll admit, I'm not sure I've been a very good father."

"It's not 'fake bait.' I told you! This is a well-established band, Dad. They have three platinum albums with Pacific Records. They tour the world and play sold-out shows at arenas. And they want *me* to play keys on tour. It's Ruby's band. Ruby wants me in it. Ruby wouldn't—she wouldn't lie to me. She's different—"

"Yes, I'm sure she's as pure-hearted as they come," he taunted. "And did you actually sign anything around this decision besides high school withdrawal forms?"

"Well, no, but they want to be totally sure I fit in first—"

"Oh, all right. So you really are throwing everything down the toilet for a slim chance at stardom. This Ruby character gets precedence over your own father, I see. What about the reputable school that wants to *pay you to go there*? Suddenly that's not good enough for you? They'll give you a degree at the end of four years. What will this Ruby give you if you even last one tour? I can argue with you all day, Kyla, and I can also tell you that if you toss aside your hard-earned opportunities for this gamble of an offer, I will not be there to support you when it doesn't work out for one completely ridiculous reason or another. You will not be able to come crawling back here. Once you're out on your own, you're really on your own. You hear me?"

My lungs and heart froze and my whole body was shivering. I couldn't meet his eyes, even though I could feel him looking down at me in a way he never had before. Then he stood up abruptly and walked out of the room. I heard him grab his coat off the coat rack and stumble on the front step as he slammed the door behind him.

I stared at the refrigerator, at a picture of the three of us sledding on New Year's Day, 1984. That was the most fun we'd had as a family that I could remember. I looked at our faces, at my enormous, goofy smile. Who was that happy little girl? She'd been gone for so long that I never really knew her.

I felt an arm on my shoulder.

My mom was next to me, giving me eyes that said she'd heard it all. I let her encircle me in her arms and I cried painful tears into her faded flannel nightgown.

"I'm glad you're getting out of here," she said. It was a statement most people would be offended to hear from their mother, but in our own sorry version of home, it was the sweetest thing she could really say. She really was a small miracle of sorts. Still supporting me through her own gigantic losses.

"Me, too," I sniffed back, feeling the last bit of hope shudder in my chest.

"Keep fighting," she added as I squeezed her. "Nothing great is easy."

"I will," I promised. And I meant it. I think.

DON'T BE SHY

MY FATHER'S WORDS PRETTY MUCH SQUASHED what should have been an astounding amount of excitement—until I left my house, town, and everything I ever knew and walked into Logan airport. There were such interesting types of people at the gate of the flight to Los Angeles, types that I didn't usually get to be around, living up in the homogenous hills of western Massachusetts. People of all ages and races, dressed as boldly as they wanted, sat around me in headphones, fidgeting with their Walkmans and flipping through magazines. I was both pained by how ordinary I looked and proud to be flying one-way to the obviously cooler coast. Something inside me was waking up, getting really excited to finally escape my boring, ordinary, small-town world.

That excitement changed to full-on glee when I got off the airplane at sunny LAX to see my name on a little sign held by a bored-looking driver. Wait, a sign for me? I wished anyone I knew could see that. Witnessing high points like this without any witnesses was like being trapped in your own good dream. No one I knew would ever understand how it felt. Suddenly, I felt lonely again. But soon after we got into the town car and drove away from the Los Angeles airport, the streets were filled with women in bold-print crop tops, tight little tummies on display, and it cheered me up again. Braids, bleach, belly rings. Hoops and sunglasses, chains, and bright sneakers—these were the stylish model types I'd never seen outside of magazines. They'd probably never stepped foot on the dreary east coast. I looked down at my faded band tee, ripped black jeans and combat boots, wondering for the eightieth time how anyone thought they were going to make me over into someone who could convincingly pull off some version of hot style.

My insecurities quickly flipped to full-on fear as we turned off the main roads and started speeding up a steep hill on an extremely narrow curving road. Great. I'd been in Los Angeles for less than an hour and I was already going to die. The driver whipped around the tight, narrow bends, chancing fate with no concern. If anyone came from the opposite direction, we were dead without warning. Just flat out dead. *Boom.* Maybe he was suicidal. Maybe he'd lived out here for so long he had a sixth sense of some sort. I felt nauseous from deep inside, flashing back to my accident with Mom. I contemplated saying something, but held my breath instead. Overgrown brush and palm trees streaked by as my clammy hands gripped at the door handle. Fast surf rock played on the radio, a nerve-jangling soundtrack for the scenario. I tried to focus on the giant houses streaking by, reminding myself I was starting a potentially dreamy chapter of life. So the introduction was a little choppy. I'd still take all my chances on it.

We finally reached a driveway leading up to a slate-gray angular house and screeched to a stop.

"534 Wonderland."

I had arrived.

Hurrying to escape the death-wish vehicle, I wondered if I might throw up. The last twenty-four hours of turbulent emotion and travel had left me in ragged shape to meet a Grammy-winning producer. The town car zoomed off without a goodbye, leaving me standing on the side of the steep road clutching my luggage like a lost tourist. Weren't LA people supposed to be more friendly? I walked across the lawn of 534 Wonderland, a patchwork quilt of shades of brown, past a dusty outdoor bar complete with chipped stools, dirty glasses, and overflowing ashtrays—a partied-out ghost-town mansion.

A catcall whistle rang out so close by that I jumped.

"Ladybird! Ladybird!"

I spun to my left to find a large gray parrot perched on the edge of a pot. The last slice of California sun was falling into the brush behind it. The bird shuffled across the rim, cocking its head sideways to look at me.

"Hi," I said, feeling somewhat stupid.

"Show me your titties," the bird said back.

I froze as it opened its wings and ruffled them.

"*Manners*, Eduardo," a raspy voice said from a cracked window on the side of the house. I squinted but couldn't see anyone inside. Standing there made me feel small, exposed, and entirely out of place, so I picked up my bags and shuffled toward the front door. The parrot hopped along on the ground beside me, which was surprisingly comforting. Even though it had just asked me to strip.

What to do at the door? Ring or knock—

Before I had to decide, it whooshed open. An older man stood before me, as thin and tan as he could possibly get, with a head full of startlingly thick, spiky black hair. He wore a dark blue terry cloth robe and flip flops and was a faded kind of handsome, his face a weathered statue that had been through a few too many storms.

"Excuse the robe. Just out of the shower," he said, his voice gravelly and low. "I'm Robert. You must be Kyla."

"Ladybird!" squawked the parrot below me. "Show me your titties!"

"Shut your pecker, Eduardo!" Robert snapped. "The one damn thing my ex-wife didn't take with her."

I laughed nervously. Ruby had told me about the ex-wife. Some French model who was notorious for heartbreak. It seemed way too personal a subject to launch into on my first day of sharing a home with an acclaimed producer.

"Well, come on in," he said, shrugging. "I'll give you the whole tour."

I stepped inside, dragging my bags behind me. I left them in the foyer lined with photos of Robert hanging out with world-famous musicians in what must have been happier, more prosperous times. The contrast between then and now was huge. I wouldn't even have known it was him in some pictures if not for the small, silver dangle cross earring he still wore.

We walked down a long hallway. He pointed out a giant kitchen, a messy rec room, and a few near-empty rooms that seemed to serve no purpose—barren spaces littered with a few items of furniture, most covered with sheets. The blankness was chilling. I was inside the most expensive home I'd ever been in, yet there was so little luxury here. Of course, I kept my mouth closed. Better that he think whatever he wanted about my first impression. Besides, I wasn't sure what to say about the coffee grounds on the kitchen counters, used glasses and pizza boxes—the only reassuring signs that someone actually still lived there.

"Not much of a homemaker," he said drily, as if reading my thoughts. I worried that my facial expressions gave me away. But Robert kept our tour moving. We approached double-padded doors at the end of the hall, he pulled them open with a grand motion. "The best room in the house."

This was it: the recording studio. My whole body shook with excitement.

I looked around in absolute awe. The walls were lined with burnt orange padding. A large microphone was set up in the center of the main room, a silver-caged bubble that looked finely crafted for the most valuable of voices. Guitars gleamed like shiny, bright-colored toys, sitting in their stands by the window to the production room, begging to be played with. A cream-colored drum kit was set up in the left corner. And in the right corner . . .

I stifled a little gasp.

"So you've already fallen for the best piece in the house."

Nothing commanded attention like the Baldwin: a ravishing grand piano beckoned like the steepest roller coaster at the amusement park, daring me to go for it.

"Go ahead," Robert said.

I hesitated, looking at his thin smile, full of distant sadness and regret. I had absolutely no clue what to do. My brain had flatlined. The whole situation was overwhelming. Why wasn't Ruby here to help with this introduction, again? She'd claimed to have an appointment. But I had no business handling this first interaction with Robert on my own.

My face gave me away again. Robert looked amused.

"Too soon? Want the rest of the tour?"

I nodded quickly.

"Alright," he said. "Better get over this stage fright soon, though. Rockstars aren't shy."

I hung my head like I'd lost the Olympics, then followed him back to the foyer and schlepped my bags upstairs. He showed me the bedroom I'd be staying in, several rooms down from his. It was more of a hotel room than a bedroom, with no distinguishing features whatsoever. It reminded me how frighteningly far out on a limb I was. There was no home nest for me to fall back on should this strange arrangement not work out.

He didn't show me his room or any of the others on the floor.

"Now go wash up and change, we're going out tonight," said Robert as he turned to leave. "You're going to meet someone really special."

My weary heart gave a little flutter. "Who?"

"Hollywood."

DON'T EAT

"So, you think you're something special, huh?"

Robert stared across the restaurant table at me, fresh vodka soda in hand. For my introduction to Hollywood, he had steered us to a small, crowded sushi house just off Sunset. On the polished wooden table, steam from tiny cups of hot sake rose in a swirl.

What kind of a trick question was this? I still had yet to put together a full sentence for the guy. He was unlike anyone I'd ever read about. I worried that I would mess something up before we even got started. For now, I was here to be a sponge, and I hoped that was enough. I didn't want him to reject me. And I definitely didn't want him to sum me up with an ugly sentence like that.

Did I think I was special? My tongue whipped around, desperate to say some snarky thing back to him, but I smiled and bit it down, hard. This was a music legend I was talking to, as well as my only chance of making it into Glitter Tears. I had no back-up plan. I wasn't even a high school graduate. The abyss was right there, just waiting for me to spiral out and fall into it. *Did I think I was special?* Of course not—and of course. It depended on which minute of which day you asked. At the moment, I'd never felt as particularly *un*-special. His question seemed to accentuate that.

No matter what, I had to play it cool. I took a small sip of the hot sake, which I hadn't been carded for, and which I'd never had before. It tasted strange, but not *bad*. Light and curious. I took another slow sip, trying to get across that I didn't consider his question anything but rhetorical, and I wasn't going to answer it.

He smiled crookedly. "Alright, you tough cookie. I'm messing with you. It's true, though. You don't up and move to LA unless you think you're something special. And here you are, holding this glittery ticket to stardom that somehow fell into your lap. Must feel pretty nice."

"Yeah, unreal." I carefully unwrapped my chopsticks, rolling up the wrapper, refusing to meet his eyes. He couldn't break me this soon. I had to show him I was tough enough to survive his questions. Tough enough to survive here.

"Well, it gets real, fast. So you better start speaking up. I've heard about you from Ruby, but who knows how much of it's true. One thing about Ruby, she likes to embellish. I'd rather hear it from you. What are you doing here?"

Ugh, he was right. I was going to have to pry my mouth open eventually or he would get rid of me. I had another sip of sake to loosen my social gears and took a stab at conversation.

"I mean, I'm here to be in the band?"

He slammed back the rest of his drink, obviously growing impatient with me. "Yeah, we all know you're here for that, but why'd you make the move, really? I hear you left behind a lot, including your high school graduation and a college scholarship."

"Yeah," I said, staring at the bamboo wall behind him, feeling something heavy sink inside. Why I made the move was a complicated issue. I could hardly bear to answer the question honestly to myself, let alone deliver a simple answer to him.

"Don't stress yourself out over there, precious. I'll tell you why you're here. You're here because this city's an international microphone. You're here because this is where artists become important. You're here because you need to matter."

Did I? Was he right or wrong? It was such an ego-centric answer. It made me mad because it was pretty much true. I immediately realized I had to find a way to become a whole lot less precious, and fast.

"Hey, you made the right move, kid. That's what I'm trying to tell you, that's how I made things happen for myself. I dropped out of high school and never went to college," he continued, grabbing his sake and downing it. "The music business takes a certain something that you can't learn in school." He finished in time to motion to the waitress for another drink as she came to check on us.

"You have to build your own path to get you where you want to go. This industry's different for everyone. I'm a man and you're a woman, so right off the bat it's harder for you to get on top. No pun there. I don't do puns, for the record. Things come out the way they come out. But you're young, smart, and soon-to-be pretty, and that already puts you at an enviable advantage. This city's a bunch of fun. A slew of trouble, too, but a hell of a lot of fun."

Again, I was at a loss. Was that supposed to be advice? It made me feel so many ways at once that all of them canceled out each other into white noise. The waitress returned with another bottle of hot sake and two bowls of miso soup.

Robert winked at me. "Miso soup is the perfect food. I hardly have room for anything afterward. Don't look at me like that. You'll see. You won't either, soon enough. Which leads me to my next point. Kyla, as a rock starlet-to-be, you need to make a few dietary adjustments. Nothing too drastic, you know. Just cut back on the food. Hey. Don't be offended, look at it this way: do you see many famous musicians that look like they eat a lot?"

I searched my magazine-loving brain. He was right. I wasn't skinny like my favorite rockstars. I guess it should have been obvious that my body weight was fair game in the "total makeover" plan. I shook my head.

"Exactly. Have you ever had an eating disorder?"

I shook my head again and looked down at my belly. My stomach rumbled in furious protest as I pushed the miso soup away.

"Good. Be sensible about it. You have the rest of your life ahead of you. It's scientifically proven that lab rats that eat less live longer. So why not be a tiny bit underweight?"

I struggled to keep my disgust separate from the face I was making, which I could only hope was bordering somewhat on *neutral*. Neutral face, neutral answers. That was the best I could do for now. "I guess that makes sense."

"I'm going to be honest with you. If you lost a little around the middle, you'd be the prettiest damn girl in this town. Now, more than any other time in your life, is the time to be thin."

I swallowed hard, stunned by both the compliment and the words surrounding it.

"Have I upset you?"

"I'm . . . surprised."

"Surprised by what? This industry is all image, so naturally we start with your weight. Believe me, you'll be happier, lighter. It's all laid out for you already. You eat like me, you'll be thin in days. That's the Robert Jeffs diet." He grinned his crooked, boyish grin at me. "I should get it published."

I stared down at the scallions floating in my miso soup, appetite all but gone. I was back in middle school, getting made fun of for the second helping of fries on my tray, dumping them in the trash and crying in the bathroom.

"My ex-wife and I used to fight about desserts all the time," he continued on, oblivious to my inner turmoil. "She had a nasty sweet tooth. Anyway, I'm sure she eats candy three times a day now that I'm not around. Probably blown up like a puffer-fish."

"There's more to life than fighting about desserts," I said sharply, angered enough to bypass my "mute" status.

"Not if your wife's getting fucking fat," he fired back, smirking.

My soup grew cold. I couldn't silence a ringing disturbance in my chest. I half-listened to Robert talk on, nodding intermittently while observing the people around us. Their good looks were mostly artificial: cover-ups, make-up, touch-ups, implants, highlights, lowlights. . . . And these strangers kept making eye contact, sharp and quick. I was getting noticed, probably because I was sitting with Robert, who looked like a celebrity trying not to look like a celebrity. I wondered if they thought I was his daughter or his girlfriend. I wondered what they made of my ratty appearance. I wondered if I would ever feel any better about myself in this town, or if it would just continue to make me feel as bad as I felt right now.

This is the first night, I reminded myself. I would find my stride and my voice. It was okay to be absorbing for now. It was okay that I didn't know how to respond outwardly to most of the awful stuff Robert said.

I concentrated on his carefully manicured eyebrows, which rose and fell to accent his points. They were mesmerizing, actually. Had their own little rhythm going and everything. Or maybe that was the sake talking. At least it was quieting my own desire to get up and leave and never be caught talking to a guy like Robert Jeffs again.

"We've got to get over to Lolita's," Robert finally said as he squinted at his watch. He sat back and pulled out a cigarette pack, offering one to me. I shook my head. A laugh danced in his eyes.

"Soon enough," he said.

THERE'S FREEDOM IN DISGUISE

THE NIGHTCLUB CROWD ROARED LOUD AS Lolita's valet opened the passenger door of Robert's car. I stepped out slowly, wishing I was already further along in the makeover process. Here, my usual shirt and jeans stuck out way more than any of the bright-and-tight outfits other women wore.

What Robert told me was the VIP entrance didn't look flashy enough to be the gateway to a "trendy" club. An unmarked black tent extended from the front door. Robert stepped calmly into the crowd, looped his arm around my shoulders and pushed through the swarm of girls with neon lips and glittered eyelids, ankle bracelets and toe rings glinting as they tee-tottered on platform heels, shooting me dirty looks. I tried to fixate on the positive: we were finally meeting up with Ruby.

Robert steered me into the bouncer, a no-nonsense muscular guy with a clipboard. "Back it up."

I took a step back as Robert said, "Omar."

The bouncer noticed Robert and broke into a smile.

"Robert, what's happening? Come on in, come on." He unclipped the rope for him and stepped aside.

"She's with me."

Omar looked me over skeptically. "She's not dressed to code. . . ."

As embarrassment burned my cheeks, I saw Robert press a bill into the bouncer's hand. "I know. Can you let it slide this time?"

I held my breath, wishing I could transform like Cinderella in the moment. We *had* to get inside. I had to see Ruby.

"All good, brother," Omar said, discreetly pocketing the cash. "Go find Katrina, she was talking about you."

"Don't blame her. Thanks, Omar."

"Omar!" someone shouted behind us.

"Omar! Omar! I'm on the list!" another voice called out.

"Shit, Robert, you let my name out," Omar said.

Robert laughed. "Sorry, man." A door opened and we were in.

All the dullness of Lolita's exterior dissolved. The interior was a glammed-up funhouse: *Alice in Wonderland* meets *Carnival of Souls*. Blue, red, and green lights trailed over the furniture and walls. We walked through rooms where California-cool-looking people danced, lounged on couches, and swung on bubble seats suspended from high ceilings while they sipped drinks out of tall glasses garnished with fresh fruit. At least it was so dark that my lack of fashion didn't stand out. I smoothed my hair and hoped for the best—until I noticed Robert had vanished. In a panic, I scanned the room, but couldn't see his spiky head anywhere. I decided it was best to stay put, so I sat down in an armchair and watched a blond girl wearing a dress so short it revealed the very tippy-tops of the back of her thighs dance with a heavy-bearded man whose large hands crawled over her butt, hypnotized and disgusted at the same time.

Someone tapped my shoulder. I looked up to find Robert holding two yellow drinks with limes. He held one out to me. I stared at it, wondering what it would do to me. Wondering if I even had a choice anymore.

"It's damned if you don't and damned if you do," he said with a grin.

"That's for sure." I took it, sipped it. My mouth puckered and salivated at the same time.

"House margaritas," he said. "The best."

We drifted into another area of the club: an outdoor patio alive with booming drum and bass beats and tropical plants. Robert moved with the easy confidence of a panther who prowled every night. He led me over to a couch with ivy draped over the wall behind it and tapped the shoulder of a blond woman with orange-rimmed glasses wearing black-light-lit neon orange fishnet tights and wristbands with stars on them. She looked oddly familiar.

"Kyla, meet Glitter Tears bassist extraordinaire, the lovely Stardust Wu."

"Oh, *hey*," she said, stepping closer.

I laughed nervously. "I didn't recognize you at first."

We shook hands awkwardly and then she studied me.

"Oh, yeah, we wear wigs out sometimes," she said in a bored monotone. She had always seemed pretty dry in the magazine interviews I'd read, so I didn't take it personally. "*So* fun."

A woman with a tall brunette beehive and thick black eyeliner walked over. A glitter tear sparkled under her left eye. It was Ruby Sky, finally.

"Hellooooo, frosting!" the beehive said as she squeezed me. I was glad it was too dark for Ruby to see me blush. "So good to see you here at last!"

And just like that, my body loosened and my vocal cords worked again.

"I love your wigs!"

She cupped my cheeks with her thin hands. "We'll find you the perfect one. It doesn't get much more fun than wig shopping."

Robert slipped a casual arm around Ruby's waist while looking in the opposite direction and she laughed and hugged him.

"How's my favorite old man?"

"Just for that I'm not buying you a drink."

"Oh yeah? Well I'm not drinking tonight, anyhow," Ruby said.

I instantly put my drink down on the table.

"Or I'll finish Kyla's." She picked it up, winked at me and took a sip.

I couldn't stop looking at Ruby. She looked so different with the wig and heavy eyeliner. And Stardust looked like a space-age supermodel or something. Was I still on the plane, asleep and dreaming? This was so much wilder than how I'd imagined Los Angeles. I hoped I'd have my own wig soon and be able to feel like someone completely new.

Ruby handed back my drink and I took another sip, wincing again as the sour citrus tangoed with my tongue. It was delicious, though.

"How are you?" she whispered in my ear. "Is Robert behaving himself?"

I looked at Robert. He looked so innocent in the moment, his eyes sort of droopy as he chatted with Stardust. He hadn't made me feel uncomfortable in a sleazy way, at least. There had been no ringing "Predator" alarm since I'd met him. I nodded.

"Hey everybody!" Ruby said loudly. "It's Kyla's first night in LA!"

A crowd of random people started cheering around us, though I could hardly assume any of them knew who I was. Ruby grabbed me and pulled me over to the DJ, climbing up onto a table directly to the right of the booth. No, she could not expect me to get up there with her. That was something I didn't even enjoy watching other people do. I shook my head and tried to back away. Ruby stubbornly held her hands out to pull me up with her. I shook my head again. There was no way I was getting up there. It would be shining a spotlight on how out of my element I was. The DJ watched us with a side smile.

"Come on!" she shouted. Ruby leaned over and spoke into my ear. "No one knows you yet, that's the best part. And if they do, they won't recognize you after we're through with you. So, who cares? Let's have some fun!"

The beat picked up to a fast shuffle. I took a bigger sip of my margarita and set it on the side table. Ruby grabbed my wrist and this time I didn't resist. I climbed up next to her as Stardust joined us on my other side. I closed my eyes hard and opened them. Still in a Hollywood club, standing on a table between two dancing pixie rockers from Glitter Tears. This was my first night in LA, but I already felt freer, with no past, a crazy present, and a question mark future.

The new version of "me" was in this band now.

There was nothing to do but keep up.

SYMPATHY IS FOR SUCKERS

"Now tell me what else I need to know about you." He sat back, vodka soda in hand, and took a long look at me.

I heaved a weary sigh. It was too late for such a loaded question.

After the club and the drinks and the dancing, my mind was a tangled mess that needed sleep. Robert and I were back at his place, and to my surprise he wanted me to sit on the patio with him. It was chilly but he'd lent me his jacket.

I was pretty surprised by how nice he'd been so far. Maybe the alcohol was making me see things from a different angle. I did appreciate that he was enabling me to be here, taking me on and trying to help me succeed at this ill-fitting, yet illustrious opportunity. I was glad I'd kept my mouth shut during our initially bumpy encounter and was dreading telling him more, but the liquor had made my tongue quicker. Who knew what I'd let loose in the later hours?

"Okay, um . . . What do you want to know?"

"I don't know, typical things you should know about someone you live with. Do you date guys or girls? Both? How hard do you party? Drugs? Disorders? What kind of issues are we working with here? Be honest. Nothing shocks me."

I looked at him, not sure where to start or how much or little to reveal. Less was still more, I decided. "Um, I don't know. I haven't partied much. Haven't really done any drugs besides smoking weed a few times. It wasn't for me. And . . . I guess I've gone out with guys before, but . . . not recently."

"So there's a story there."

I remained silent, willing him to not press this one.

"You can tell me," he said. "C'mon. We're buddies."

I thought hard before continuing. It took a lot to say it to him. I hadn't said it to anyone, yet. Maybe Robert would help me feel better about it, though. He'd been through much more than me. Maybe he'd make me think it was small-time. Or normal.

"I guess I've only had bad experiences."

Robert sat up.

"Did something really bad happen? Do I need to kick someone's ass?"

I felt simultaneously misunderstood and exposed. I could spin the usual stories that used to work on Jenny. Stories about manipulation, pushing, pressuring; scratchy skin and clumsy fingers. Which was all true, but so was the fact that I'd gotten myself into those bad situations despite the fact that I didn't want anything to do with the guys. I was what they called a "prude" back home, potentially a "dyke" as well, but I wasn't ready for Robert to know any of that. I just wanted to be left alone. So I shook my head.

"Did you at least slap 'em good?"

That made me smile. "No . . ."

"We'll get you slapping soon."

"I don't know how. Never have."

"Every woman's got a natural inner slap. You'll see."

He lit another cigarette.

"What about you?" I asked.

"Hell no. I'd get my ass sued fast. If you own anything, you don't slap women around here, no matter how badly they ask for it."

Oof. I guess that answer was at least better than the alternative. I pressed on, hoping to keep the attention away from me for the rest of the night. "I meant with partying, dating and stuff . . ."

He scanned the Hollywood skyline sprawled beyond his yard. "Well that's a complicated question, seeing as there are so many things that need explaining, or they make me sound really bad."

I nodded like I understood. And I did. He didn't appreciate being on the spot, either. We had finally reached a checkmate situation and that was fine with me.

"Ladybird!"

Eduardo flew from around the corner and perched on a keg tap on the bar. He cocked his head at me.

"Show me your titties!"

"Where did he learn that?" I blurted out in disgust.

Robert waved him away, ignoring me. "Get lost, bird."

"Aren't birds supposed to sleep at night?"

"Who knows? He does what he wants, has the spirit of the ex-wife," Robert muttered. He drained his drink and looked distressed for a moment. I looked up at the starless, light-polluted sky, feeling my mind stretch far beyond its usual limitations in the extremely foreign environment. There was a different kind of darkness in this place. For one terrifying moment I felt the full weight of how much I was about to learn and how it would change me. Fierce goosebumps popped up on my arms.

"I'm basically a good person who's been bad places," Robert finally said, returning to the conversation that had been dead for what seemed like minutes. "I've set the world on fire a few times, been up and down and to too many Chinatowns to count."

What was *that* supposed to mean?

He got up and went behind the bar to fix himself another drink. He motioned to ask if I wanted one and I shook my head. It was definitely going to be a long night. I was so jet-lagged, too. I hoped I wouldn't fall asleep mid-sentence.

"You've got to drink more," he said. "Otherwise you'll make me feel like ten times the alcoholic I like to consider myself."

I laughed.

"Seriously," he said. "I don't like that."

There it was, another little alarm bell that he was pressuring me. I wasn't used to pressure from older people who weren't my teachers or parents. It was scary. My first impulse was to strike back, but I still couldn't be flat-out rude. He was fixing me up so I'd be stage-ready in a matter of weeks. What was the better answer than *hell, no*, again?

"I'm sorry, I'm just getting used to everything," I said carefully.

"I pity the fool who pities me," he said. "And don't apologize for your smart choice not to get completely plastered your first night with a stranger in a strange place."

A stranger in a strange place. He was right. What I was doing was actually as crazy as it felt. I was in a realm I knew nothing about. Maybe I had been too quick to come here. Maybe I should be begging my father to take me back. Maybe—

"You seem to have a level head for your age. Which is rare in these parts." He laughed drily, took another drag, followed by a sip from his glass. Me? Level-headed? "I'm curious to see how you're going to shape up," Robert staggered on. "Gotta knock you around a bit. We don't take kindly to squares." At that, he laughed and tipped his cigarette into the ashtray, dropping it entirely.

"I don't feel any shape at all," I said sullenly. And I didn't. I never had. Yet here I was, being more daring than ever, and somehow being called a square. He was obviously testing me on the first night. I had to hold up. Stay cool.

Then things got really weird. At first I thought Robert was trying to wink at me. Then I realized his eyelids weren't blinking in unison anymore. His left eyelid was going down after the right one. It seemed he had almost completely passed out until he jerked up in the chair and looked me dead in the eye, again. What was he on? Would he never go to bed?

"You're . . ." He searched for his words. "Upholding your virtue is going to take way more effort than it's worth. You'll see."

He kicked back the rest of his drink and stared into the empty glass for a moment.

"Go to bed," he said sharply.

His tone was a slap that stunned me. Then he went silent, staring down into his glass as if he'd fallen under a spell. I stumbled inside and up to my room, steeped in shock and jet lag. I had managed to survive my first day in LA. Barely.

RECORD EVERYTHING

Eighteen. That random age that a human being is considered grown and capable of individual consent, but is still actually a baby inside. Like a baby grand piano, but a baby grown-up. Maybe it was all the books I'd read, but I'd always felt pretty mature for my years. My grandmother had called me an "old soul." But in this environment I was so blindingly aware of how young I actually was. Robert kept pointing out my inexperience. I wanted him to see me as—well, not quite an equal, but someone ready to be on his level. I felt uncomfortable as I replayed all the subtle put-downs, and took a long time showering and organizing my stuff.

It was nearly lunchtime when I finally made it downstairs. Robert was in sweatpants and a T-shirt at the kitchen table, feet up, smoking a cigarette and drinking coffee while paging through a magazine. The smoke curled out of the open window behind him, blending with the colorless haze of the Hollywood hills morning.

"Good morn—er, afternoon."

He flicked his cigarette ash into a large stone ashtray shaped like a hollowed-out bottom of a pyramid.

"Coffee's next to the fridge, assuming you drink it," he said without looking up.

"Thanks." I didn't, but now was undoubtedly the time to start. I poured myself a mug and looked in the fridge for a bite to eat. It was empty aside from a quart of skim milk, a couple take-out boxes, and some assorted condiments. I closed the door and stood there with my coffee mug, examining the Chinese take-out magnet. The buzz of the caffeine began to overtake my hunger. Robert was right. Dieting at his house was going to be easy. There was absolutely nothing to eat.

"Alright. Enough lollygagging. Let's hear you play," he said abruptly. Before I had a chance to react, he glanced at the clock and stood up. "C'mon," he ordered. "I have people coming. You either play for me, or you play for all of us."

That settled it. I followed him into the studio, my heartbeat revving up as we got closer. It's not like I had great reason for being nervous, I wasn't auditioning or anything. Still, Robert had worked with so many incredible musicians it made me unsure if and how I'd make an impression.

"I'll be listening from the control room," he said. *Good*, I thought. If he wasn't in the room with me, it was easier to pretend he wasn't there at all.

Once seated at the Baldwin, I felt a sudden, welcome sense of home for the first time since leaving my parents' house two days ago. The smells of my old piano at home came back to me: birch, some implacable smoky scent, must, and dust. I stared at the gorgeous creature in front of me: a perfectly groomed, shining horse ready to jump as high as I dared. I poised my fingers over the keys and plunged into the unfamiliar board.

The press of my fingertips struck crystalline notes deep in the instrument's throat. Like finding water after being lost in the desert, I rejoiced in the songs that were best friends to me, forgetting about Robert, forgetting about Hollywood, forgetting about it all. I sailed away on my tunes, thrilled to be playing again.

As I let my hands drop into the last chords of my favorite set, I pressed the sustain pedal down and let the notes ring out long before looking up. Half an hour or so had passed, maybe more. I'd been so wrapped up in playing that I had no idea if Robert was even still listening. Through the glass I saw he was in the control room talking with two other guys. I tried to slip out into the hallway but the studio door was locked, somehow. I pulled at it and finally looked back into the control room. They were laughing now. Robert pressed something and his voice surrounded me.

"Where do you think you're going? Get in here."

I forced a grim smile and entered through the heavy padded door to three guys grinning at me. One of them had a bunch of faded tattoos and spiky bleached hair. When he smiled, a metal tooth winked.

"I'm Ollie, gorgeous," he said to me, and held out a hand.

"Mike," said the other guy, who had a long brown ponytail.

"I was asking Robert where you came from," Ollie said.

"Boston," Robert answered before I had a chance.

"Marvelous," Ollie said.

"You sound British," I said.

Robert smirked. "They're from Brooklyn. That's one of their tricks. They think it snags the birdies," Robert said with a fake British accent. "The accent gets chicks," he said in his exasperated voice when I still didn't get it.

"Don't listen to him," Ollie said. "He's full of absolute rubbish. So, tell me more about yourself," he continued, motioning for me to sit on the couch. I stayed put, feeling uncomfortable and wondering again where the hell Ruby was. Really, I had come to be with her, rehearse with her band, right? And here I was stuck having to hang out with these strangers. This wasn't my idea of any kind of makeover. This felt like straight up objectification. *Look at Robert's new plaything* sort of thing. I briefly considered my options: be rude, be quiet, or be charming. I went for the middle ground.

"Back it up, Ollie," Robert said. "She's good."

"Too good for me?" Ollie said with a thick grin.

"He's a bullshit artist," Mike said. "We apologize."

"Your songs are more mature than I expected," Robert said. "How did you get so good at lyrics?"

"Uh, I don't know. I read a lot of poetry."

"That was a lot of emotion to come out of someone so . . ." He trailed off, looking to the side, but I caught the amusement in his face. My insides twisted in embarrassment. "Well, inexperienced."

"And how old are you, gorgeous?" Ollie chimed in.

"Lay *off* it, Ollie," Robert said immediately.

"Jeez, Robert, what're you crawling up my ass for?"

"She's here for business."

"Yeah, you're all business, aren't you," Ollie shot back.

It was funny that Robert was acting sort of paternal. It made me think he liked me, maybe, but in what kind of way still wasn't clear. At the moment, he looked conflicted about something. I held my breath and willed my tongue to keep still. Meanwhile, Robert was giving Ollie a stare that shut him up. I wondered briefly how rough Robert's track record with women was, how much I didn't know and didn't have the experience to even imagine.

As if to purposely disrupt my thoughts, he turned around and pressed a few buttons. My song, "Fights like Tonight," poured out from the speakers. I'd never been recorded professionally before. I'd made a few bootleg demos off a four-track recorder I bought at a garage sale, but that was it. It was eerie to hear myself so clearly, as if I were actually playing in the room. I stood there and listened in a strange state of shock. I'd expected to be embarrassed. But hearing myself well-recorded was a completely new sensation for me. I was enchanted by my own song from the other side. I loved how I came across through the musical mirror. Robert pressed another button when it finished and I shut my eyes, bracing myself for any comments to deflate my excitement.

"I reckon she'll be running Ruby out of a job, soon," Ollie said. I laughed in surprise. It wasn't like I was in competition with her. Was I? It honestly hadn't even occurred to me.

"Nah. She's too good for Hollywood," Robert said, then chuckled. "But I guess we're working on that."

THERE'S NO LOOKING BACK

I WAS TRAPPED IN THE RECORDING studio for hours, watching Ollie and Mike lay down some machismo rock as Robert worked the soundboard to turn their raw ideas into new tracks. Their angry sound was like salt on the wound of Ruby not calling all day.

Just after sunset, she finally blew in like a fairy of the night, all bubbly and beautiful in a shimmery purple halter top and maroon satin miniskirt, gushing on about some party we were going to. She sorted through my scrappy collection of clothes while I showered.

The warm water pelted down hard on my shoulders and I imagined washing away all the anxiety and uncertainty that clouded me. Sure, I'd been kept in the dark all day. But what could I expect from Ruby? A timed-out itinerary of what I was supposed to be doing at Camp Robert Jeffs? I had to roll with the chaos, because that's what the cool kids did. They didn't care. They didn't obsess. They didn't wait by the phone for *anyone*.

So, we were going to a party. I could handle a party, not that I had loads of experience. I'd avoided the party scene back in Northampton. It was mainly a bunch of wasted guys pawing at the girls who put up with them, desperate to sleep with them. But even I knew those parties weren't comparable to the kind of parties that Ruby Sky attended out here.

Wrapped in a towel, I reentered the bedroom to find all of my things spread out on the bed. I kicked myself for not asking Jenny to let me borrow some of her clothes. Guess I just assumed that I would show up in LA and instantly be presented with a fantastic new wardrobe—like Ruby would have Robert's closet stocked with trendy new outfits for me or something.

Ruby stared at the bed, shaking her head.

I folded into myself with humiliation. "Not too much to work with, is there?" I finally managed to get out, voice wavering. I remembered the look I'd gotten from the bouncer the night before and willed myself not to break into tears.

She flipped her bubbly demeanor back on instantly. "Don't worry! We're going shopping this week. This is fun, you know, this is the stuff you'll laugh about later. Like, remember that time you first got to LA and had to put together something to wear to Ian Somer's party?"

I couldn't have heard her right. "Ian Somer? The—"

"*The* Ian Somer. Yes. He's a good friend."

This was much, *much* more of a big deal party than I'd even thought. "My best friend Jenny worships Sting Ray. They aren't touring or anything anymore, are they?"

She shook her head. "Ian had a lot he needed to sort out and the band fell apart while he was battling his demons. . . . You know, typical, over-glorified, heavy metal drama. I'm sure they'll make a documentary about it one day."

She shrugged and picked up a black jean skirt.

"Let's start with this. I think I have some tights in here that will make it more exciting." She snapped open a small aqua trunk I hadn't noticed at her feet and all sorts of colorful fabrics popped out.

I examined my shapeless jean skirt while she picked through scarves, stockings and gloves. "I wore this to a concert three years ago," I said woefully. "I'm not even sure it fits."

"With these," she said, ignoring me and pulling out a pair of dark-and-light-pink striped stockings from her trunk. She grabbed a fuchsia V-neck tank top. "And this. *Now strip.*"

Something went quiet inside. I sucked in, dropped my towel and did as I was told. There was a flicker in her eyes as she watched me get dressed in my underwear. I felt modest but bold at the same time. I could feel her eyes on me, but couldn't tell what she was thinking. As I slipped the fuchsia top on she shook her head violently.

"Ugh, all wrong!" Ruby got up and tore the shirt off of me, throwing it into the corner of the bedroom. She scratched me with her fake nails in the process, leaving a glaring red line across my torso. I didn't acknowledge it, or even dare to breathe as she pulled a black tube top out of her trunk and threw it at me. I held it up. It looked like an eight-year-old's swim top.

"What, you never saw a tube top before?" she asked impatiently, coming over and whipping the top away from me before I could respond. "C'mon, girl." She motioned for me to turn around, then held my arms up above my head and took off my bra. I went rubber, giddy and vulnerable in her physical command. She slipped the tube top over my hands, pulling it down my face and neck then finally tugging it over my chest like she was trying to fit a scrunchie over a tree trunk.

"Okay, perfect, now let me see . . ." She pulled a long, shimmery pink scarf out of the box and looped it around my waist, tightening it under my chest to make my boobs pop out even more. This seemed to satisfy her at last. Though I could barely breathe, when I looked in the mirror I saw someone that I never expected to see. I saw a babe.

"Wow, you made it look like I actually have a rack!"

"Yo, cherry pop, you *do*, you just don't know how to accentuate it."

I shot attitude back at her through my stare in the full-length mirror.

"Wait!" Ruby searched though the heap of clothing and eventually pulled out two black arm-length lace gloves knotted together. They looked like perfect examples of something I would never wear.

Still, I undid the knot, slipped them on, and looked in the mirror.

"Wow."

"I know. And we haven't even started your makeup and hair yet." She grinned. "Stardust always used to say I should be a stylist if the band didn't work out. This stuff is really fun for me. And you're a really blank canvas so it's even more satisfying."

I knew what she meant, but it still hurt. *A blank canvas.* It was why I was so nervous about meeting the band. Jeremy and Slinky seemed unapproachable. They probably wouldn't even notice anyone who didn't have multiple piercings and tattoos. Jenny had begged me to get my nose pierced before leaving, but I'd resisted, knowing it was silly to get your nose pierced—*real quick*—out of fear. Plus, it would probably get infected or something and then I'd look gross *and* dumb. She told me it was this kind of overthinking that had gotten me into this predicament—this emergency dash to LA to get an image makeover before going on tour with a famous band. She said if I'd committed to some piercings and tattoos—"stamps of legitimacy for musicians" as she called them—I would've probably been able to stay in Northampton to at least finish high school. But instead, my "blank canvas" self had to go to LA immediately so they could have enough time to pierce, starve, dye, and mash me into someone who looked and acted as if she belonged in a cool band.

I sat very still and quiet as Ruby took her time coloring in my face with her makeup. It was a nice, calming feeling as she moved the brushes and wands over my face like a professional, finally selecting a dangerous shade of dark pink lipstick and dabbing it on my lips. Then she sat back and admired her work.

"Saucy vixen. Perfect."

"Can I look?"

"Of course."

I turned around and was immediately floored by my reflection. The earrings she'd put on me, big, sparkly music notes, made the first dazzling impression. Then I noticed my smoky, silvery eyelids. I was definitely more "city" than I'd ever looked before. In fact, the only traces of the Berkshires I could still detect were my flushed cheeks. My mom always said we Bells were "sunshine kissed."

The thought of my mother deflated me. That was why I had really left; to get far enough away from my parents' sadness in order to have a chance at finding my own happiness. And suddenly, that felt really, really selfish. I choked up.

"Everything all right, lemon drop? You don't like the makeover? Too much?"

Ruby's voice shook me back to reality. Too late for regret.

"No! I love it. I was . . . remembering something from home."

"Oh no, there's no use looking back now," she said. "It'll only trip up your transitional flow. Let's go show this stupid world the new Kyla Bell!"

I went back over to the mirror and stood before it, trying to hold back tears with the wonder of the transformation. Ruby had swept my hair up and knotted it high on my head, leaving a few loose tendrils to curl around my face. It made me look older or something, more sure of myself. It was exciting and made me crave more change. I wanted to try different things, wear bolder styles, stretch my emotions. I wanted to be an adventurous musician, too. I wanted the whole wild roller coaster ride.

When I came downstairs, Robert was sipping a drink at the island in the kitchen. He looked me up and down and turned to Ruby.

"Always knew you were a good witch."

Ruby grinned and flipped her hair. "I go both ways."

PARTY LIKE THERE'S NO YESTERDAY

I WAS BUZZING ON A DANGEROUS cocktail of excitement, an empty stomach and adrenaline-laced anxiety as we left for the party. Ruby drove a pink Jeep Wrangler with the doors and rooftop removed. I sat on the fuzzy pink cheetah-print seat and fastened my seat belt, trying not to freak out about all the open air by fixating on the gadgets inside the car. A dashboard bobble-head of Mad Martha, the lead singer of the famous punk band HyperZ. A lips-shaped air freshener—"*Outdoors Scent*"—which made me smile. A constellation of glow-in-the-dark star stickers across the airbag.

"You dig my ladybug?"

"Yeah!"

"You should try driving her sometime. You have a license, right?"

"Yeah, but . . ."

"You don't drive?"

"Right."

"Why, again?" She started the engine.

Because I half-killed my mother last time?

"Long story," I sighed, not ready to transfer the weight of my past onto Ruby yet.

"Hang on!" She giggled maniacally as the engine caught and Mad Soda pounded out through the speakers. We zipped down the canyon at the fastest speed yet. Palm trees and busy restaurant patios blurred by, spinning my nerves into fizzy adrenaline. I clung to my seatbelt like a parachute, pressing into the furry seat cover, my closest option for a security blanket. I caught a glimpse of myself in the side view mirror and tried to cringe less as we sped through the streets, cool air rushing all around us. How could I be this upset about home when we were headed to Ian Somer's party in Malibu? I forced myself to switch gears—I couldn't let myself be robbed of the buzz I should be feeling.

I'd heard Malibu was the most exotic and rich area of Los Angeles, and as soon as we crossed the city limits, it lived up to expectations. Endless ocean that crashed right into cliffs. Bulb-lit beachfront clubs. Fancy sports cars and flashy motorcycles. It was everything it had promised to be, but strangely anticlimactic at the same time. There was something common about Malibu. The jutting canyons covered with trees vaguely resembled a terrain that seemed familiar. But the ocean air that clung to my skin like a cool film kept me aware of how very far from home I was.

As we pulled up Ian's long gravel driveway, my jaw dropped. The house was a Gothic stone fortress built into the cliff, jutting out like an eerie mirage. The beach-side castle loomed like an impending nightmare. Probably *everyone* would notice how out of my league I was. The clothes and hairdo were the easy parts. But conversation? Character? I had no idea where to start. My cool factor depended on staying quiet.

"Deep breaths." Ruby looked amused and squeezed my hand, making me conscious of how cold it was. "It'll be fun, really."

I stared at the giant slate walkway, lit-up mermaid fountain and bushes trimmed into perfect triangles. I knew Ruby was trying to comfort me, but she was also assuming I went to parties. I did not. And even if I did, they definitely wouldn't be at the richest kid's house. And that kid's house was probably the size of this one's bathroom.

As we entered, the hot press of the party enveloped me. Flames of flickering torches brushed the room with light. Brass candlestick chandeliers hung on heavy chains from 20-foot ceilings. Everyone looked as gorgeous as movie stars. They probably were, but I wouldn't know it. My parents didn't have cable or even a VCR. Ruby seemed oblivious to the staggering greatness of the scene, taking my hand and pulling me toward a guy who was tall and exceptionally thin, even thinner than Robert. It was *the* Ian Somer—dressed in a silver and black suit with his salt and pepper hair combed back in a low, tight ponytail, his eyes fixed on the tan brunette next to him until Ruby sidled up and whimpered, "Stop hitting on my girlfriend."

"Look who we have here," Ian Somer's voice was so creaky it was hard to believe he'd been the raucous singer of a popular heavy metal band. He stared at Ruby like she was the only person at the party now. The brunette looked annoyed. She clearly wasn't used to losing someone's attention. But Ruby was bottled lightning, there was no contest.

"Ruuuubyyyy Skyyy," Ian said. "Her name like sex on my lips."

"Ian!" She pushed him playfully and he almost fell over. "This is Kyla, my new keyboardist."

"Hey," I said lamely. "Cool party!" *Oof.*

Ian studied me for a moment. "She's cute. And young."

"And oh-so-fresh on the scene," Ruby didn't miss a beat. It was getting weird.

"Freshest I've seen in a while," he said approvingly. "What, did you fly her in yesterday?"

"Pretty much," Ruby said.

"Fabulous," Ian said, grinning. His teeth were so large and unnaturally white they looked fake. I caught myself staring and looked away quickly.

Was this all I was to them? Some wide-eyed, dumb-hearted, sell-myself-to-the-highest-bidder type? It was so hard to know the right way to react, especially when no one out here seemed to understand me at all.

My head was spinning. I wanted a drink. No one cared. They had already moved on to another topic.

"Jeremy and Slinky here yet?" Ruby asked.

"Yes. Those two already made off with a couple of my Brazilians," Ian said. "I think they're out in the courtyard by the pool, smoking themselves into a psychotropic haze."

"Of course," Ruby said as she rolled her eyes and laughed along with Ian. The brunette still glared but it didn't matter: she didn't exist in Ruby's reality.

"Come find me later," Ian said, blowing Ruby a kiss. "I have a surprise for you. And make sure fresh meat here doesn't get hassled by Anthony. He'll smell her from a mile away."

Ugh. *Fresh meat?* And who was Anthony? My mother's weird warning, *watch out for the wolves from the west,* echoed in my head.

Ruby's eyes flashed. "Well, any offspring of yours is bound to be disastrously horny." She was being flirty again, and I was surprised how fake she suddenly seemed.

Ian grabbed her waist and gave it a squeeze. "She's right," he said to me.

"I'm always right." Ruby twisted free, grabbed my hand again, pulled me away from the thin silver wolf, and dove into the crowd.

We made our way past counters filled with platters of the tiniest yet most delicious snacks, platters of miniature corn dogs and tiny triangle cucumber cream cheese sandwiches. I stared, suddenly hungry, but Ruby didn't even glance their way. She whisked me away before I could even snag a carrot stick, out through sliding glass doors, and into a huge inner courtyard. Palm trees and blooming jasmine drooped around us, a fragrant California jungle. Ruby led me toward the deck of a gigantic, glowing, blood-red pool.

Suddenly, she ducked behind a bush and pulled me against her. "There they are, over there," she whispered, pointing. "Let's have some fun!"

I looked over and spotted Slinky—instantly recognizable because of his shaved head and his height. He and Jeremy were standing with three tan, tall, gorgeous women, smoking cigarettes and talking. Whatever Ruby's idea of *fun* was, at least it might distract me from being the misfit of the party.

"Okay, here's what you do," Ruby said into my ear. "You walk over there and ask Slinky why he locked you in the trunk of his car."

"Wait—*me?*" I laughed as if she were kidding. She reached over and messed up my hair a little. "Hey!"

"Perfect," she said. "Except act even more angry."

"What?! I don't know how to act!"

"Shhh! You do." She stared into my eyes and put her hand on my cheek. I nodded as slightly as I could to keep her hand caressing my face. She had command over every single nerve in my body and she knew it. "It'll be *so* worth it, I promise. We do stuff like this to each other all the time. It'll be like your initiation into the gang, okay?"

I had no choice but to say yes and carry out the mission as best I could. I bit my lip and stared at the group across the pool. One of the Brazilians had her hand on Slinky's arm. Slinky was so animated in conversation that it didn't last there long. Ruby gave me a little push toward them. I sucked in as much air as I could and headed over, thinking about the improbability of me being able to pull this off. Then I thought about my father and the anger kicked up like a restless dog waiting for me to pick up a leash. A deep scowl took over my face.

Jeremy noticed me first, his eyebrows lifting to alert the others. They turned to me as I took in a ragged breath.

"Hey." My voice cracked as my nerves kicked in. "Slinky!"

"What—"

I forced the words out as he morphed into my father in my mind, trying to keep me away from my dreams. "Did you *really* expect to get away with keeping me locked in your trunk?!"

They all stared at me in disbelief.

"Um, who are you and what the *hell* are you talking about?" Slinky said.

"Whaaat?" one of the women said with a heavy accent. "Don't speak to this poor girl this way."

Slinky's eyes widened. "I don't know this chick."

I stood there heaving shallow breaths. The crowd buzzed around us as the woman with electric blue eyeshadow dug her nails into Slinky's arm.

Slinky knocked her hand off him. "Ow! What is this?!"

"Let's go find real gentlemen," she said to her friends, shaking her head as they flitted away like a charm of hummingbirds.

Jeremy shook his head. "Slink, you really don't know this chick?"

Slinky scowled at me. "No, but she's sure as hell on some messed-up drugs."

By the time I'd fully comprehended what I'd done, I was hearing familiar laughter. I watched their concern dissolve as Ruby finally emerged from her hiding spot.

"*Damn it!* Shoulda known you were behind this." Slinky stabbed his finger at her.

"I had to think of some fun way for you to meet the newest member of the band!"

Jeremy chuckled and ran a hand through his shaggy faux-hawk.

"So you're Kyla," he said, smooth as a radio deejay. "Nice."

"Yeah," I said sheepishly. "Nice to meet you guys."

"Wish we could say the same," Slinky mumbled.

"Oh, don't be sore." Ruby gave him a shove and he recoiled. She seemed strong for someone so petite.

"*I* thought it was funny," Jeremy said. "Dude, did you see how fast those chicks dropped us? Worse than that time I almost fainted at Red Light Lounge."

Slinky cracked a stubborn smile and I felt relief. Maybe he wouldn't hate me forever. "Not funny," he said grudgingly. "That was messed up. They think I'm a psycho now."

"Oh, *so* sorry, your hotshot-ness," Ruby said, frost in her words. "I thought you had a sense of humor. Who cares about the model-of-the-month club?"

Jeremy looked at me in admiration. "Well, I'm glad Kyla's got some balls."

I stood there smiling blankly like the pawn that I was. His first impression of me had been Ruby's creation. Everything from my wardrobe to actions, even down to the lines I spoke. The usual Kyla wouldn't have caught his eye, let alone had "the balls" to impress anyone. I almost felt bad for going along with Ruby's plan and starting us off on such an artificial note.

"Who needs a drink?" Ruby asked, attempting to soften things back up.

Jeremy and Slinky simultaneously held up empty glasses. I nodded in eager agreement.

"Why don't you and Kyla go get them," Ruby said to Slinky.

We all knew what she was trying to do. I held my breath, preparing for the sting of his rejection, but Slinky just shrugged and headed inside.

Slinky moved with the balanced, ready-for-anything ease of a skater. He had a way of running his hand over his buzzed head like he was self-conscious, but I caught him checking himself out in every single reflective surface we passed. He wore excessively baggy jeans and a black T-shirt that clung to his wiry frame. His eyes were as intense as the magazine photos depicted, complete with long, thick lashes that only a few guys seemed to be gifted with.

Slinky didn't say anything to me. I stayed close by his side like some kind of awkward appendage and took the drinks he gave me to carry. We paused in the kitchen so he could grab a couple of mini-burgers off a platter and pop them both in his mouth at the same time. I really wanted to eat snacks too, but definitely not in front of all these people. Besides, both my hands were full. He scanned the party while he chewed and I stood there feeling mortifyingly wrong by his side, my stomach growling at being so close to what it wanted, but still denied.

He wiped his mouth after a gigantic swallow. "How 'bout this place?"

"Totally rad," I said lamely. He didn't respond and I was so hungry I turned my mute button off and babbled on, hoping to distract myself. "I really love the—"

"Place is a shit show," he interrupted, gawking at me as if I had said something crazy. I froze. Then he snorted, "C'mon."

Back out by the pool, Ruby and Jeremy were talking to two older men puffing on cigars. Ruby sniffed the drink I gave her and made a face. "Whiskey," she said, and I knew to never give her whiskey again.

"Slinky ordered it," I said quickly. I had no loyalty to him.

"Of course he did," she snapped, putting her drink down. "He's into petty revenge."

She smoothed her halter and recomposed herself in an instant.

"Kyla, this is Eli and Mark from Source Records," Ruby said. The balding man named Eli moved next to me. His thin, pale lips were stuck in a pucker like he'd had too many margaritas.

"So, Kyla, what do you play?" he asked, breath peppered with cigar.

"Keyboards," I said hesitantly. I took a huge sip of my drink. My throat started to burn and my eyes watered. I struggled not to cough.

"Let me see your hands." It was more of an order than a request as Eli seized my left hand. His skin felt strange and papery on mine. I struggled not to shudder. He stretched my fingers out and studied them as I took another big sip of my drink with my free hand, relishing the burn this time. It overpowered the weirdness of an old man stroking my hand. Ruby was watching me closely so I fought the impulse to reclaim my hand. I felt like a horse being appraised, wanted to tell them all to buck off.

The party was shaping up to be one awful scene after another. I knew I had better get used to it if I wanted my future to last. Ruby's eyes affirmed my thoughts. I took a deep breath and managed a small smile as Eli looked at me with a sunken stare.

"I can tell you must be good. These are very artistic fingers."

Ew. What was there to say to that terrible line but, "Really?"

"Yes. I've seen a lot of hands, trust me. I can also tell you haven't been in LA very long."

"How?"

"Your nails aren't manicured."

"Oh," I said, annoyed enough to retract my hand.

"That and you seem scared out of your mind." He laughed and the rest of them joined. I was appalled but tried to conjure a smile instead of crumble and fall through the cracks in the patio.

My head was reeling from all the whiskey and awkward interaction. I looked to Ruby, hoping she'd help me out with some more direction, but she was already walking away with the other Source guy. As they disappeared into a swarm of people in the kitchen, I felt a hand on my arm.

"Don't worry, I'll take care of you until she's back," Eli said lasciviously.

It took all the control I had not to shiver as I realized we were being "left alone." I couldn't take much more of this 70-something-year-old record executive hitting on me. My drink was almost gone. And probably no amount of alcohol would make me feel okay if he touched me again.

Jeremy glanced over and I shot him a look that said *please help me.* He was my last chance at getting out of this without burning bridges I never knew I'd be standing on, especially so soon. Amusement flickered through his expression and to my great relief, he wound his way over to us.

"You and Eli getting acquainted?"

"Yes, I'm unabashedly hitting on your cool new band member," Eli said with a cackle that made me cringe deep inside.

Jeremy's laugh was a short, explosive burst of sound. "Yeah, she seems cool now," he said. "We'll see how she holds up when we get into rehearsals."

"Indeed," Eli said, as if he knew exactly what Jeremy was talking about.

I shot Jeremy a confused look but he was busy sharing a knowing one with Eli. Then they looked over in Ruby's direction. It seemed like a warning that Ruby was difficult and hard to please. A warning that if I didn't do well in rehearsal, Ruby might even drop me. I had no idea how she operated at the "workplace." My father's warnings floated back to me as I drained the rest of my drink.

"Drinking harder tonight, are we?" I heard a familiar voice say. Relief rippled through me as I turned to see Robert standing poolside, vodka soda in hand. Compared to Eli, Robert was a saint.

"Hi!" I surprised both of us by flinging my arms around him. He seemed pleased at my enthusiastic greeting.

"Well, well," he said approvingly. "Looks like I'm already behind."

As Eli and Jeremy exchanged hellos with Robert, I tuned them out, searching the crowd for Ruby's purple pigtails. I had to get back to the one person I felt safe standing next to, or I was definitely going to get myself into trouble.

"My date seems to have disappeared," I heard Robert say, and refocused my attention on the men around me.

"Powdering her nose?" Jeremy smirked.

"She better not be, not without me," Robert said.

"I have to find the bathroom," I said, anxious for a reason to get away. "What does she look like? I'll tell her you're looking for her."

Jeremy, Robert and Eli laughed and exchanged glances.

"Don't worry about her," Robert said. "She'll be back around soon enough. But grab me another drink on the way back out, will you?"

I nodded and headed back into the house. The party seemed to have doubled in size. A guy in a suit was pulling trays of red Jell-O shots out of the fridge. He saw me watching and handed me a large cube. I thanked him and sucked it down, enjoying the tingle.

When I finally made it to the black marble bathroom, I stared at myself in the mirror for a while, trying to find a face that didn't scream "lonely and weird." No matter how I shifted my face, my eyes kept giving me away.

But how do you change what your eyes contain?

The only answer that came to mind was *more alcohol.*

Back at the bar, women with way more sex appeal than me laughed and flirted with the bartender, rendering me nonexistent. A bottle of vodka was just within reach. I contemplated swiping it, but I hesitated.

"Take it," a voice said as if inside my head.

"No," I replied automatically, turning around. A guy with long, curly hair and very curly eyelashes was daring me. His playfulness was refreshing—like a burst of oxygen after walking around in outer space for the last hour. I liked him immediately.

"No?" He raised his eyebrows. "C'mon . . ."

"No way," I said, smiling reflexively.

"Then allow me." He reached over the bar and grabbed the bottle. The bartender turned right in time to see him set the bottle down in front of me. My limbs turned to jelly. But then, to my surprise, the bartender turned back around like he hadn't seen a thing. Curly hair winked at me, then grabbed a few cups off the stack and scooped some ice into a champagne bucket.

"Impressed?" he asked.

I nodded, back on the mute button.

"Good. Now come join me for a drink in the cabana."

I hesitated. I didn't want to be running off with another stranger. Excuses churned in my head, and my face gave away my concern.

"Of course," he said, hitting his head in mock frustration. "Where are my manners? I got so caught up in the mystery of your shimmering aura that I forgot to introduce myself. I'm Anthony. You are . . . ?"

"Ian Somer's son?"

He burst out laughing. "I never knew I had a brother."

I rolled my eyes. "I'm Kyla."

"Kyla. I like that name, it's different," he said. "C'mon, Kyla, follow me."

I was starved for a friend. His use of my name and overall charm were appealing. Plus he knew almost everyone at the party, which made me trust him more, but also made getting outside a very slow process. He gave people real hugs, and women and men noticeably perked up under his gaze. There was something about him. . . . I started to think his sweater had superpowers. It was thin and gray and looked snuggly soft. He was an attentive lead, never losing me through thick parts of the crowd even though I was a timid follower. As he led me outside, he said, "You need to learn to be more assertive."

I didn't know what to say, but squeaked out "Okay," which made him laugh as though I'd said something hilarious.

The cabana was empty as if it were waiting for us. Anthony gestured at a pile of floor pillows surrounded by candles glowing on tall candlestick holders. I sat down on a cushion and tucked my legs to the side, trying to act casual.

"So, Kyla. You're a musician," Anthony began.

That freaked me out a little. "What, you're psychic?"

"Your earrings kind of give you away."

"Right." My hands went up to the dangling music notes on my ears. I hoped he couldn't see me blush.

Despite his elite status, Anthony seemed nicer than anyone else at this crazy party. As he poured us drinks, I hoped—I *prayed*—his intentions were not what they usually ended up being when guys were singularly nice to me.

"Who did you come here with?"

"Ruby Sky."

He looked questioningly at me. "Friends?"

"Not exactly. Well, I guess we are," I stumbled, "but she asked me to join Glitter Tears for their next tour, so that's why I'm here. In LA, I mean. But, I guess the party, too." It was the most anyone had let me talk in a while and my tongue was tripping over itself.

"How old are you? If you don't mind me asking. . . ."

This tired topic again. "Eighteen."

"Seriously?"

"Uh, yeah . . . Why is that a big deal?"

He grinned. "It's not a small deal."

I took a sip from the glass he offered me, hoping the topic would blow over. The drink was strong, but I was beginning to appreciate strong drinks. They really did take the edge off. I felt more relaxed than I could remember ever feeling one-on-one with a guy I didn't know. I'd thought for a long while I was going to be permanently turned off to guys, but there was maybe something about this curly-headed charmer. I wasn't crawling away from him in my mind, anyway. I was actually pretty cozy.

"How old are *you*?" I asked, feeling bolder.

He laughed it off. "You're getting more assertive already."

He rubbed my thigh, sending invisible fingers tapping up and down my spine. I didn't hate it, but I wasn't sure about it, so I shivered and took another sip of my drink.

"Cold?"

"No," I said. "Well, maybe a little. I thought LA was supposed to be hot all the time."

He laughed. "It's the desert by the sea. Dry heat days and crisp, cool nights. Let's warm you up, though." He pulled off his sweater and handed it to me. I stared at his tan, toned arms, his hairless nipples, his sculptured abs. I didn't know a man's body could be . . . sensual. They'd been different degrees of ugly and unappealing to me before. I couldn't stop staring.

"It keeps you warmer if you wear it," he teased. I shook my head and pulled the sweater over my head. The fabric was even softer than I'd imagined. "There. You look warmer."

"I am. Thanks."

Anthony laughed and slid closer, putting a bare arm around my shoulders, giving me a squeeze and a wisp of his body odor, which was cinnamon-y and spicy. The premonition of him making some sort of move fluttered up inside me. He leaned closer and I felt the heat of his breath flash across my neck. Paralyzed, mesmerized—whatever he was doing, I didn't move away. He started kissing and gently biting my neck and earlobe, whispering into my ear how sweet I smelled and tasted. His cheeks and lips were so soft. I closed my eyes and felt parts of my body stir with a strange new mix of pleasure and panic.

A very wry voice broke us up. "Aren't you two a sight for drunk eyes."

Anthony pulled away and I opened my eyes to see Ian and Ruby standing in front of us.

"Typical. Just typical. Wonderballs meets new girl in town, twenty minutes later he's half naked and she's letting him nibble her neck." Ian shook his head. "I thought I warned you to keep her away from him," he said to Ruby, following with an abrasive burst of laughter.

Ruby fixed a cold stare on me. I felt silly and caught and tried to shoot her a "Whoopsie, what am I doing?" smile, but it came out a mangled choke-face.

"What's all this about?" Anthony asked haughtily.

Ruby shifted her gaze. Her smile was a warning. "You know, Anthony, not to give you pointers or anything, but the next time you want to seal a deal you might want to choose a more private spot."

"I don't appreciate that insinuation." Anthony stood up. "We're hanging out, having a nice time of it, and you two show up and start scolding us like we're two thirteen-year-olds about to pop each other's cherries."

I scrambled to stand up, confused and ashamed. The ground wasn't so steady under my feet. Ruby's stare was really unraveling me. Was she jealous? Had he put something in my drink to make me like him? Was this a normal reaction to drinking on a totally empty stomach? Or was I just not used to any of this, any little part?

"C'mon, Kyla," Ruby ordered. "Robert's occupied for the evening so I'm taking you home now. I'm tired."

I nodded and started to take off the sweater.

"Keep it, beautiful," Anthony said to me. He gave me another touch on the arm that sent flurries through my insides. "Stay warm, all right?"

Ruby shook her head and marched toward the house.

"Thanks," I said to him, wishing that he'd asked for my number as I trailed after Ruby.

Back in the Ladybug, we drove in silence. Ruby didn't even play any music.

"Did I do something wrong?" I finally got enough courage to ask when we pulled into Robert's driveway. By that point I'd decided it was better to be chastised than ignored.

She just waved coldly at me, and backed out of the driveway as soon as I got out.

Well, this is it, I thought. Another attempt to abandon my own skin resulting in failure. No matter what, I couldn't figure out the right moves with these people. Every day was a ticking countdown on the inevitable bomb of my attempt to "make it" in LA. Robert's words floated back to me as I let myself into his empty ghost town mansion. *Damned if you do and damned if you don't.* If that was the way it was, then I would rather be damned if I do. And that at least gave me the bravery to walk through the giant, dark house alone, eventually crawling into the bed still wearing Anthony's sweater. The confusion I felt in so many places and ways finally broke me down and thundered out.

I sobbed myself to sleep.

DRESS TO KILL

EVEN WHEN I WAS ASLEEP, I couldn't relax. I awoke the next day from feverish dreams to the rustling of the intercom. My stomach growled, a response I had to agree with.

Robert's voice crackled through the speaker by the light switch, "Anyone alive in there?" I let out a low moan. My mouth tasted sour and my head was heavy. "If you can make it downstairs, I have something for you."

A surprise from Robert? That got me moving. Downstairs was brighter than normal. Had there always been no curtains? I squinted as I entered the kitchen, feeling dizzy, and held myself up with the counter. Eduardo was standing on the island, pecking at dry cereal scattered over the swirly marble surface. The patio door was open and Robert walked over, shirtless and glowing from sun intake. His ribcage was alarmingly pronounced and apparently he shaved his chest. He wiped his brow and poured two cups of coffee, dropped a few ice cubes in, and yawned.

"Your girlfriend called. She's running a little late for your big shopping spree," he said as he handed me a cup. I glanced at the clock: twelve-thirty. Took a sip of coffee. Bitter. Not good. Robert was watching me. He took a box out of the cabinet and slid it across the island. Sugar. I dumped some in, spilling a bit.

"Sorry. Don't feel well," I mumbled.

"I suspected as much, and have just the thing to fix that." He walked over to the liquor cabinet and pulled out a bottle of vodka. I groaned. Robert grabbed a jar from the fridge and poured some murky red mixture in with the vodka. I squinted but the jar wasn't marked. "The Robert Jeffs hangover cure. Fixes you right up. You'll be drinking again in a few hours."

He set the glass down in front of me and I stared at it suspiciously.

"What is it?"

"Don't think. Drink."

I stared at him. What kind of a catch phrase was that? He was the strangest example of a "role model" ever known. But he was also my only guide through the rocky territory of the LA music scene. And I felt so awful I'd try anything.

"Do it."

I raised the glass up to my nose and took a whiff. It smelled like hot sauce and vinegar. *Gross.*

"All at once," he said. "Straight down the hatch. Who's the pro, here?"

I pitched the mystery mixture back, gagging at the salty, sour taste as my throat fought it down. The stuff was something nasty. The bathroom was right around the corner, and I briefly considered running to it.

"Give it a minute."

I sat at the island counter, gloomy and grimacing, and took a sip of coffee to kill the taste. More bitterness, then a blissful lump of sugar hit my taste buds. Sweet relief. I poured a little out straight from the box into my hand and licked it up.

Robert nodded at me. "This is progress."

He sat down at the table and lit a cigarette, putting his feet up on a chair. His stomach skin gathered into the tiniest rolls. It was hard not to stare.

"You're not having any?" I croaked out.

"I can handle my substances," he said. "It's non-actions I'm no good at. You know. Not drinking. Not smoking. Not sleeping around."

Robert paused to take a drag and I continued to study him, wondering exactly how much he had lived through, as he stared out the window and seemed to consider the years. I got the feeling that—like me—Robert lived in the past. It made me feel sad for him—he had so much past to regret.

"They say that most people who move to LA end up alcoholics and addicts," continued my teacher of all things non-scholastic. "I remember how hard I tried to be the exception to that cliché, but there are clichés everywhere you turn, here. They catch you before you even know what you're running from. I've dodged as many as I can, but screw me if it isn't damn near impossible. It's like the smog, there's no escape, it's everywhere . . ."

His thoughts spun out fast. As he spoke, he held a lighter under his hand, flicking it and moving his fingers back and forth over the flame. The air filled with the sickly smell of burning hair. I wondered how long I should sit there and let him burn himself. But was it my place to tell a man forty years older than me to stop playing with fire? "Real leather doesn't burn," he said.

Thankfully, chaos interrupted. "Afternoon, you crazy cats!" Ruby called from the hallway, her sing-song voice injecting relief straight into my body. Robert put the lighter down and made a fist with his hand. As if casting a spell, everything tornadoed on cue: Ruby danced into the room, a bright and vibrant whip of energy. I jerked up and spilled coffee all over the counter. Eduardo spread his big gray wings and cried, "Mayhem! Mayday! Murder!" as he flapped off through the open patio doors.

But Robert sat eerily stone-calm through it all.

Ruby grabbed a towel off the counter to help with the spilled coffee. She looked at it, wrinkled her face, and dropped it. "Gross!"

"What do you expect? This is a bachelor's pad," Robert said.

"I mean, *gross!*" Ruby said. "C'mon, Kyla. We're out of here!"

Thankful for the sudden exit, I rushed out after Ruby and jumped into the Ladybug without hesitation. She seemed to be back to the Ruby who loved me, not the shut-down ice queen who had dropped me off last night, and I was more than happy to roll with that. Her bright purple locks whipped around her face as we cruised down the steep, narrow street covered in a canopy of eucalyptus. I clutched the sides of my pink fuzzy seat and breathed deeply, trying to relax.

"*So* ridiculous he doesn't have a housekeeper," she said, turning toward me. I couldn't see her eyes behind her giant heart-shaped sunglasses. "He's not clean, I'm warning you—if you haven't noticed already."

Ruby made a daring left turn and some slick-o in a Corvette honked at us. She gave him a wave and smiled. He shook his head as he sped away. "Kill 'em with kindness," she said. "A cliché for a reason. Nobody gives a friendly girl much crap."

"Robert was just talking about clichés," I mumbled, closing my eyes as she took a steep turn down a side street, almost taking out a jogger in the process. "He seems really depressed."

"Oh, I know. He has such a complex about that," she said emphatically. "I think it's being alone that's making him so down on himself."

"Ruby? What really happened with his ex-wife?"

She sighed. "It's been three years and he still can't move on. I'm worried about him. He keeps losing weight, too. I beg him to keep some food around, but he refuses to go grocery shopping. I don't think he's gone once since she left. He's really sensitive even though he acts tough. I'm sure you've noticed. Maybe starving himself is his weak attempt at being suicidal. Robert may be a master in the studio, but he's a total baby when it comes to women."

This didn't add up. He seemed to have plenty of charisma. "What do you mean?"

Ruby turned onto the busy street crowded with shops and cafes. "He has no problem getting chicks, but he gives them way too much power once he's involved. You know. He's a Pisces. He's never content by himself. He always needs someone around to devote himself to."

"Really? He doesn't talk about his ex like he liked her that much."

Ruby pulled past a vacant parking space and started backing into it.

"Please. He absolutely lived for her."

"Who is she, again?"

"I thought you knew. Linda Crosby. The model in all those Yodi Yo ads."

"With the marsupials?"

"Yeah, the totally weird animal lingerie ads. That's her."

"Wow."

"He wasn't happy when he was with her, either." She backed the Ladybug up to the curb and put it into park in front of a tattoo parlor, taking her lipstick out and redoing her perfect, vampire purple lips in the rearview mirror. "She treated him like crap, demanded all these treatments and vacations, and he kept giving her what she wanted. She became his purpose in life. It was kind of disgusting to witness. I have no idea how much she helped business, but he was doing better than ever in the studio at the time, so at least he didn't go bankrupt. He was convinced that she was his ultimate muse, responsible for the success he'd worked so hard his whole life for. All they'd do was hang out with her crazy young friends and do blow." She glanced at her sprinkle donut watch. "Crap! C'mon, we gotta go meet Lex. We're running *really* late."

We got out of the car, but I wasn't at all done with the subject.

"So what happened? C'mon!"

She took my arm and squeezed it.

"Look, don't bring up this stuff, obviously. He gets really upset talking about it, so I figure it's better if I tell you so you don't ask him or something."

"I swear, I won't bring it up."

She tugged me across the street. "So anyways, he was hanging on despite being almost 30 years older than her. And—oh, did I forget to mention she was 19 when they started dating? Ha. Yeah. So anyways, some Swedish model named Alfonso moved to LA for pilot season, and the next thing you know, Linda left Robert after only being married for six months. Keep the pace up, buttercup!"

I was dragging. The story was worse than I expected, plus I still didn't feel tip top—though I admittedly felt better after managing to keep the terrible hangover drink down. Ruby seemed amused by my reaction. "Oh, come on, it's the same story, it happens all the time. Anyone could see it coming. . . . Well, anyone but Robert, apparently. But the week she left, he had a really bad episode and hasn't been the same since. He's been getting worse, lately."

"What do you mean?"

"Oh, there he is!" Ruby squealed, taking my hand and pulling me toward a very pastel café. An impeccable guy wearing designer jeans and a baby blue Polo shirt sat outside with three paper cups on the table next to him. He had beautiful features that looked painted on from a distance. Dark, full lips. Lashes so thick it looked like he wore eyeliner. *Was* he wearing eyeliner? It was so hard to tell with LA guys.

"Lex, my darling summer moonlight," Ruby squealed.

"The radiant Miss Ruby," he said, smiling. They embraced as I stood there, staring at the shape and color of his amazing heart-shaped lips. "Always so good to see you!"

He turned to me. "Hi, Kyla! I've heard *so* much about you. I'm Lex." He offered me his hand and we shook. "Oh, she's going to be *fun*," he said, looking me up and down.

"A real fixer-upper," I said dryly, which surprised everyone, but I was tired of being the poor little suburban girl referred to in the third person. Plus, the day's start had me on thin ice. But thankfully they laughed.

"Funny, too," Lex said. "Love that biting East Coast sarcasm." He handed us both a cup of coffee, which I was learning how to appreciate more with each cup. I took a sip.

It was the best thing I'd ever tasted, hands down. Some kind of half cocoa half coffee creation. Pure magic.

"What is this?!"

Lex winked at me. "A mocha, baby. This place makes the best. So, first thing we have to do is buy you an outfit to go shopping in."

I laughed. They didn't. "Seriously?"

"Yes. We need a good base outfit to show the salespeople, so they can use that as a springboard to show you things in your style. And so they don't treat you like you don't belong there. These people can be really snobby, trust me."

We headed into a cool-looking shop called *Scream* on the corner of the street. Club music boomed from speakers. Mannequins proudly posed on tables in trendy outfits. The salespeople were all wearing headsets which made them seem like they were producing a fashion show.

"But I thought *you* were picking my outfits," I said, suddenly afraid.

He laughed. "Isn't she adorable? I don't have access to what these stores keep in their back rooms for the big shots. Depending on how well you're dressed, they'll pull out the gems for you. If you look like you don't care about fashion, they'll ignore you unless forced otherwise."

As if to further prove his point, the saleslady headed straight past me over to Ruby and asked if she needed help.

Lex turned around. "Does it look like *she* needs help?"

Seven stores and hundreds of dollars on the band credit cards later, we were sitting out on the patio of a Mexican restaurant for happy hour with Stardust. I was utterly exhausted and starving, but it seemed I was alone in that. Nobody even looked at their menus. I gnawed on a few corn chips to take the edge off. Ruby and Stardust both ordered big lime green frozen margaritas that came with little umbrellas in them. Lex was drinking a beer and talking about some actress he'd slept with the night before, which was confusing. I'd assumed he was gay, judging by his totally platonic vibe whenever he poked his head into my dressing room. Now he was swigging beer and going on about the complicated bra this girl was wearing. Maybe he was "off duty" now. Maybe he could see through me. Or maybe he was still hiding parts of himself in the straight life smoke and mirrors.

I looked down at my new "shopping" outfit. The black jeans were tight, so tight that some of my belly hung over the top, which made me suck in constantly. They did make my butt look better than ever, though, I had to admit. My top was sleeveless, a shimmery black V neck cut long, blissfully hiding the fact that the jeans were barely buttoned. And the thigh-high boots were practically glowing. I wasn't hating the new look. It transported me from myself. It let me hide better.

Ruby passed me her margarita.

"Have a sip!"

I took my second sip of alcohol before the sun went down that day.

"You know who was interested in this young pop tart last night?"

My stomach flipped as I braced myself for her to bring up Anthony and last night's events that had mysteriously turned Ruby cold at the party. I had hoped she'd let it go since she'd been nice to me all day as if nothing had ever happened.

"Who?" Lex asked.

"Eli Goodman," Ruby said.

"Isn't he, like, seventy?" Lex asked, crinkling up his nose. I was grateful someone else was as disgusted by it as I was.

"Well, it certainly doesn't hurt business," Ruby said.

"He was so creepy," I said. "He wouldn't let go of my hand."

Stardust passed her drink to me. "What did you do?"

I looked down. "Nothing."

"Smart girl," Ruby said. "He could very well be producing our next album. He's already told Kevin he's interested. Which is why," she paused and we stared at her, waiting. "Igavehimyournumber," she let out fast in one breath.

I waited for her to acknowledge she was kidding. She avoided my stare.

"Really?"

"Yes, Kyla," she snapped. "And to be honest, he probably won't call, but if he does, you'll probably accompany him somewhere and be a pleasant date. It's no big deal."

"But . . . He's older than my *father*," I said.

"Get used to it," Lex said, rolling his eyes. "Old men know no limits here."

"He probably exclusively dates teenagers," Stardust said. "You can't tell us this is news to you, that older guys date younger."

I sat back and thought for a moment, still somewhat in shock. "Back east they flirt a little, but I don't think any of them think they actually have a chance."

"They have more than a chance around here," Lex said. "Them and their piles of money. It's hard for a young buck like me, competing with all these sugar grandaddies."

I shut my eyes, fighting the disgusting image of Eli going in for a kiss. My eyes popped open in horror to find Ruby watching me, reading my thoughts again, and laughing.

THERE'S ALWAYS A PILL FOR YOUR PROBLEMS

"You LOOK LIKE A STRAWBERRY CUPCAKE!" Ruby exclaimed.

"That's pretty much what I feel like," I said, staring at myself in the bedroom mirror.

"Ahh, I want to eat you! Do you adore it?!" she asked, eyes wide and glitter tear sparkling in the bathroom light. She played with her hair so the shiny deep purple layers fell messily around her face. "You're my counterpart. We go together. It's perfect. Kevin's gonna be so into it!"

I grinned, though I couldn't imagine Kevin being into anything, let alone my new hairstyle: hot pink bob with bleach blond tips, curled under my chin, producing fantastic movement when I shook my head. My part was to the right side now, and my reflection felt foreign. The whole world around me was now framed in pink hair. It felt like a wig, one so pretty and awesome I would hesitate to buy it for fear of not being able to pull it off. The stylist had morphed me into someone worthy of a band, a magazine shoot, even a place onstage with touring musicians. I'd never felt less like myself in a way I liked.

"It's pretty cool," I said. "My parents would hate it."

"That's why they're three thousand miles away." Ruby tickled the back of my neck and grinned at me in the mirror, which made me realize she had not yet spoken about *her* parents. That topic felt "off limits."

Finally, I had new and appropriate clothes to wear to tonight's big magazine party. Ruby effortlessly oozed style with a bright blue sailor dress that ended high-thigh, navy and white striped leg warmers, and tall combat boots that seemed to be anchoring her small frame.

I told Ruby I could dress myself but she insisted on helping again, which I certainly didn't mind. She picked me out a short, fun party dress with thin, sparkly silver belts around the waist, one that she found during our shopping spree. It was much more feminine than anything I'd ever bought on my own, but now that I was so distant from old self, I could wear anything I wanted.

"Put it on," Ruby urged.

I started to undress. She sat on the bed and watched me.

"Are you sure this isn't too dressy?" I said.

I stood there in my underwear and bra, noting that this time, I didn't feel self-conscious—partly due to my new body, which, after just three days in Hollywood, was already tighter than it had ever been, and partly because Ruby seemed to enjoy watching me undress. At least she seemed to, and I liked her watching me undress.

"Your eyes are witch light framed by the pink hair. You're a total bombshell."

I beamed and tossed my hair a little. Ruby stood up with the dress in hand, brought it over and handed it to me.

"You're even more amazing than I thought," she said, standing close as I stepped into the dress and pulled it up over my legs. "You're such a chameleon, and that's the number one thing you need in the business, the ability to shape-shift, and *fast,* and you have it in a way I've never seen before. Look at you. Who wouldn't believe you're in Glitter Tears?"

We looked in the mirror and it was true, we belonged together; the two shimmering bottom colors of the rainbow. There was a connection forming between us that felt similar to my dreams of flying, terrifying and thrilling and absolutely intoxicating. I wanted to stay in the sky with her forever.

"When I first met you, I immediately saw your over-whelming sugar cup potential," Ruby continued, caressing my shoulder. I was practically purring as I looked into her eyes. "You were thirsty for a new life. I could see the flicker of a stifled flame. That's been me before."

I shook my head. Was she finally going to talk about her past?

Ruby shrugged as if it was irrelevant. "What I'm trying to say is that you've bloomed so much in a matter of days. I saw the way your eyes lit up back in Boston when I spoke about this life, and now you're, like, totally living it and combusting with that excitement. It feels so good to be around that kind of energy."

She moved behind me and tugged my dress in, zipping it up for me. I closed my eyes and smelled the honeysuckle vanilla scent that wafted off her. I remembered being in Boston, hugging her goodbye on a street corner in the slushy cold, unsure if I'd actually ever see her again and smell that wonderful scent of hers.

A sudden sweep of dizziness and stab of pain caused me to falter.

"Oh, I . . ."

My eyes began to cloud up and I had to take a break from standing. I crumpled onto the bed with piercing cramps so strong I could hardly breathe. Ruby sat down beside me and started to rub my back in circles.

"What's wrong, sugar muffin?"

"Don't know," I mumbled, turning over to lie on my back. My blood was doing weird things in my body, and my face felt hot. "Cramps. Tired."

"Lie back. Breathe."

I stared up at phantom blood cells exploding against the whiteness of the ceiling as I tried to breathe deep and slow. Was I going to faint? Where was I, really? Was I really in my own life? I had lost the mental map of my surroundings. Nothing was familiar. It was as if I was floating through a hazy atmosphere for the last however many days and suddenly realized there was no oxygen.

My stomach made a very loud gurgling noise.

"You're hungry."

"Maybe?"

She lay on her side next to me and ran her fingers through my hair.

"It's okay. So many changes all at once."

Her touch had some strong magic. Ruby stroked me all over until I felt the blood flow gradually even out. She rummaged through her purse, opened a bottle of pills, shook one out, and went to the bathroom. When I finally managed to sit up, she reentered the room with a glass of water, sat down beside me, and offered me a capsule, half-brown and half-blue.

"What is it?"

"It's Dexedrine. I call it 'Dream.' Little booster for the body. It's harmless. Doctors give it to practically anyone. It manages your appetite and gives you energy."

I held the pill and stared at it for a minute. Thoughts walked cautiously through my head. Wouldn't it be better to eat a little something? Could I say no? What would happen if I took it? I didn't want to faint at the party. But Ruby knew better than me, didn't she? I placed the capsule on my tongue and washed the thoughts and pill down with water.

"Good girl," Ruby said, tickling my back.

THE INDUSTRY GETS INCESTUOUS

RUBY WARNED ME THAT THIS WOULD be the first time I'd
experience one of the darker sides of being in the spotlight:
paparazzi. It was a *Cranked* party—a popular music magazine
event. Red carpet and flashing bulbs in our faces. Fans and
journalists wanting to talk to Ruby and the rest of her gang.
I'd be noticed and questioned, but she advised that most of
my answers should be as short and cryptic as possible. Ruby
didn't want me to let people know who I really was and where
I came from. She thought I wasn't ready for that kind of
exposure, yet. She told me to have fun with my answers, but
not to reveal anything personal about myself. "In this town,
casual liars always have the advantage, chickadee."

But as much as she'd prepped me, nothing—I mean, no
amount of forewarning or scenes from movies or television—
could have prepared me for the explosive whirlwind of chaos
when we stepped out of the limo together as a band for the
first time. The crowd outside of the hotel lobby was a flock of
drunken peacocks: colors, feathers and heels, fashion dares,
stares like we were naked and dreaming. The pillars of the
front entrance were lit up with electric rainbow colors. The
fountain between them sprayed rainbow-lit drops over

marble mermaids. Red carpet lined the makeshift wall decorated with *Cranked* logos that stretched from the side of the entrance to the lobby inside.

We made our way to the red carpet. Ruby went first, followed by me, Stardust, Slinky, and Jeremy. Stardust had on a strapless tight yellow dress with a gold lightning bolt across the chest and shiny green boots. The guys were wearing matching ripped-up tuxes, their rebellious uniforms for "high-brow events."

I struggled to stand tall in the heat of the lights, poised against the swelling and swarming on the other side of the rope, people pitching questions and compliments at us as we made our way slowly toward the lobby. Blinding flashes snapped in our faces. I tried as hard as I could not to look like a rabbit hovering under the shadow of an eagle. My heartbeat was scary intense. It helped to focus on Ruby's press-on smile that conveyed sexiness and confidence at the same time. When I tried to smile like that, it felt phony.

We stopped outside of the lobby and posed together in front of the biggest group of cameras. The flashes were going off like microwave popcorn and I felt woozy. I grabbed on to Ruby's wrist to stop myself from swaying and she grabbed my arm and squeezed back, smiling so brightly at me that I felt a natural smile return to my face and I could look back into the faceless mob of photographers.

"Glitter Tears!"

"You guys look smokin'!"

"Hottest band ever!"

"Slinky! You're the sexiest man alive!" a woman called out. Slinky flashed his iconic model face, rubbed his head in that self-conscious "who, me?" way, and the crowd laughed.

"How 'bout a comment on the upcoming tour?!"

"*Perpetual Twilight!*"

"Who's the new girl?" a guy called out from the side of the big cameras. It suddenly became all quiet and everything seemed to slow down.

Ruby winked at me. "Kyla's on the keys!"

"Hot pink's hot!" someone else said. Laughter broke out and I looked at the ground. For a moment it seemed to be a mean joke. Then I remembered that I was a reinvented being, maybe even "hot" by Hollywood's standards. Ruby squeezed my waist as reassurance.

"Hands off, she's mine," she sang, and kissed me right there on my lips.

The crowd cheered loudly and bulbs started to explode again. Ruby whispered very quietly, "Don't look so shocked, doll. Publicity stunt," and pulled away.

I tossed my hair and smiled shakily as we continued inside, but I was walking in quicksand. It got harder and harder to move as a quiet terror unfolded inside me. *What had just happened?* The kiss, my first female kiss, was with the one and only Ruby Sky, *and* it was captured by who knows how many paparazzi. I was blind to the room temporarily, hoping I'd make it through the doorway on my own. I held my head in my hands and pressed my fingers to my eyes for a moment, seeing only tiny black explosions.

"Yo," Stardust said quietly, pulling me aside. Apparently, she caught my discomfort. "Don't worry about it. I know it seems like a big deal now, but everyone forgets everything pretty fast around here."

I stared at her honest eyes, her shimmery gold eyeshadow. Did she really know?

We pushed into the ballroom. People were milling around tables set with red and black tablecloths, the same colors as the *Cranked* logo. I looked up and there were over fifty crystal chandeliers hanging from the incredibly high ceiling. Did such a room even exist in the entire state of Massachusetts? There was a band setting up on a stage at the front. I narrowed my eyes to see. They were fussing with their cords and doing mic checks. Was that..?

No, it couldn't be. Ruby hadn't said anything.

I grabbed Stardust.

"Is that Eyes Wander setting up?"

She looked at the stage.

"Oh, yeah. It totally is."

We moved through the crowd as fast as we could. People checked me out as I brushed past. It was a totally new experience for me to be "eye-catching." My heart beat strong inside my chest, fueled by the intense looks of strangers. I was annoyed by how good it felt to be admired.

As we edged closer, I could see Ruby talking to someone who was bending down onstage. Brian. I felt a surge of something strong grip my chest.

He caught sight of us and waved.

"Hey, Stardust."

"Hi, Brian. Didn't know you guys were playing."

"Yeah, neither did we until a few hours ago. Who's your friend?"

I swallowed. Did I really look that different?

Ruby turned around as Brian's eyes fell on me. She smiled.

"Don't you even recognize your own discovery?"

I gave him a little wave and his face shifted as he realized who I was.

"Oh my *god*. Kyla!"

Brian staggered back a little, pretending that I'd struck him. We laughed. He got down from the stage and walked over to give me a hug that somehow felt like home. When he pulled away we looked at each other and I tried to stop clenching my jaw so tightly. Why was I so nervous?

Ruby bumped hips with me and then threw an arm around Brian's waist.

"Impressive, isn't she?"

"Incredible. How long have you been in town for—a few days?"

"We work fast." Ruby answered for me, letting out her Tinkerbell laugh.

He stepped back and looked me up and down. It didn't feel creepy like it did with other guys. Just complimentary. "Sure do. You ladies are a perfect trio, now."

"Hey! Troop Rainbow Brite! Over here!"

Calvin had caught sight of us, yelling from the edge of the stage. We waved at him and Tommy. Maybe it was kind of over-the-top, the outrageous combination of bright colors between us. I still felt self-conscious about the pink hair.

Brian glanced at Ruby, who was looking at him in a way that made my guts go through a meat grinder. He put his arm around her and squeezed. "Here we are, surrounded by you gorgeous girls. Where are the Glitter Tears guys, anyway? Jeremy owes me. He lost a bet, big time."

"They ran off to the courtyard as soon as we walked in," Ruby said. "We're gonna go find them!"

But drinks first, thankfully. We grabbed bright blue martinis before making our way out to the patio courtyard. The sweet liquid calmed me, along with the palm fronds hanging low, roses and jasmine blooming from the side gates. People were gathered around wrought iron tables lit by lanterns with candles. Cigarette and weed smoke tangled through the fragrant spring air. Ruby was headed toward a group in the corner when I stopped. She noticed and turned back to me.

"You okay, sweet tart?"

"My teeth are clenching. It's weird. I feel weird talking to people like this."

She nodded. "The Dream does that at first. It'll even out soon. Have some of your drink. Never underestimate the power of a blue drink. And, here . . ." She walked over to a guy smoking by himself at a table in the corner. She said something to him and I saw him hand her a couple of cigarettes. Ruby came back over, handed me one and grabbed a candle off the nearest table.

"These help a lot."

I didn't really think about it. I was caught off-guard by Ruby being the person handing me one, not Robert. I didn't even know she smoked, but here we were, now was as good a time as any to try. I put it in my mouth and she held the flame up to the end.

"You have to suck in to light it, silly."

Doing this, I immediately coughed. She lit her own, put the lantern back on the table, and studied me.

"Don't tell me this is your first cigarette."

I hung my head like I was admitting I still wet the bed.

"Holy crap, and you're living with Robert. I'm shocked he hasn't given you a habit to match his yet."

My mouth tasted of burnt chemicals. It wasn't quite what I'd expected, but it did give me something to do with myself besides drink too fast. I took another sip of my drink and watched her smoke, trying to mimic her movements. It was really hard for me to keep from coughing, though. I had to take baby puffs and barely inhale.

"So these are supposed to make it better?"

"Sure. Gives you something to do with your mouth and the movements relax your jaw. Here, let me teach you how to inhale."

Soon after, she left me smoking at a table partially hidden by palm fronds to say hi to her friends. She'd tried to bring me along, but I had no interest in meeting people at the moment and the drug had given me enough confidence to finally turn down an invite. My skin felt too tight, my muscles too tense. My brain was racing and something felt very wrong about the night. I was familiar with anxiety on many levels, but this was a new plane. She was right about one thing: I certainly wasn't hungry anymore. Just restless and lonely in a place full of people too exciting for me.

I couldn't believe she'd kissed me like that after calling me "hers" in front of the world. What would people think? That I was Ruby's new pet? That I was some little lovestruck lesbian that had gotten into the band for a romance with Ruby, not my actual talent? Thoughts whirred and I felt more and more trapped in a corner. How would my parents react? How would Jenny react?

Jenny.

I had tried to convince Jenny to practice kissing with me once when we were much younger. She had been totally grossed out by the idea. The crinkle of her nose had never been so insulting. Was she going to think I had been harboring a secret crush on her the whole time we'd been friends, now? *Had* I been harboring a secret crush on her the whole time we'd been friends? I didn't think so, but I was so confused at the moment that I wasn't sure. The Ruby kiss happened and no one talked about it afterward, but I felt pretty stunned by the sudden exposure of what had previously been my most well-kept secret. Or had I only been fooling myself? Could Ruby have seen through me the whole time? Could everyone? Was I totally and hopelessly transparent?

I wrenched up and away from the smoke-filled patio, pledging to see Eyes Wander's set and then somehow get home before I made a bigger fool of myself. There was a lot to be figured out. It really pissed me off, Ruby throwing me into the headlights like that. But I knew I wouldn't stay mad at her long.

In truth, I already missed her by my side.

Apparently, Ruby didn't feel the same way. She seemed happy to chat with her friends on the patio for a long time. Stardust, my savior of the night, took me around to meet people inside. I smiled too widely and ground my teeth, which prompted her to finally take me over to the snacks table and give me a few celery sticks to gnaw on. That made me feel a little better until it happened: I saw Ruby giving Brian a pre-set kiss to the side of the stage. A kiss with the same lips I'd just had on mine. But theirs wasn't a light, fluffy kiss like the staged red-carpet peck—it was a real kiss that made them seem hungry for each other. A darkness gnashed up within me so alarmingly I immediately rushed back to the patio to find another cigarette.

NEVER FALL (ALL THE WAY) IN LOVE

"So Ruby disappeared."

Robert and I were having a "nightcap." In truth, I didn't need another drink. I'd had three drinks and the "Dream" pill still hadn't worn off. My mind was wide awake but my body felt beyond exhausted. Robert was wide awake as well, and a strong honesty seemed to be coursing through both of us. I felt strangely close to Robert, sitting with him late at night on his patio. It felt like the end of the world, us two sitting up above Hollywood, talking it out over the city lights below, a silent symphony of twinkles. It made me want to write a song. Robert's eyes approved as he lit the cigarette dangling out of my mouth. I inhaled and managed not to cough. Progress, I guess.

Robert lit his own smoke and kicked his feet up on a chair, finally getting around to the subject I had been dying to bring up. "Yeah . . . She and Brian are magnets. Can't stay away from each other."

"I noticed."

"Jealous?"

I frowned and he let out a dry laugh. "That's a 'yes.'"

Sighing, I flicked my cigarette. I was starting to realize that most people probably smoked for the action of it.

Certainly not for the taste. "I don't see why I would be. It's just a weird feeling. Uncomfortable."

"Well, she's your everything right now."

I shifted uncomfortably.

"Well? Isn't she?"

How had he pegged me so quickly? My fears about being more transparent than I thought were confirmed. I was speechless. To deny my planet-sized crush on Ruby seemed pointless at this point, but I wasn't ready to expose my inner feelings, either. Or maybe—maybe I was. Maybe it would feel great, freeing myself from this anxious cage that I'd felt trapped in all night—all *life*, really. On the verge of breaking out, I struggled for an appropriate opener to share with Robert.

Robert ran his hand through his hair. He looked stoic in the shadowy light of the full moon filtering down onto us. "Kid, are you that much in denial? You should see the way you look at her. I'm surprised she puts up with it."

"What do you mean?" I was shivering as though suddenly naked.

"Let me spare you a lot of trouble, Trixie. Never fall all the way in love. And *definitely* don't go falling for any of these people."

"I don't understand. '*These people*'?"

He took a long drag and let the smoke out slowly.

"You don't want to date actors, and you don't want to date musicians."

"Why not?"

"Entirely too scattered and egotistical. Reflect for a moment. Musicians have the god complex. They think they're divine beings. They need to be everywhere, and they need everybody to be in love with them. Trust me. You don't want to be involved with anyone like that."

"But . . . *I'm* a musician."

"Yes. You're an aspiring musician, and you're different *now*, but who knows how date-able you'll be once you get some time in the spotlight. Trust me, babe. I've seen enough people go through the fame flip and end up upside-down and inside-out. You don't even want to know what I'm talking about. Take my word for it and date people on the other side of the cameras. You'll thank me later."

He sipped his drink and tapped his fingers against the lawn chair.

"I don't get it," I said. "I thought you were all about musicians."

"Well, yeah, that's why I know what I'm talking about. I've been involved with more musicians than anyone," he continued. "For decades, I was basically a musical pimp. All the little singer-songwriters were falling all over me, letting me control them like puppets. Why wouldn't they? I knew how to make them as glorified and glamorous as they saw themselves. But what I didn't have was willpower. Absolutely no willpower at all. And when you don't have willpower, things don't last. When I was in the eye of the tornado and all the beautiful young bombshells wanted me . . . Who can say no? What on earth could make anyone say no to that? It feels like the reward for all the years of struggle and hard work—that force that makes everyone want a taste of you."

His speech, combined with the cigarette, was making me dizzy. We had started out talking about my current situation and suddenly we were deep into his past. I was surprised at how outwardly observant he could be for someone who seemed to shift every conversation onto himself.

"But it's not as sweet as it seems," he continued. "You end up with messy situations. Many, many messy situations. Musicians are insane, you know, most of them battling warped egos, nasty addictions, abusive pasts—In other words, *they got fucking demons*—but unfortunately, they're also entirely too charismatic for anyone's own good. They've got magnets coming out of their fucking asses and they recklessly shake them at anyone with eyes. Hate to break your heart, here, sweetheart."

Did he really think he was breaking my heart? That this was all news to me? For a moment, he almost reminded me of my father. I really hadn't expected him to go on a tirade about musicians sucking. I realized my cigarette had gone out and stubbed it into the ashtray, pretending to be fine. Casual Kyla, shrugging her shoulders. *Whatever.*

He shot me a skeptical look, then shifted his gaze out over the cityscape.

"I mean it, Kyla. Don't shrug it off because you're one of them. You don't operate that way, *yet*, but you'll see . . . You, too, will use and use, jump from one person to the next, leapfrogging up the goddamn side of a mountain, always headed to the highest point possible. And you'll swear you mean it. They all swear they mean every fucking thing they say and do along the way. They create these perfect ice-sculpted moments, only to melt them in the heat of what comes next." He paused, and for a second I thought he was going to start crying. Then he sniffled like he had a cold and continued on with passion.

"You're left with these meaningless spots of time, these beautiful, heartbreaking, hollow images. And then you're a haunted person, and the ghosts of your past never leave. All it takes is a few chords of a certain song to backflip me into bed with a woman who swore her love for me was as real as her heartbeat. And look where we are now. Strangers in separate worlds."

Robert shook his head, got up, and walked over to the patio bar to fix himself another drink. He paced back and forth for a little, the shadows of his thoughts darkening his eyes even more. There was nothing to do but sit back and let him go on.

"Everything comes with a history. And the taste of the past rarely mingles well with the present."

We'd taken a wrong turn, somewhere. What had almost turned into my first honest discussion about my sexuality—for once, I had the right combination of courage and curiosity to maybe actually open up to someone about it—had turned into a monologue delivered by the most broken man on earth. Not only did I not feel included in what he was saying, but honestly, I couldn't relate at all. I'd never really dated *anyone.* I hadn't even pretended to like any of the wannabe posers back in my hometown. But now, thanks to Robert, all I felt was fear of the future, fear of dating, fear of moments that would *"prove so hollow later"*—although I sort of knew what he meant already, if I really let myself think about it.

I felt a strange urge to hug Robert but didn't want to actually move. He came back over finally, sat down and closed his eyes. He was resting, or maybe remembering something. I watched his pupils dart around under his paper-thin eyelids. I realized I was fidgeting so much I'd ripped a nail. I tore the rest of it off, causing sharp, unexpected pain. When I'd gotten my first manicure, they'd forced me to get "tips" even though the fake nail extensions made it impossible to play piano. Ruby had assured me that I'd get used to them, but there was really no way. I examined my torn nail bed, bleeding at the top. Maybe I'd rip all the fake tips off for a real "punk rock look" that would be the final touch on the image part of this bizarre makeover.

Robert's eyes suddenly popped open and he stared directly at me. "You want to know the worst part about being with musicians?"

I shook my head. I didn't, really. He ignored me and went on.

"When you're trying to forget them, you still have their catchy little fucking songs stuck on repeat in your head."

I'd had the chorus from "Sweet Excuses" on repeat in my head since Eyes Wander had closed their set with it. I thought about Ruby, probably somewhere dark with Brian, and the ugly energy rattled in my chest again. Robert must have felt it, too.

"It's a good thing *your* songs aren't catchy," he said to me, and winked.

"Is it?"

"Go to bed, before I try to make out with you."

I didn't need more of a reason than that.

GET PUNCTUAL OR FIND ANOTHER GIG

IT WAS FINALLY HAPPENING, THE REASON I was actually here, what should have been the main focus but had hardly come up until that morning: band practice. We were going to play together. As a band. For the *first time*. The rehearsal studio was in North Hollywood, which was in someplace called the San Fernando Valley. I was still so far from understanding the layout of Los Angeles, sprawled lazily between canyons, valleys, and ocean beaches. Robert had something in his car called a *Thomas Guide* that had maps of the entire city in it. The thing was the size of a phone book.

North Hollywood was a completely un-magical area. The constant thrum of motorcycles and trucks wasn't good on a headache. Strip malls featured stores with signs that promised things like "CA$H FOR JWLRY." The stale air was like the taste of last night's cigarettes. It all added up to one giant, pretty unattractive place—depressing and desperate. The few people on the sidewalks seemed staged in an attempt to make it seem more real. Faceless walkers in hooded sweatshirts, hats, and baggy jeans. Everything about it was creepily devoid of glamour.

I looked over at Robert dragging on a cigarette as he turned onto Oxnard from Laurel Canyon.

"What's up with this place?"

"This is where people come to make porn, score drugs, and rehearse with their bands." Robert glanced over at me. "I see you tensing up over there. You can't get an STD or a meth addiction just from passing through."

"I'm not, I wasn't—"

"Let me guess," he said. "You've never seen porn."

"Um . . . Not really."

"Typical. Sign up for music education and end up having to teach sex ed."

Was he calling me a prude like everyone at my high school? I didn't want to know. "Don't bother."

"Oh no?" he said, playful as I'd ever seen him. "You're already an expert? Please, elaborate."

I looked out at the sidewalk, embarrassed, and then the nerves kicked back in as we pulled into a large lot. Jeremy was slouched up against the graffitied side of the warehouse, smoking like he owned the world. He was his own vision of celebrity, wearing a tight white shirt with torn, paint-splattered jeans, and baby blue Ray-Ban sunglasses.

I hopped out of the car, eager to abandon the porn conversation. Robert honked and peeled out of the lot, which was empty except for several deserted shopping carts and a few cars. No sign of Ruby's pink Jeep.

I looked at Jeremy up close for the first time in daylight. He had little creases in his forehead and some stubble. His eyes were a shade lighter than his hair, which was jet black and very curly. I felt warm toward him, remembering how he'd saved me from the old creep at the party the other night. I'd read that he was half-Italian, half-African-American, and originally a jazz drummer from New Orleans—which I had never been to, but knew was a wildly different place. I didn't have much to say on any of that, being a so-called clueless and cultureless white girl from suburban Massachusetts—still, I wanted to get to know him better, especially since we were about to play together.

"Sooo . . . You're the backbone of the band, right?" I said, quite un-slickly. *Great start, Kyla.*

He offered a polite smile. "Ironic that my back's in such bad shape these days."

"That's right—you were in the hospital. How's it going?"

He stood up straighter and cracked his neck. "Alright, I guess. Have to wear this stupid thing when I play now, for a little while they said. Makes me feel like an old man." He lifted up his shirt to reveal a white brace around his torso.

It was a somber sight. "Aw, no. Are you in pain?"

"Only when the drugs wear off." He pulled a bottle of prescription pills out of his pocket and shook his head as he popped one. "I hope this doesn't slow me down too much."

I liked hanging out with Jeremy. He didn't try to act any certain way and he didn't make me feel like I had to, either. Shooting the breeze with him was way breezier than I'd expected.

"C'mon, I'll show you around. Maybe we can jam a little before they show up."

Jeremy pushed the double doors open and we walked into a church-sized musical shrine of sorts. The walls were painted a deep shade of green and vines hung from pots next to the row of high windows that circled the space. Sunlight streamed into the room, hitting different spots on the ground, creating a patchwork effect on the black carpet. There was a water fountain, a kitchen, a vocal booth, and—in the main area—the most instruments I'd ever seen together in one gigantic room.

I hurried over to check out the keyboard. It was a Roland stage piano with weighted keys, all 88 of them, with a nice finish. I hit a few notes and nothing happened. Sheepishly realizing it wasn't turned on, I fumbled around for the power switch on the back. Jeremy grinned at me when I looked up. Busted.

He picked up his sticks and dove immediately into a fast rock beat. I stared down at the keys. It was strange to play standing up. It was even stranger to play with a drummer, but as my fingers moved over the keys I gained more confidence. It was kind of like playing with a much cooler metronome. I started putting notes together as I never had before, really letting loose. I could tell Jeremy approved because I kept catching him looking at me and then he'd close his eyes and nod.

We'd been jamming for a little while when the door opened. I fell out of my trance to see Ruby and Stardust entering the studio.

"You guys sound so good!" Ruby said excitedly as she walked over to my side. "We heard you as soon as we turned into the lot." She had on a little white vest and her purple hair was loose and flowing over her shoulders. The glitter tear was the only makeup she had on, and once again, I softened seeing how uniquely beautiful she was as she looked around the room.

"Do you like that board?" Stardust asked.

I nodded enthusiastically. It really was better than any I'd played. "It feels so real!"

"Slinky's not here yet?" Ruby raised her voice to Jeremy. "I thought he was coming with you."

Jeremy held up his hands. "Last I heard, he was picking something up downtown and then coming here."

Stardust plugged in her silver sparkle bass and began plunking some ominous low notes. Jeremy took a towel off a rack behind him and wiped his brow. It made me feel good that he'd broken a sweat from our jam, even though he was a jazz guy and had probably been humoring me.

"Well. What am I supposed to say? Typical?" Ruby tossed her hair and stalked over to her microphone.

Jeremy shot me a look I wished I hadn't received. I stared at a mandala poster on the wall that also seemed dramatically out of place. There was some piercing feedback and I turned my attention back to Ruby, who was busy adjusting her mic stand.

"That useless jockstrap. We're not waiting for him," she said angrily. "Let's go."

I glanced up at the clock above the side door. Hadn't she been thirty minutes late, herself? I quickly focused my attention back on the keys in front of me. Even without Slinky, this was still sort of the big moment I had been waiting for, a chance to feel I'd really earned my current reality.

"Have you been practicing the new songs?" Ruby asked.

I nodded, trying not to appear nervous. I'd meant to rehearse at Robert's more before our first practice, but I'd been so busy and distracted . . . *Sweet excuses.*

Jeremy came over and said, "Check, check," into Ruby's mic. Nice and clear, no feedback. Stardust stomped on a distortion pedal and turned her back to all of us. Then Ruby picked up Slinky's guitar and stepped up to the mic.

"*Insecurity / I'm VIP / Won't you let me in for free,*" she sang into the mic as she strummed the guitar slowly, the opening to the first song off *Perpetual Twilight*, "Kill Me." She seemed satisfied with the mic levels, nodded at Jeremy, and he returned to his kit. Ruby cleared her throat and nodded again. He tapped his sticks and we launched into the song headfirst.

It was exhilarating to play with these pros, making music that sounded so good, and so much more exciting than my own songs. There was a hurricane of energy coasting through me when we finished.

I wiped my hands on my jeans, swallowed hard and looked at Ruby. *Uh-oh.* She seemed like she was deciding what to say to me.

"Okay! So, Kyla. What did you think of that?"

What did I think?

"Um, you guys sound really good," I began nervously. "I was thinking I could add to my part, make it a little more complex or something, maybe?"

"Okay, good. I'm glad you said it so I didn't have to. Needs the most work in the chorus. Right?" I nodded quickly, trying to act like I was thinking the same thing. "Great. If we're on the same page this should work fine. So, let's try it again?"

I nodded. I was supposed to do what now? I looked at Jeremy but he shrugged and looked away. This was worse than I'd expected: zero guidance or instruction, totally winging it, failing miserably. Ruby was about to find out what a mistake she'd made—a big, fat, expensive mistake— bringing me out here.

"Jeremy, could you bring it up a little more on the second chorus? I don't want it to sound the same as the first, it has to be ten times the intensity."

"Can do," he said like he was asked to go check the fuse box or something. I made a note to try not to take her criticism so personally. She was particular and I hadn't exactly found my place in the band musically, yet. I couldn't count on it to be an instant transition, especially not with the amount of nerves I was juggling.

Thankfully, Ruby came over and showed me on the keyboard what kind of part she was hearing. Her ideas sounded a lot better than mine. A lot fancier, too. I hadn't known she could play both guitar and piano so well. She knew exactly what she was doing on both instruments. What was it like, to be so multi-talented and in-command? What did she see in me? Whatever it was, it wasn't going to last much longer if I didn't pick up the pace.

"It doesn't have to be that exactly, but you see what I'm going for?"

I had been nodding so much I felt a neck cramp. Ruby opened her mouth, seeming to be debating saying something else, but then we all heard the double doors bang open and watched Slinky slink into the room.

"Sorry dudes, traffic was gnarly. I almost bailed on my car and skated here."

"You're an hour late."

"Yeah, yeah, I know. Let's not have a big conversation about it. I'm ready to go."

Ruby's back was to me so I couldn't see what face she was making, but I could still feel the reaction: ice cold. I glanced back at Jeremy, who raised an eyebrow. Ruby walked past Slinky to the bathroom and slammed the door behind her. Slinky shook his head, went over and picked up his guitar, tapped a few pedals with his red sneaker, ran his hand over his head, and strummed one long, distorted chord.

"Drop that beat, I'm ready to go," he announced like he was the star of the band.

"I need more coffee." Jeremy said pointedly as he got up and went over to the kitchenette. Stardust and Slinky started whispering conspiratorially. I felt confused and alienated from them all, so I turned the volume down on the keyboard and tried to figure out Ruby's version of the part. Under the circumstances, it was almost impossible to remember.

Ruby burst out of the bathroom, grabbed her purse, and beelined for the door.

"Aw, c'mon, what the fuck," Slinky said.

She stopped and turned toward him. "No. Fuck *you*. The next time we rehearse, you're either early or you're not going on tour," she said. "I can't deal with this egotistical bullshit all summer. Get punctual or find another gig."

The doors slammed shut behind her. Then the Ladybug started up and sped away.

"Shit," Slinky spat and kicked his amp over. We all heard something break inside.

I'd never seen Ruby act that way before. She was petite but could certainly be scary. Jeremy gave me another look and I felt my stomach twist up.

"I don't have to put up with this," Slinky snarled as he threw his guitar into the stand. It tipped over too, making screeching, dissonant feedback as he strode out. We heard another engine catch and the car drove off.

Stardust put down her bass and unplugged Slinky's guitar. "Wouldn't be a band without drama."

That wasn't enough for me. "She won't really throw him out, right?"

Jeremy shrugged. "It's been threatened before, but he's still here, isn't he?"

That was all the reassurance I was going to get.

STAY READY TO RUMBLE

AN UNSETTLING GLOOM FOLLOWED ME AROUND like smog, enhancing my disillusionment. Though I was technically on an exciting adventure, there was something really off about the whole setup. I wasn't sure what I was or wasn't allowed to do. I was at the mercy of those around me or I was out of a place to live. It was implied that I had to go along with everything on Robert or Ruby's agenda or else I'd basically be homeless. That left me with surprisingly little free will within this world of freewheeling rock stars. It seemed like a large portion of my duties was to make them feel better about their habits and lifestyles by mirroring them. What *I* wanted didn't matter to them in the slightest.

Personally, I was dying to go see some hip hop shows. The underground scene was alive and thriving in LA, unlike western Massachusetts. The dark and twisted rock scene Robert pulled me into had so far only fueled my desire to escape into the uplift of a fat hip hop beat, and absorb the strong, rhythmic poetry of rap. Robert was all about heavy metal at the moment, so I was pretty much forced to act interested regardless of how much I didn't enjoy it.

Gazzarri's on Sunset Boulevard overflowed with leather-clad tattooed guys with either long or spiky hair. Tough chumps with big hands pounded their fists into each other and shouted at the stage. Robert had given me a tip to "dress dark" but with my hot pink hair I felt like an Easter marsh-mallow in a drawer full of knives.

When Robert offered me a drink, I marveled at how there didn't seem to be any "nights off" in Hollywood. It was a Monday and people were tossing them down as if they'd been working hard all week. I could relate a little, I guess. I was worn out from the weekend, especially after the very draining rehearsal in which we hadn't accomplished a thing. Ruby's temper was so easy to trigger. New worries pushed at the edges of my temples, worries that fell away with the first few sips of a stiff drink.

I felt lost in the jungle of the wildest wood—Hollywood drink in hand, empty stomach, suddenly craving a cigarette to uncoil the tension inside. I bummed one from Robert and went out on the street to get a minute to myself. The little moments of solitude while stuck in other people's scenes were windows to imagine who I would be if I'd come here on my own, what people I would have chosen to hang with. Would I be the girl with pink hair smoking by the side of Gazzarri's? Definitely not. Or would I be, say, a brunette in baggy jeans, chain wallet and a T-shirt, working late at Book Soup and then skating home to play my keyboard and sing to myself? Maybe.

But would I rather be her?

Cars streamed by on Sunset Boulevard, lit up by neon signs. The air was heavy with the smell of exhaust, urine, and alcohol. After a week of life in LA, I still wasn't at all comfort-able, constantly bombarded with these larger-than-life characters so dynamic and powerful that my own personality and dreams had been temporarily wiped out. These days, everything was either impossibly high times or ground zero. I was officially on the roller coaster.

Woohoo.

A girl in a neon windbreaker and leggings with wrists full of jangling bracelets came up next to me as she held out flyers to people. "Come see Warped Minds at the Roxy next Friday! Five dollars! Hey, take one!"

For the most part, people ignored her. A guy with half his face tattooed like a bionic man took one and tried to get her number. She flew out of the situation effortlessly, using her overenthusiasm as a shield. She noticed me watching her, smiled, and held out a flyer. "Hey! You should come!"

"Thanks." I took the flyer with an encouraging smile, even though I knew I wouldn't be there. She seemed to be giving me flirty eyes.

"Got another cigarette?" she asked, blowing a bubble with bright pink gum and frosty pink lips.

I was considering what to say when Robert stuck his head out of the doorway. "Hey, lightning fingers, get in here. They're about to go on!"

I handed her my half-smoked one. "Here you go."

I felt agitated as I trudged inside. I'd almost made my first friend on my own, here, in Hollywood. She was cute, sweet, and into music. Damn Robert. But he was the only family I had out here, so I let him drape his bony arm around me and shout into my ear, "We're going up front, stay close." He held onto my shoulder as we pushed through the crowd. I bumped into arms and chests and choked out a few *excuse me*'s that dissolved into the throbbing air. We were suddenly only a few feet from the front of the stage that smelled like a moldy gymnasium.

The band entered from the back in a cloud of dry ice. They wore orange prison uniforms and had all-black instruments—the drum kit even had black cymbals. The screams rang out, strobe blinked on in full effect, and the band launched into their first song. I wasn't prepared for the crowd to erupt as it did. I felt Robert's arms hover around me, a skinny force field against fans as they started springing into a mosh pit. I'd try to move, only to be bumped back into the frenetic circle.

Then the stage went dark. A heavy guitar riff ripped through the darkness. People started to chant "Slay! Slay! Slay!" I glanced back at Robert, who looked oddly young and alive in the sweaty pit of raw energy. He kept his eyes on the stage as someone screamed. I could see the outlines of the band members in the blackness, frozen. People chanted harder and harder. I'd been to shows with mosh pits before, but this was different. This felt dangerous. A frenetic energy rippled through me and I started looking for a way out of the crowd. I knew something was about to go down.

A strobe flashed for a millisecond and the orange-jumpsuited band members were standing straight, stiff as flagpoles. Robert's friend Manny began a drum roll. Darkness again. Amplified cheers. The beat picked up. Another flash and they were bending over slightly. Darkness again. Deafening shouts. My heart roared in my ears. A longer flash, the band was now crouching. Darkness again. An explosive snare roll broke out, the lights flooded on throughout the whole venue, and the band jumped up as music boiled out of the speakers like overcooked syrup. As the crowd erupted I tried to escape. A slow-motion fist flew straight at my face. Then everything went dark.

WEAR BRUISES LIKE BADGES

OUR FIRST PHOTO SHOOT AS A band was in a huge downtown loft with skylights and abstract paintings on the walls. As soon as I saw Ruby I wanted to turn and run the other way. She was paging through a notebook on a couch, a mug in hand, dressed in a black lace corset and petticoat. She looked up, saw me, and set her mug down immediately. Her mouth fell open a bit and we stared at each other in mutual woe.

Stardust walked into the room, munching on a carrot stick. She had on a ruffly number that hugged her slender body in all the right places. "Slinky and Jeremy are loving the burlesque theme. They found these hats in the wardrobe room—"

She stopped short and flinched at the sight of me. "What happened to you?"

My hand went up to my left eye. Ruby got up off the couch and came to my side, her delayed concern more reflexive than genuine.

"Yes, what happened? Are you okay?"

"I'm sorry. We were at this show last night—"

"Who's *we*?" Ruby asked quickly.

"Robert's friend was playing Gazzarri's."

"Metal Mondays Manny? Ugh, I should have known!" Ruby moaned. "Anytime he's involved, things get jacked up."

"Well there was this really crazy intro to one of the songs and some guy freaked out, started swinging, and caught me right in my eye."

"When Kevin sees this—"

"Kevin sees what?" a male voice asked as if on cue.

The three of us turned to see Kevin walk in the front door. At first he stared at me like he didn't know me, then his face darkened. "What the hell happened to you?"

I covered my eye quickly. "Had a little accident last night."

"Yeah? I think you took your rock 'n' roll makeover too far," he said, looking sourly at me in my "casual" outfit of tight black jeans, platform boots, and a see-through black mesh shirt with a hot pink lace bra underneath. "Were you aware you're supposed to be photographed today for the feature in *Strings & Stars* when you decided to get into a fist fight?"

"Makeup will cover it," Stardust said to my aid.

"Well, what are we waiting for? Get her in makeup *now*," Kevin said. "Ruby, can I speak to you outside for a moment?"

Ruby nodded, conveying her disappointment with me as she walked by. They went outside and shut the door behind them.

There was a painting on the wall with a little brown dot on the bottom and a mass of colorful larger circles at the top, like balloons let loose in the sky. I felt like the brown dot, so tiny and different—unable to float.

Jeremy and Slinky entered wearing bowler hats and suits. When they saw me they broke into schoolboy grins.

"Damn! Check out the shiner on Kyla," Slinky said. He walked up and squinted at me. "Guess I've got competition for official problem child of the band."

"News flash: you've officially been beaten," Jeremy said.

"Our band should really be called Ruby and the Fuckup Fairies," Slinky said.

"What did Kevin say?" Jeremy asked.

"He's outside talking to Ruby right now," I said morosely.

They looked at each other and burst out laughing.

"And I always thought pianists were tame . . ." Slinky shook his head and looked at me in admiration.

Jeremy got serious for a moment. "Who did this to you?"

"Robert took me to Gazzarri's last night. The crowd was outta control, and I caught a loose fist in the face."

"It happens," Slinky said as he walked over to the kitchen area. The counter was covered with delicious-looking sprinkle donuts and to-go cups of coffee. Drinking coffee to take the edge off didn't exactly work. I wished there was some sort of alcohol. And although a little food would probably have a similar comforting effect, I wouldn't be caught dead in public with a donut in my mouth. Kevin would fire me on the spot. Now, where had Stardust gotten the carrot stick?

"This is Amber, the makeup artist," Stardust said as she walked in with a really skinny girl with blond hair. Slinky straightened up and immediately started rubbing his head, his hilarious tell. Amber seemed oblivious to Slinky-turned-schoolboy. She walked right up to me and tilted my head toward the skylights, studying me while snapping gum that smelled like artificial strawberry.

Finally, she said, "Yeah, I can work this down." She let go of my head and flashed me a quick smile. "I like a challenge."

Slinky was in love. "Is that right?"

She ignored him. We went into a large room with more skylights and a wall of windows overlooking a park. Against the wall stood a dresser littered with makeup, topped by a vanity mirror lined with little round bulbs. Amber gestured toward the chair.

"Sit down so I can fix this asshole's handiwork."

"It wasn't—"

"You don't have to explain. It's my job to cover up this stuff, not ask questions."

She got to work. Twenty minutes later she had it covered completely. I could breathe a little easier. Ruby and Kevin walked into the room with another guy holding a camera.

"This is the best I can do," Amber announced, tilting my face around again.

Kevin squinted at me. The photographer was sweaty, scrappy, and unshaven. He came near me, breathing heavily.

"Step into the light, sweetheart."

I obeyed. He studied my face closely.

"The camera will still pick up some of the purples, but I can keep the bad eye out of most of the shots."

Kevin turned and left the room without saying a word. The photographer hurried after him. Ruby sat on a chair across from me with her arms tightly folded as Amber continued dusting my face with powder. It was obvious that I needed to beg for more forgiveness.

"I'm really sorry, Ruby."

She cooled down somewhat, maybe because the makeup artist did such a miracle job. "I know, it's not your fault," she said. "I should've reminded Robert to take it easy with you last night. Kevin's really worried about you, though. I spent the last however many minutes convincing him that things are actually going well, the black eye's a fluke."

I felt a big "but" coming so I held my tongue. Ruby looked at herself in the mirror and ran her fingers through her hair. Her makeup looked especially good. The smoky eye shadow made her eyes look seductive on a supernatural level.

"But I had to tell him about practice yesterday, and he said it sounds like we have a lot of work to do before the tour. I didn't think so originally, because the parts you wrote to my last albums fit so well. I understand, though, the new stuff has a different vibe to it. It's okay. Don't go getting frown lines. You're doing your best and I realize that. I told Kevin that a lot's getting thrown at you. He's just nervous that you're not going to be able to handle it. I told him that wasn't even the case. I told him this would be the last incident, and he said it better be . . . or else he'll find someone else."

"Oh no," I said, my voice coming out a whisper.

"Oh, yes. You know how he is."

No one spoke. My mind went fuzzy.

Ruby wanted me to promise something that I wasn't sure I could deliver. I shook my head, stuck at war with myself. The black eye couldn't be less my fault, and yet they were already threatening to call me off because of it. What kind of people was I dealing with? Hadn't Ruby bothered to explain to Kevin that I was at the mercy of Robert's nightly exploits? I winced in pain, still recovering from the night before. My head hurt from the moment I woke up.

Ruby tapped her fingers, staring at me, waiting for me to let her know how I planned to deal with this. I couldn't meet her eyes. She was too fierce, too beautiful, and it was all too much.

"Should I talk to Kevin?" I finally blurted out.

"No, I did the talking for you," Ruby said. "He has to run to a meeting now anyway. Just try to keep yourself out of rough spots from now on, all right, honey cakes?"

"Yeah. Will do. Thanks," I mumbled. It was as good a promise as I was capable of at the moment. I looked up from my hands to meet her eyes but Ruby had already left the room.

Amber handed me the tube of concealer with a sympathetic glance. "Keep it."

The photographer set us up to pose in his main studio, which was painted white and lit from all angles. The theme was Victorian burlesque. Ruby had changed several times and was now wearing fishnets, a shredded black lace and blood red corset with a short drape skirt, a lace and pearl choker, and black lace gloves. She held an unlit cigarette in a white pearl cigarette holder and her lips and nails were painted dark red. Jeremy and Slinky had accessorized their black suits with bowler hats, suspenders, canes—and for Jeremy, a well-fitting pair of spectacles. Stardust had settled on wearing a burnt orange corset and black petticoat with her signature orange glasses. The stylist had put me in a tight, pale pink satin dress with black trim and a push-up bodice that somehow made me the bustiest of the bunch. I could hardly move or breathe, but I supposed that was fashion.

The photographer positioned us around vintage furniture he had rented for the shoot—pale cream satin-covered chairs, a long maroon velvet couch, a few embroidered gold cushions, and a brass candlestick holder that sat on a chestnut table. I sat between Stardust and Jeremy on the couch, Stardust's hand on my shoulder, Jeremy's cane across both of our laps, hooked around our thighs. Ruby sat to the side on her own throne, staring off into the distance, and Slinky stood behind the couch, monocle to an eye, raising an eyebrow, hand on his chin.

After a few shots, the photographer tried other arrangements.

Stardust, Ruby and I sat on the couch, Jeremy behind Ruby with his hands on her shoulders, and Slinky kneeling before her with his cane hooked around his neck.

Another: Stardust and I sat in chairs on both sides, while Ruby laid across the couch, Jeremy and Slinky both posed above her, staring down at her while she looked into the camera with a queen's confident stare.

The hardest pose: the photographer had me kissing Ruby's hand, on my knees before her, while she looked up into the sky and the other band members sat around us, staring at us. I wondered what that one was about. Had he heard something?

After forty minutes it felt like we'd been working for hours. The photographer seemed perfectly content playing musical chairs all day. I marveled at how easily the rest of the band seemed to turn into props, not caring how much he moved them or what he barked at them—mainly directing them to change their expressions. I had a much harder time not taking his commands personally.

"Kyla, give me a hard look, you're too soft, you look embarrassed."

"That pink hair doesn't make you a girly girl. Give me the look that says you could kick anyone's ass. Let that black eye shine through, show us the bad girl who gets into bar fights."

"I have to ask Pinky for the third time: stop looking so nervous. You're a big, bad rock star, people need to fear and respect you, not think you're some good girl who woke up to find herself in the wrong band."

The guys laughed at that. Slinky muttered, "Nailed it," and I felt the burn. Jeremy gave him a small punch in my defense, for which I was grateful.

"Great, now you're as pink as your hair."

That set Slinky and Stardust off on a giggle spree and I blushed even harder. The only experience I'd had in front of the camera was school portraits, and they never asked you to change into horribly uncomfortable clothes, get into degrading positions and to somehow also look cool while managing all that.

"I *don't* want to have to do this again," Ruby said in her chilly tone.

From that point on, no one spoke again until the photographer got his "money shot."

FIND COMFORT IN THE CHAOS

BACK AT ROBERT'S, I WASN'T SURE how to loosen the tightness in my chest. All I'd been trying to do was fit in, but it had been much more complicated than I expected. Ruby seemed to be a walking landmine. Nobody was holding my hand, and even though I was doing the best I could to keep up and go where they wanted me to go, do what they wanted me to do, I was already on my last chance. I'd been so distracted by everything that I hadn't had much time to think about my family situation back home. It was sort of this weight I carried around with me, personal pain buried in a locked, sunken chest, but that wasn't enough. By now, I had hoped to lose the key.

As I floated around wondering what to do with myself, I noticed Robert's bedroom door open a crack. I'd been curious to peek in there since the first day, so I knocked lightly and pushed the door open. To my shock, it was as blank as the other rooms downstairs. There was nothing on the walls. The bed was a mattress on a metal frame in the corner, dirty black sheets, unmade. The bedside table held a phone, a roll of toilet paper, and a lamp. The closet door was open and crumpled clothes and shoes spilled out. The desk:

a few scattered papers, business cards, and pens. No letters, no books, even. I felt goosebumps pop up at the nothingness of it all. The room was absolutely empty of personality. I closed the door and continued down the hall to the staircase, even more unnerved and tiptoeing even though there seemed to be nobody home. I racked my brain for something to do, some way to feel more comfortable, and the answer finally hit me.

I could release the stress the only way I knew how: find the piano and play.

I entered the recording studio through the double padded doors and felt another wave of awe at the grandness of the room, so clearly created to capture great music. I sat down at the piano and ran my fingers over the keys, tickling the beast with the most exquisite laughter. The sound pumped fresh energy through my blood. I knew I should practice songs from *Perpetual Twilight,* but I wanted to enjoy playing for a little bit, and didn't especially care how silly or unformed the melodies and lyrics were. I felt a new song bubbling inside me, ready to burst out.

After dancing with a few A-minor chords I stumbled across a melody, cleared my throat and began to sing. I continued, the chorus unfurling itself out of nowhere. I played with the melody for a while, losing track of time in the thrill of creating something stronger than what I'd written back in Massachusetts. This crazy environment was obviously affecting me on the outside, but now I saw how it was changing my internal parts, rewiring my creativity. It felt like I had grown in at least one positive way. If this band dream ended, I still had myself, right?

By the time I got up from the piano bench, I felt recharged.

Robert was smoking in the kitchen when I came in. He looked dejectedly out the window at a ripe orange sun hanging low in the hazy sky.

"Hey, Robert . . . You okay?"

He sighed and looked back out the window.

"Sometimes I get this feeling—this sickening, tightening feeling—that not even all the drugs in the world would be enough to make me truly feel okay."

I shook my head, speechless. I didn't even know how to begin to respond to that. He shrugged.

"Just do us both a favor and don't end up like me."

What a haunting thing for my mentor to say—though the truth was, I wasn't sure what to call Robert, anymore. Maybe he'd given up on me. Maybe he'd given up on himself. He started mumbling incoherently. I held still, trying to make out what he was saying. After a tense minute he stood up, pulled up his sweatpants that barely held onto his hips, and stood there awkwardly for a moment.

"Coffee?" I asked, for lack of better conversation options.

He shook his head.

"Sorry," I said, not sure what I was apologizing for. "Should I make some?"

Robert ran his hands through his rumpled hair and down over his face, pulling at his skin, which looked paler and looser than usual.

"Mi casa, su casa," he said flatly.

He stood there, glowering at me, as I fumbled around, opening cabinets, looking for coffee filters. I needed coffee like never before but I didn't want to ask him where anything was or ask him to do anything for me.

Finally, he walked over stiffly, yanked open a drawer, and

slammed a package of coffee filters on the counter. Then he went to the freezer, grabbed a bag of coffee beans, and slapped it on the counter so harshly it burst open, sending beans ricocheting everywhere. I gasped.

"Don't let the fact that I have badly suppressed emotional problems get in the way of my hospitality," Robert said coldly. Before I could respond, he stalked out of the room, pounded up the stairs, and slammed his bedroom door shut.

I shivered. What a chilly shadow of a human being. All at once, I felt homesick. My parents' kitchen suddenly seemed like the coziest place on Earth compared to this one. After somehow brewing some excessively strong coffee, I took a mug of the steaming black liquid up to my room, shut the door, and picked up the phone.

I had been too nervous to call anyone from home yet, afraid they had seen the photo of the staged kiss with Ruby wherever it had been published. I had no idea how long those things actually took to circulate.

My hand shook as I dialed Jenny's number. When she answered, her voice made me feel like myself again for the first time since I'd left home.

"Jenny!"

"Oh no way, you're alive!"

"Yeah, I'm so sorry I haven't called," I said. "It's been nonstop."

"Shut up and tell me everything already!"

Where to start when so much had happened?

"You have no idea how much I've wished you were here. There's so much to make fun of, it's painful."

"I'm sure you've got better things to do than be cynical," she said. "Start with the band. What's going on with you and

Ruby? How are the other members? Slinky, Stardust, and the drummer's name is Jeremy, right?"

Had Jenny seen the red carpet kiss? I ignored her question about Ruby for now, and distracted her with other band stories. "Yeah. They're cool, I mean, I think they like me all right. Ruby had me pull this crazy stunt on Jeremy and Slinky the first time I met them, you would have been so proud. We were at this party at Ian Somer's place, and—"

I was cut off by a mind-shredding scream. I held the phone away from my ear until she stopped.

"What do you *mean* Ian Somer's place? You can't just *say* that!!!"

"Oops, I guess that part should have come first . . ."

"You met him? In person?!"

"Uh-huh, yeah, I met him. He's cool, but in a sort of creepy way."

"Um, he could be as sleazy as he wanted to be, I'd still jump his bones," she said. "Holy shit, Kyla, did you pounce on him or what?"

"No, of course not," I said. "He's *old*, Jenny."

"He's a total legend! Who the hell cares what age he is?"

I debated whether to say anything about Anthony at first, but then I let it out to continue the distraction. "Well, I did kinda almost make out with his son—"

"Anthony Somer? I *hate* you right now! Why am I not there to strangle you? You *almost* made out with him? What, did you have an idiotic change-of-heart at the last minute?"

"No, I . . .well, we sorta got broken up by the party. He gave me his sweater, though. It's yours if you want it."

"Um, if you give me his sweater, I am yours for LIFE."

"Yeah, it's all yours."

"What a friggin' dream life. This is too much. You've got to call me more. My life's as boring as it gets. I need to hear about this stuff."

"I know, I seriously haven't had more than a couple hours to myself. People don't take any nights off here. It's insane, Jenny. My head is this big whirlpool filled with coffee, fizzy water, and vodka."

"You've been partying every night?"

"Yeah, pretty much. It's so weird. You know, I've been drinking, and I've hardly been eating, and even done—"

"Kyla!" She sounded genuinely shocked. "I know you're feeling pressure to become cool overnight, but . . . what are you doing to yourself over there?!"

"I know, I know," I said, suddenly realizing she would worry about me too much if I told her the truth. "I take some pills for energy, you know, prescription stuff. And I've lost a little weight for the image thing. No big deal—"

"Listen to yourself—"

I remained quiet and she sighed.

"Ugh, I sound like my mom. Christ. How does that happen? It's a pre-programmed script in my brain. Sorry. I know you're going through LA rock star boot camp or whatever, but make sure you don't get sloppy, okay? I want my best friend intact for these adventures."

"Thanks," I said. "It feels really good to talk to you." I paused, finally thinking of a way I could test if she'd seen the paparazzi picture of Ruby and me without actually asking. "And about my hair . . ."

"What did you do to your hair?!"

The anxiety lifted. She hadn't seen it yet.

"Well . . .it's short, and hot pink . . ."

Another shriek, this one shorter than the last. "Hot PINK?! I wish I could see you. This is torture. I'm staring at Bootsie's little face right now, and he's so confused, he's whimpering because I keep jumping up and down and screaming."

I laughed. I could see her in her bedroom with Bootsie, her British bulldog, on the floor, head cocked. It made me miss her even more.

"You'll see it soon enough," I said, wincing. Jenny loved magazines. She'd know everything before long. I wasn't sure how she'd react, so I was glad I had a chance to talk to her before it came out.

"Oh, you are too much, Kyla Bell."

It was nice to be too much for a moment, instead of too little.

WHAT HAPPENS IN THE CLOSET STAYS IN THE CLOSET

RUBY DECLARED IT WAS TIME FOR a girls' night out, so Stardust and I went to yet another party with her. I scarcely knew what day it was, and had no idea which neighborhood we were in, but I was glad to get away from gloom-and-doomy Robert for a night.

Like an East Coast summer, you never knew which way the clouds were going to shift with Ruby Sky. It appeared that all was forgotten from the photo shoot at the moment, and the hot sun of her affection was beaming back out at me from her glitter-dusted eyes as we raged it up. Someone started up a pie-throwing contest and decided I had to throw first. A guy handed me a pie pan filled with whipped cream and I stared at the poor young woman whose head was stuck through the hole in a board twenty feet in front of me. A crowd had gathered on the porch, waiting, watching and cheering. Ruby and Stardust stood to my right, cups of punch in their hands.

"Do it already," Stardust said.

I nodded, concentrated, and threw the pie. It hit the guy standing next to the target square in the crotch. There was an eruption of laughter.

"That's where her eye goes!" someone shouted. More laughter.

"Oops," I said, quickly stepping aside. Stardust was up next. Ruby and I moved back to a spot next to an inflatable moonwalk and she handed me the drink we'd been sharing. "This party's pretty fun!" I said, sipping the strong fruit juice and vodka concoction and feeling happy for the first time in what felt like a long time.

"Yeah," Ruby said absently, staring at something behind me. I turned to look.

The guy I'd hit with the "pie" was approaching with a scary big smile. He was short and cocky, tan and muscular. I'd overheard someone saying earlier that he'd been voted off a live dating show called *Slam Pig: The Next Generation of American Sluts*.

"So, doll, you gonna help me get cleaned up or what?"

I was taken aback and slow on the uptake. Thankfully, Ruby circled her arm through mine and took over for me.

"You seem like a big boy. I'm sure you can handle it yourself."

"Aren't you that singer chick? Ruby something or other?"

"Yes! And you must be that pie dude, charming something or other."

He grinned at us. "Hey, you both can come help me out, you know. I'd dig that."

"Oh, *totally*," Ruby said. I looked at her in surprise and she smiled, hushing me with her eyes. "Tell you what. We'll meet you in the bathroom."

"Really?" He stared at us like we were free ice cream on a hot day. She nodded and stuck her head into the nook of my neck, nuzzling me. My heart revved. She smelled so delicious, like spun sugar, jasmine, and honeysuckle.

"Mmm," she cooed, echoing my sentiments as she emerged from my neck.

That got the guy excited. "Which bathroom? The one off the kitchen?"

"Yeah," she said. "Give us a minute."

He nodded excitedly. "Righteous."

Ruby laughed and whispered something into my ear. I didn't hear what she said but her warm breath tickled so I laughed too. He stared at us for another moment, nodded again, and I heard him say, "All right!" to no one in particular as he made his way toward the kitchen.

I took another sip of our drink. The jungle juice was sickeningly strong, but not as strong as my attraction to Ruby. The combination, though? I was a goner.

"Are we really gonna do this?" I asked.

"No, silly," she said. "Of course not. We're gonna let that tool wait there for us."

"Oh. Okay."

"You disappointed?" she teased.

I laughed uncomfortably. "No!"

"Not convinced." She took my hand, pulling me behind her as she headed past people bouncing on the moonwalk. We went into the house through a side door and she led me down the hallway. I was hardly conscious of what we were passing or who was around us. All I was aware of was her soft hand enclosed around mine and the waves of giddiness as the alcohol worked its way through my system. I wanted to move her hand all sorts of places. I wanted to be in a room with Ruby, and Ruby alone.

Ruby pushed open a door to what turned out to be a bedroom and we entered. There was a single light on next to the bed. It was a girl's room; pink bed sheet set, shelf of assorted heels, panties and tights hanging on an air-dry rack. The room was smoky with incense, blasting me back to the past with the familiar sandalwood scent that filled so many hippie shops in Northampton.

"What are we doing?"

"We have to hide. And I need a pick-me-up."

She let go of my hand, sat on the edge of the bed, and started looking through her bag. I sat down next to her, hoping for another Dream pill. I wanted my hunger stabs to go away again, and I could use a little energy. With a dinner of popcorn to hold me down, the jungle juice was making me woozy, fast.

But what she pulled out this time was a tiny cobalt blue vial.

"Time for you to meet cocaine," she said calmly. I was instantly curious. I'd never seen it or done it before. "You're going to try it sooner or later, and I'd rather it be with me," she continued.

"What will it do?"

"Same thing as the Dream, basically, except it's stronger and you feel it quicker." She carefully knocked the white powder out onto a book and used a card from her bag to break it up. I watched with a combination of excitement and nerves as she pulled out a twenty-dollar bill and rolled it up. She made four little lines and bent over to sniff one, letting out a pleasure gasp when she finished. I accepted the rolled-up bill that she offered and pressed one of my nostrils shut like she'd done. As I inhaled the line I remembered a kid I'd seen snort the contents of a green pixie stick and become the hero of summer camp. He'd had green boogers afterward, which he'd shown off proudly.

My eyes watered and I sniffled loudly as I felt something drip down the back of my throat. I swallowed hard, tasting nastiness. Ruby patted my arm.

"Good girl," she said, bending over to do another line.

When we'd finished, she brushed off the book, put it back, and got up. I remained quiet, my thoughts racing off as I watched the centerpiece of my current obsession, Ruby Sky, open the closet door to reveal all kinds of colorful fabrics. She parted the clothes and beckoned me with her fingers. I approached cautiously, feeling a heightened sense of curiosity. Ruby grinned and pounced on me, and suddenly we were down on the dark floor of the closet. She held me against her as we lay entangled in a nest of dresses. Her chest was pressed to mine, and I struggled to breathe as my whole body flipped on like a thousand-watt bulb against hers. The strong substance coursed through me, pressing outward. I was going to burst out of my skin.

"You're so sweet, Kyla," she said, stroking my hair and face, running her fingertip up my cheek and down my jawline. It felt like she was tracing the pattern of a heart. "You're so pure. Sometimes you remind me of myself when I was younger."

Though a simple statement, it felt monumental somehow. My voice came out a whisper. "Really?"

She pulled me in tighter, arms encircling me as if to contain me, starting a tingling fire in my lower torso. She was so close I felt her heartbeat through her chest pressed into mine and smelled the punch on her breath, sweet and strong. "I wonder why the types of relationships we want the most as kids come to us later in life, when there's so much more to be confused by," she whispered.

I had no idea what she was talking about, but suddenly found the courage to ask. "Ruby?"

"Yes, cream puff?"

"What were you like as a kid?"

She went quiet, fingertips halting, and I worried I had killed the mood. I worried I had bad breath. I worried I couldn't breathe like this for much longer. A panic set in through the silence. I focused on her heart, strong and rhythmic compared to my fluttery, jittery one. I focused on breathing and tried to calm down.

"I was an anxious child," she finally said just as I started to sit up. "My parents split up when I was five, and I hated living with my mother. She was an addict, but she won custody of me because she had her mother's house to live in and my father could barely afford to buy an RV. I used to call him every night after she passed out and beg him to take me away. My dad was a writer, wrote short stories that sometimes got published, but he didn't have any money because he refused to get a full-time job. Anyway, one night it got really bad, my mom's boyfriend did something awful after she'd passed out, and I ran away, called my dad from the corner store, and we took off."

Ruby's breathing grew more shallow. I was thankful she didn't go into more detail. I didn't want to go anywhere that dark in the past. The whole world seemed to be shut off and far away from the warmth of the closet. She pinned my arms down, pressed her chest to mine, traced tiny circles on my cheek, moved her mouth dangerously close to my lips. I felt like we were tucked in some sort of alternate electric paradise.

She continued in a dreamy, fairy tale voice. "From then on, I bounced around the West Coast with my father, eating at soup kitchens and stealing from thrift stores. We were always on the run. It's just another LA story: from the trailer to the top. That's why I stayed here, why I still love it. It's, like, the only place where that's possible. In most cities, poor kids don't have a chance. Here, it's almost an advantage, you know; it means you're more authentic and driven than the competition."

I nodded. I would have agreed with anything at that point. I never wanted to leave the closet, the soft press of her body against mine could go on for days and I'd be happy.

"You feeling okay?" she asked.

"Yes," I said. I didn't say that I had gone off to heaven in her arms, and that she should never leave me. I didn't say that I desperately wanted to kiss her everywhere. I thought how ironic it would be to have my first full encounter with a female inside an actual closet. It was surprising that I had *any* vocal restraint in the state I was in, but oddly it seemed that I'd become more acutely aware of things.

"Thanks for listening, babe. I don't tell many people that stuff."

She released my arms, sitting up and taking my head in her hands. She tilted my face up so I could look into her eyes, shadowy and sparkly in the dim light.

"You are so amazing," I said quietly.

"So are you, buttercup," she said. Her hands encircled my neck, thumbs pressing under my ears, lips so maddeningly close to mine. I hoped she couldn't feel how hard my heart was banging against my ribcage. I wanted her to kiss me so badly I was about to find the courage to do it first, but I was also hyper-aware that would mean things would shift dramatically between us—maybe even ruin all that I had to hope for, career-wise. Did it have to change everything, though? At the moment, I almost didn't care. I just wanted her with every fiber of my being.

A bitter nasal drip suddenly filled the back of my throat. I swallowed uncomfortably and reflexively made a face.

Spell broken, Ruby let go of me. An involuntary sigh of disappointment escaped my lips as she got up and offered me her hand.

"I was crushing you, poor thing."

"I didn't mind," I said instantly, embarrassing myself with the earnestness of my tone.

She laughed in the face of my vulnerability. It was the cruelest, harshest laugh I'd ever heard, one that warned of imminent trouble. One that probably could have told me everything I needed to know, had I been listening.

"Listen, be a good girl and keep this all between us. Okay?" she said, slapping me lightly on the cheek before she headed back to the crowd, leaving me alone and forlorn in her wake. She didn't look at me again for the rest of the party.

DYSFUNCTION RUNS DEEP

GLITTER TEARS WAS BACK AT IT again, trying to have a rehearsal. So far, the atmosphere was even weirder than last time, but at least we were all present, just waiting on Ruby.

I felt on edge and hoped my playing wouldn't reflect that. Or maybe it would be a good thing. I had heard that playing angry helped, sometimes. Frustration pressed at me and I had no idea how to kick it away.

Jeremy crouched by the mixer, adjusting some knobs.

"What's going on?" Stardust asked.

"*Aagh*, one of these effects is screwed." He stood up. "I think I got it, though."

Slinky emerged from the bathroom, wiping his hands on his jeans. "Let's be all warmed up when the princess gets here."

Stardust frowned. "She said she was coming early. She had a kink in 'Flamethrower' she wanted to work out."

"Huh," Jeremy said. "Well, I haven't heard from her." He sat at his drum set, pulled out some brushes, and started playing a fast jazz beat. "I'm gonna keep messing around till she gets here. Wallace wants me to do a set with him in Brentwood this weekend."

"Jazz fusion sucks." Slinky plugged in his guitar and strummed the opening chords to 'Faded.' Jeremy ignored him and kept playing jazzy, syncopated beats. It was a total musical mismatch, but I kind of liked the way it mirrored the off-beat energy of the room.

"What do you think they put in this stuff?" Stardust asked from over by the fridge, a can of Wild Child energy drink in her hand.

"Crack," Slinky said. "The hippies chug it when they run out of blow."

I went over to the kitchen to get myself some water. There was a magazine open on the counter. I stood there thumbing through it while drinking and *boom*! There was an interview with none other than Ruby Sky of Glitter Tears.

"What's this?" I asked.

"An article that ran a few weeks ago," Stardust said from over by her bass.

I checked out the cover in awe. It was the new issue of *Amped*. I hadn't seen it yet. There was Ruby looking impossibly hot, crawling on the ground in a black and purple bodice that matched her hair. She had black glitter on her eyelids as well as her tattoo tear. "*Glitter Tears Glam Girl*" was the headline.

I flipped to the interview and started to read. It began with the writer's commentary: Glitter Tears was as true as rock gets, refusing all trendy fads, keeping it authentic. Ruby's vocals were sexy and perfectly wound like everything was thrilling to her. Then Ruby spoke about the story behind the *Perpetual Twilight* album, how she wrote it in a little studio in London with only one window, out of which it seemed to perpetually be twilight.

The article went on to mention the other members of the band. Stardust Wu's parents were two first-generation Chinese engineers. She grew up in Santa Monica and dropped out of design school as soon as the band took off. Jeremy, a jazz-trained New Orleans percussionist, auditioned for Glitter Tears as a joke, but the joke ended up being that he could play Ruby's music better than anyone else. Slinky was originally from Orange County, and was not just a famous lead guitarist but also, of course, a pro skateboarder and sex icon for teenage girls. The writer seemed a little jealous of Slinky, speculating that "perhaps his ego keeps his guitar technique from being brilliant."

I laughed inside, betting Slinky hadn't even cared to read the article. Then, something toward the end made chills run up my arms and legs. Ruby mentioned a new band member on the keys. She didn't specify who it would be, only that "he'll be an excellent addition to the upcoming tour."

I put the magazine down and looked over at Stardust and Slinky.

"You guys?"

"Yeah?" Stardust said hesitantly.

"Who's the keyboardist Ruby mentions in the article? Was there supposed to be a guy going on tour with you?"

Stardust sighed and leaned her bass up against the wall as Slinky strummed some fast power chords and sang, "She finally found out, she finally found out," in a high-pitched screech.

Stardust hit him. "Shut up, stupid." She came over and sat down at the kitchen table, making a face. "Okay. I'll tell you some stuff before Ruby gets here." She glanced at the giant clock in the shape of a bass clef over the front door and shook her head. "She's never this late."

I sat down, already dreading the conversation we were about to have. Jeremy and Slinky continued to jam with their heads bowed, clearly wanting no part of our discussion. My leg bounced up and down as I waited for her to start.

"Okay," Stardust pushed her orange glasses up on her nose and tucked her hair behind her ears. "So, Ruby had lined up another keyboardist before you. His name was Mike. He was a recruit from another band, Dixie Cup. They're still unsigned, they kind of suck. Mike's clearly the most talented. He was already a Glitter Tears fan, he's this femme guy with a blond ponytail. Ruby got him in to practice with us and he was working out all right, but then . . . Ruby got involved with him. Things between them got hot fast and then went down in flames."

She took another small sip of her drink. I needed details.

"What happened?"

"Brian came into town and she disappeared for a little while. She usually does when he's around. But Mike freaked out. He was pretty nuts for her. He ended up going over to her place and spying on her."

"No *way*," I said.

"Way. He saw Ruby and Brian together and . . . things got messy. Now, he's not allowed to come within five hundred feet of her, but apparently he couldn't handle that, so he left town. I think he went back to Michigan to live with his dad."

"Wow. That's crazy."

"Actually, it's typical," she said. "The lawyer said, 'Oh, yeah, I know the guy to help you out, he finalizes hundreds of restraining orders a week.' A week later, it was a done deal."

"So there's a lot of psychos around here."

She let out a short laugh. "A restraining order doesn't necessarily make someone insane. There are a lot of obsessive artists, it's always a fine line."

"Yeah," said Slinky from across the room where the guys had stopped playing and I hadn't noticed. "Ask Jeremy." He burst out in a high-pitched laugh. Jeremy threw a drumstick at him and he dodged it easily.

"Jeremy has a restraining order?" I asked quietly, afraid to hear the answer.

"My ex is the crazy one," he said. I turned to face him. He tapped the cymbal with his index finger. "Whatever. She wouldn't mail me my stuff so I had to go get it myself. It's actually a really boring story."

"Sure is when you tell it," Slinky smirked as Jeremy gave him the finger. I turned back to Stardust. It was a lot to digest, but I could tell by her expression she wasn't finished yet. I looked at the clock again. An hour had passed since rehearsal was supposed to begin.

She shook her head. "Look," she continued matter-of-factly. "I love Ruby. We all love her. She's our queen. But you need to be aware that Ruby's pretty reckless with people. I've been meaning to talk to you about this after you two disappeared at the party last night."

I looked away, unsure what to say. Pretty sure my deep blush gave enough away for me to remain quiet. I felt guilty even though we hadn't actually done anything, maybe because of how badly I wished we had.

"What happens between you two isn't only your business," Stardust continued briskly. "We're all going on tour in a few weeks. We're going to be together every day, all day. What you do now, how you handle the relationship, will affect all of us. It was hard enough finding and losing Mike in a matter of months, but we're all glad he's gone, because dealing with the two of them on the road would have been way worse."

Thoughts whirred and crackled in my head. I wasn't sure what to say. How much did she know? How much did I not know? How long and how much had I been keeping myself in the dark about what was happening between Ruby and me? *Was* anything happening between Ruby and me? This conversation was the closest I'd gotten to validation that it was.

"Nothing happened," I finally managed to get out. It sounded like a pathetic lie, even to me.

Stardust finished her energy drink, burped a little burp, tossed the can into the garbage, and continued. "Then don't look so panicked, Kyla. We dig you, but it's obvious that Ruby's got a hold over you. Maybe nothing's happened so far, but things could go wrong fast, you know? I'm not trying to freak you out, just trying to prevent a lot more unnecessary drama for us all to have to deal with."

"What do you think's going to happen?"

Stardust shot me a "get smarter" look. I stumbled on, although I couldn't believe we were having this talk, that these words were coming out of my mouth. "I mean, you think something's going to happen . . . between me and Ruby? Because, um, I thought she likes guys."

"She likes who she likes," Stardust said matter-of-factly.

My heart zoomed with possibilities and I tipped my water glass, spilling water onto the open issue of *Amped*.

"*Damn it*," I said with a little too much emotion.

"Quit scaring her over there," Jeremy said. "Everything's gonna be fine, Kyla. We believe in you."

"I, for one, am all for lesbos," Slinky said, still strumming at his unplugged guitar. "I say go for it. Onstage."

"Oh, shut up, bonehead," Stardust said to him. "Such a tool," she muttered under her breath.

"I heard that, Dusty," Slinky said.

"Good," she said sharply. She got up and went over to the phone by the kitchen sink. "I'm calling Ruby again."

I excused myself and went into the bathroom. My reflection in the mirror was once again showing a lost girl searching for a clue. I was so far out to sea that I couldn't even see the shoreline of myself. I wished I knew what to say to these people who were far more in the know than I would ever be. They all probably thought I was a ticking time bomb, and now I definitely felt like it.

What Stardust had said was true. Ruby did have a hold over me. She was my stunning superhero. She'd rescued me from my sad little existence. How could she not have all the power?

The fact that she hadn't shown up for practice produced more gnashing teeth anxiety. I could feel her presence stronger than ever, even though she wasn't there. Sometimes the only person in the room is the person not in the room. Her absence was a dark thundercloud over us all.

Maybe it was my fault she wasn't there. Was she upset about our moment in the party closet? She'd seemed distant ever since. But no, it couldn't be my fault this time, nothing had actually happened. But what was Stardust talking about, being careful about how I handled the relationship? I wasn't "handling" anything, and certainly didn't have the backbone to deny Ruby anything. . . .

When I came out of the bathroom, thoroughly un-soothed, Stardust had her purse on her shoulder. Slinky had put his guitar away and Jeremy was packing up his cymbals.

"We're out," Slinky said. "This is on her, this time."

Coming over to refill his coffee mug, Jeremy shot me a tight smile. "Don't stress. It'll work out. It always does. You'll get the hang of the swings. You just have to be flexible."

I wondered if I could be much more flexible than I already was without turning into jelly and completely slipping through the cracks.

THE PAST WILL ALWAYS HAUNT YOU

THAT NIGHT, ROBERT AND I DROVE along Sunset Boulevard listening to the dissonant wailing of The Bell Tops, sharing a stiff drink out of Robert's driving thermos, deep in the search for Ruby Sky. We'd done a drive-by of her cottage on Beachwood. We'd checked a café on Gower where she liked to write. The next stop was the Sunset Strip's Rainbow Bar and Grill. Robert said it was a legendary place where people went to meet others in the music industry. He went there strictly to drink.

We valeted the car and walked up to the entrance. A variety of Hollywood characters—actors, musicians, groupies—sat on the front patio, cigarettes blazing, drinks in hand. The guy at the door was an older Italian mobster type in a suit with a droopy nose and silly putty skin. He nodded at Robert and didn't ask me for ID.

Inside, I fell in love with the vintage charm of the place. Rainbow Christmas lights and countless photos of famous artists decorated the walls. A giant stone fireplace blazed at the front of the dining room. Circular red vinyl booths were crowded with people. Glistening pizzas perched on stands on the tables, and the whole place radiated with the smell of pizza and garlic and French fries. My stomach twisted with desire.

"No Ruby and no open tables," Robert said. "Let's try the back patio."

He greeted the tattooed bartenders and tough-looking waitresses as we walked past the kitchen out to the patio with a separate bar. A high cocktail table with two chairs was open in the corner. "Perfect," he said, and he pulled out a chair for me.

I sat down as Robert went up to the bar for drinks. Three women who were dressed like they had just finished shifts at a strip club were perched in front of tall drinks. They were gorgeous, but I had to look away because one of them kept chewing on her fake fingernails and it turned my stomach.

"Here we go, lightning fingers," Robert said, returning with our drinks.

"I think that's my favorite nickname I've ever had," I said.

"Well, I can't say you're the only one I've called that, but you're the one who likes it the most," he replied with a smirk.

I rolled my eyes and sampled my drink. I was starting to expect the initial punch of the first sip, learning to enjoy the fizzy aftershock of dizziness. I couldn't help but wince as I took another sip. It seemed there were only two types of drinks in LA: strong and stronger.

"What's wrong?"

"My stomach's so empty that I feel drunk already."

He stood up. "I can fix that."

Robert disappeared and reappeared so quickly it seemed almost suspect. He was carrying a wicker basket with a napkin in it. Several tiny loaves of warm bread were nestled inside.

"Thanks! Here," I said, handing him one.

He shook his head and held up his hand. "I don't do bread," he said. "Hangs off these old hips."

I sighed and took a tiny bite as something caught my eye at the bar, a woman who could have been Ruby from behind. The lighting was so dim I couldn't tell if her hair was purple or brown. Robert turned to follow my gaze. She twisted her head and it became instantly apparent that it wasn't Ruby, so when I looked back at Robert and he had gigantic saucer eyes, I was confused.

"What? It's not her," I said.

"Yes it is," he said, his voice almost a whisper.

"No, I can see her face from where I'm sitting, and it's not."

He gave me such a chilly stare that I shivered.

"I think I'd recognize my ex-wife from two hundred feet away, let alone ten," he said, his voice flat again.

My eyes searched the room again and I spotted her: Linda Crosby had appeared in the doorway past the bar, looking tan and tantalizing in a thin white dress over lace leggings and boots. Her hair was long, loose, and professionally sun-streaked, and seemed to move separately from her body like a bunch of restless grass snakes. She didn't fit in among all the salty rocker types on the patio, and a lot of them had taken immediate notice. She stood in the doorway, pondering her next move, when a striking guy with dark stubble came up from behind her and kissed her bare shoulder. She hadn't seemed to notice Robert yet.

Which was good, because Robert was frozen in a particularly hideous expression, like he'd stepped in dog crap or something. His despair permeated the air.

"Should we—?" He waved me silent and finished his drink in one swallow. If jealousy was the emotion painted all over his face, it was a color I hoped I'd never see again.

Linda and the guy made their way to the bar. She was staring straight ahead but not really seeing anything. In her mind she was probably miles away, sipping martinis on a balcony in Malibu. I wondered why they were here. They looked like they'd come straight from some yacht party photo shoot or something.

Robert stood up abruptly just as one of the women standing next to us drunkenly tried to pass a tequila shot off the bar to her friend and sloshed some on Linda, who whipped around angrily to see him standing there. I stared at her, hypnotized by her unearthly, air-brushed looks. She and Robert held each other in a steely eye lock. She finally broke it to check me out. I wondered why she was paying me the slightest bit of attention, let alone giving me a catty look, until I realized she thought I was his date.

Robert shattered the silence.

"What are you doing here?"

She threw her head back and let out the tinny bounce of a fake laugh. "What am I doing here? That's actually a good question. This place isn't my style. Greg likes it for some silly reason."

Greg, presumedly the stubble guy, had his back to us and was busy ordering drinks from the bartender.

"Dating down. I'm shocked." Robert said dryly.

She flashed Robert a sharp-knife smile. "And I see you've gotten yourself a cute little no-name. She's young—very young. Poor thing must think you still have it."

He held her in a level stare. "She knows I've never been worse."

Her face shifted ever-so-slightly. "Well. Guess you've had your time. Don't be so hard on yourself. That's how it goes.

You rise and then you fall. Dating younger girls doesn't help you get it back. You of all people should know that."

Linda looked like—and even seemed to speak like—a robot; totally cliché lines, completely devoid of emotion. Her date turned around with two drinks in hand. "Here you go, babe," he said as he held the drink out for her. She didn't take it. He noticed Robert and me and raised an eyebrow. "What's up?"

Nobody answered for a moment, letting his question hang stupidly in the air. Then Linda said, "Greg, this is my ex-husband, Robert."

"Oh, *heavy*."

Robert's eyes remained on Linda the entire time. "Well you're still a raging bitch. That doesn't go away no matter how many brainless models you date."

Greg put the drinks on the bar and stepped closer to Robert. He was pretty ripped, but Robert had a few inches on him. "Hey, do we have a problem, man?"

Robert punched him faster than I'd ever seen anyone get punched, a blur of fleshy movement, and then Greg was on the ground holding his nose. Blood streamed through his fingers, creating a dark liquid bloom on the front of his shirt.

The iciest smile slipped across Linda's lips. "You and the teenager belong together."

As people swarmed around Greg and Linda, Robert grabbed my arm and we hightailed it through the patio. Robert grabbed his keys from the rack as the valet guy rushed toward us.

"Hey! You can't do that!"

Robert pushed him away and he fell over as we tore across the parking lot to where the car was parked. I barely had time to jump in before Robert accelerated and the car roared out of the back of the lot.

We raced up Laurel Canyon so fast I had to close my eyes. Even in the California heat, I was shivering. I dug my nails into the side of the passenger seat, the surprise sucker punch on replay in my head. We climbed the canyon in silence. The city lights flickered and twinkled down below as if everything was going to be okay. That was the thing about LA that scared me the most so far: everything looked so good from the outside, but was malicious in so many hidden ways.

DISAPPEAR WHEN YOU CAN'T DEAL

ROBERT HADN'T COME DOWN FROM HIS room. Ruby still wasn't answering her phone. I didn't have any of the other bandmates' unlisted numbers. Part of me wanted to call home, but I didn't have anything good to tell them and I couldn't bear to hear my father's told-you-so tone. As restless as I'd ever been, I paced back and forth in the kitchen, debating whether I should go knock on Robert's door. I finally decided against it. Seeing him like that at the Rainbow had shook me.

I needed to get out of the house. We swung by Ruby's place yesterday on our search, so I knew where it was. Without thinking too much about it, I wrote a quick note telling Robert I'd gone on a mission to Ruby's house. Cursing myself for still not having found the courage to drive since the accident with Mom, even in these dire conditions, I took off on foot for Ruby's bungalow.

It felt great to be on my own as I walked down Laurel Canyon in the smoggy sunshine. The air was thin and dry and I started to feel more normal. I could walk at my own pace, enjoy my surroundings without anyone steering the conversation or naming the destination. No one even knew where I was. It dawned on me how much relinquishing all control had to do with my ever-increasing anxiety. I vowed to get out on my own more and make more of my own decisions. It felt like I could breathe right for the first time in weeks.

By day, the city looked larger and more sprawled out than after dark. I wanted to call LA home. Was there space for me here? The guilt about leaving my family—especially my mom—hit abruptly, slamming me into panic again. I'd never have taken the jump on my own if I hadn't been offered a hand from across the country. Ruby had somehow opened up my tightly packed box of secret desires. On one hand, it was unfathomably exciting, and on the other, I had no idea how to handle it. Daydreaming was definitely better than day*doubting*, however. The escape was in the distraction, and without Ruby around, reality was pressing in too hard.

Ruby's bungalow was at the bottom of Beachwood canyon, nestled between giant palm trees and blooming roses. You could see the crooked, iconic Hollywood sign from her street. Bright white and pink blooms were dripping off the rose bushes, hanging their heavy heads of petals, shimmering in the sunshine. I stepped around the sprinkler, enjoying the mist on my neck and face. The whole place felt very cute—pale purple paint on the exterior of the house, lace curtains in the windows, a brick chimney that ran up the side. I'd have guessed that a grandma lived there if I didn't know it was Ruby's place. It made me love her even more that she chose to live in a cozy bungalow instead of the bigger, flashier places she could afford if she wanted. She'd said she would never feel comfortable in a big house after living in an RV for all those years. She liked to feel the walls around her.

Her car still wasn't in the driveway but I went up to the window next to the door and peeked in anyway. The living room was full of parlor furniture. On a wide, oval-shaped mahogany table in the center was a partially-assembled jigsaw puzzle, but there were no other signs of life. I felt like a trespasser peeking in, not much different from her last obsessive keyboardist, Mike. I backed away from the window, hurried to the front door, and rang the bell.

A few long minutes went by without a sound from inside. But I wasn't leaving until I found her. She *had* to be in there, I could feel her close, and I would do whatever it took to make sure she was all right. I followed a brick path that snaked around the house, through a few lovely vine-covered arches. Under the last one, I became caught up in a spider web and I shivered and struggled to brush it off, twisting my head in the process, where I glimpsed a side window partially cracked open—no screen. I snuck up and strained to hear what was going on inside.

A harpsichord rang out—broken chords with a haunting melody above it. The recording was fuzzy and crackly. I stood on my tiptoes and peered through the window at a very messy bedroom. The bed had huge, ornately carved wooden balusters, and the mess that covered the mattress reminded me of my bed back home—a lumpy nest of sheets, clothes, and papers. Next to an old dresser sat the source of the music, an antique brass phonograph. Sunlight bounced through a crystal hanging in the window, creating fragments of drifting rainbows on the walls.

I pushed the window frame up as far as it would go. The nostalgic old record jangled my nerves. Gathering all my strength, I hoisted myself up through the window, then careened forward onto the rug with a thud. My hands dug into the soft shag carpet. An overwhelming scent of vanilla honeysuckle perfume mixed with something strong and sickly, like decomposing yogurt. The phone dangled off its hook from the bedside table.

Something in the bed moved, knocking a bunch of clothes and papers to the ground.

"Ruby?" I croaked, my voice a shrill bullet through the stuffy room. A tangled purple mess of hair emerged from the nest, followed by Ruby's pale, squinting face. She looked at me, her eyes wet and spacey—two glossy planets, far, far away.

"Kyla?" she murmured.

"I came to check on you."

I slowly approached the bed. "We're all worried about you. You missed practice." I said all of this gently, noticing how puffy her face was, deep imprints of pillows marking her cheeks.

"Am I awake? Or dreaming?" she said again, wiping her eyes.

"You're awake." I shook my head and sat carefully on the edge of the bed, knocking a belt, a bottle of prescription pills, and a few stockings to the ground. "I'm so happy to see you," I said in a gentle tone previously reserved for my mother.

She sat up a little more, sniffed, and wiped her face on her sleeve.

"It's happening again," she said in a muffled, morbid whisper.

"What is?" I asked.

She didn't answer. I leaned in closer. "Ruby, what's happening?"

"I messed up," she said. "I can't go through with it again, I can't."

"I'm here to help you," I said. I knew from experiences with my mother that it was better to support than press for details. "We'll fix it together, okay?"

"You can't," she whimpered. "Nothing can make it right. I can't do it again."

She dissolved in sobs. I stared at a photo on her nightstand of her and Brian at some event on the red carpet, taken a few years ago. They were holding hands and both appeared to be supremely happy. But here in this room, a terrible sadness hung in the air around us. I took a tissue from the box on her nightstand and tried to give it to her, but I couldn't find her hand under all the stuff on the bed.

Minutes passed as I waited for Ruby's tears to die down. I glanced at scattered bottles of pills, resisting the urge to read their contents. I wondered how many she had taken but I couldn't badger her, she was far too fragile. At the moment, it seemed unlikely that she would be able to get herself out of bed.

It didn't matter. At least she was here beside me, alive and awake.

When she finally reemerged from under the sheets, I couldn't look at her without feeling hopeless. Her face was not Ruby Sky, but a totally different person. Her eyes were darker, wilder. They reminded me of the trapped squirrels in the attic when my dad set out Havahart traps.

"How did you get here?" she asked suddenly.

"I walked."

Her eyes widened. "All the way from Robert's?"

I nodded.

"You're nuts."

"You've been missing for a couple days. I had to find you."

She shook her head. "Someone's come to the door a few times, too, but—*Wait.* How did you get inside?"

I looked over to the open window. The sun was going down in the pink-purple sky beyond the rose bushes.

"The window?" Ruby's voice raised and she offered a weak laugh. Although it was a lot drier than her usual tinkle it was still a relief to see her smile. "You're even more rock star than I thought."

I blushed. "I love your place."

That made her laugh again, stronger this time. "My room is unfit for human life."

"It reminds me of my bedroom back home. I really love your old phonograph. And this bed is so cool."

She reached out to touch a baluster. "This belonged to my dad's sister Rose. She died while giving birth."

Her face paled and she looked about to be sick.

"Ruby? Can I get you anything? Water, a cold wash towel, a trash can?"

"No, cupcake," she reached out and took my hand. Her skin was clammy and her fingers gripped mine tight. "Thanks. I'm actually glad you're here. I can't help it, I shut everything out when I . . . I get really sad."

"I understand."

Ruby's eyes seeped into me in that way that again reminded me of my mom. "How do you understand?"

I looked down at our hands interlaced over a striped sock.

"I help my mother a lot when she goes through . . . sad times."

It was the first time I'd brought her issues up to Ruby. I didn't want her to be scared that I had emotional problems, too.

"Has your mother been through a tragedy?"

"Yes," I said. "Well, there was an accident that, um, brought out psychological issues."

Ruby sighed. "Who *doesn't* have psychological issues, is what I want to know."

I gave her a half smile, relieved at her response.

She squeezed my hand again, then let it go and propped herself up. "Look, Kyla, this may sound strange, and I'm sorry about your mom, but I'm sort of glad to hear it. It makes me feel like you're able to handle more. You know, I wanted to tell you, but I wasn't sure you could take it."

"Tell me what?"

There was a big pause in which every single terrible thing she could say ran through my mind. Every single thing except the words: "I'm pregnant. *Again.*"

My mouth fell open but I shut it quickly and tried not to look too shocked. "It's so awful, you don't even know," she went on, her words speeding up. "A few years ago, I decided I didn't want to be on birth control anymore. You know, like, why do *we* have to take the hormones that screw our bodies up? Men would never take anything that had such nasty side effects. But it turns out that I should have protected myself, because men can walk away from a pregnancy, and women can't. That's the simplest fact of life. And maternal mortality runs in my family. But the abortion was a horror story on its own because they messed up and didn't put me all the way under for the procedure. I still have nightmares about it. I learned the hard way to protect myself all the time, no matter what. Then I went back on the pill, even though I'm way more of an emotional train wreck when pumped with progestin. But—"

She broke off and I watched her body wrack with stifled sobs.

"But somehow, I screwed up and I'm pregnant *again*. And it's too awful, too awful to deal. And right before the tour! What am I going to do?"

She folded forward and I held her starving kitten body in my arms, scared that I wouldn't be able to ever find the words to soothe her, afraid that she was going to break her own bones with her crushing sobs. I held her for a long time, my own mind so overwhelmed that it kept shutting down and then jerking itself back on again with every twitch or shudder of her ribcage.

I wanted to ask her who the other responsible party was, but deep inside I already knew by looking at the picture of her and Brian next to her bed. When the crying died down she saw me staring at it.

"He can't know," she said softly. "I can't bring myself to tell him this *a second time*."

"Why not?" I asked. "I'm sure he'd want to help."

"No," she said. "It's too much . . . I'll do this on my own. He won't be able to look at me ever again if I tell him. It took such a long time for us to come back from the first time."

"Well you're not alone," I said more fiercely than I meant to. "I'm here for you."

"I know you are, angel cake." She twirled a lock of my hair around her index finger, tugged it gently, and let it go.

"Ruby? Are you and Brian . . . together?"

She sighed so sadly I regretted asking immediately. "We'll always be together, but we'll also always be apart. We are what we can be, when we can be together."

The simple explanation of a clearly complex relationship struck a nerve. I wanted to protect her from this nebulous yet constant part of her life. Someone she felt that continually connected with no matter how many times he failed to protect her from his end. Struggling not to sound too judgmental, I said, "Do you like that . . . situation?"

She took a shuddery breath. "It's complicated, but it's also the relationship that makes the most sense for us."

I bit my lip. It was time. I had to say the words that flowed from the cavern of my immeasurable fixation on her.

"Ruby, I want you to know I'll always be here for you. Always, no matter what, okay? I'll never leave you." There. Short and sweet and no big deal, right? I hadn't come off as too grandiose or needy—

She smiled thinly. "And I appreciate it, Kyla, but I'm going to have to ask you to take off for now. I'll be in touch. I need to be alone right now. I'll deal with everything."

Oof. She totally steamrolled me and clearly rejected my tender offer of lifelong commitment. Still, I couldn't help but whine, "Why?"

Ruby rolled her eyes. She'd suddenly shifted back to a fully alert, sharp-tongued queen. "Look, I've been through worse than this on my own, and I can't really be responsible for making sure you're okay when I should be making sure I'm okay—"

"You don't have to make sure I'm okay! I'm saying—"

"I need to be alone now," she said, firmer this time.

I couldn't tell what hurt more, her frosty tone or the way she was practically pushing me off the bed. I stood trembling above her, panting in my own fury at being too young, saying the wrong thing, always being the green girl. I felt out of control, stumbling out on a limb, achingly blind from within.

"I won't let you shut me out," I stammered.

Ruby stifled a yawn and pushed me further away. "Go. It was a mistake to tell you. You're falling apart already, and now it's going to be one more weight on my chest. This is why I don't do this."

I was stumbling, free-falling. "I'm not trying to be a weight. I'm trying to be *here* for you, Ruby. After all, I'm only here *because* of you."

This seemed to set her off even more. "Kyla, I never asked for your help, so don't go reeling into some messy headspace about this being your problem. God, you said you could handle it. I'm sorry I told you. Now get the hell out of here before you go all psycho on me!"

Her words whipped me across both my flaming hot cheeks. Was she already comparing me to the last keyboardist? How had things come to this? Was I turning into him? Ruby really was impossible. No one had a chance at getting in. But how did Brian keep doing it? By always being one foot out the door at the same time?

"And leave the way you came in, I don't feel like getting up to lock the front door behind you," she snapped, disappearing back into her nest. The only sign of her was the slight rise and fall of the sheets as she breathed, rustling stockings, papers, and panties. I stood there for a moment and watched the rainbow light waver and dissolve toward the bottom of the walls with the waning sunset. Then I climbed back out through the window and vowed to stop chasing the stormy Ruby Sky across the jagged valleys of her dysfunction.

BAND IS FAMILY

LIFE HAD GONE FROM WEIRD TO downright spooky, somehow magnified by the constant sunshine and heat. Robert still hadn't come downstairs since the night of the sucker punch. His cars remained in the garage, and I occasionally heard his toilet flushing. I thought I could hear him mumbling to himself sometimes when I'd hover outside his room, but I couldn't get the nerve to knock and see if he was okay.

The truth was, I was scared. He might scream at me. The incident with Ruby reminded me that I shouldn't push myself on people. I couldn't bear to go through another blow-up. I was exhausted all the time yet had trouble sleeping at all. My appetite had almost entirely disappeared. I was currently surviving on coffee, awful-tasting tap water, fists of stale cereal and cocktail nuts, topped off with the cigarettes Robert had stashed in the kitchen.

Alone in the bathroom I confronted my unrecognizable reflection, struggling to find a way to see myself as worthy of any positive thoughts. There were fleeting moments I saw myself as someone I could feel sort of confident about, but mostly I found nothing but flaws. My face was all wrong. My brain was scratchy. I'd never felt flatter inside, stuck in this weirdo wonderland populated by twenty-dimensional cartoons with sinking boatloads of issues. I bent forward, rested my head on my arms on the edge of the sink, and stared harder. The mirror wasn't telling me anything I wanted to hear.

The more weight I lost, the edgier I felt inside, the darker my moods got. Everything was ill-fitting or off in some way. There was no comfort to be found anywhere, in anything. I was struggling to connect with a self I remembered from back East, a shred of something that felt familiar, but all I saw was some strange pink-haired girl with dark circles under her eyes, a slouchy poser stuck in a permanent panic attack.

There was a lot of time and fuel for fresh material for my journal, though. I listened to music in the studio as loud as it would go, scribbling away. Sometimes I'd put *Perpetual Twilight* on and listen to it, not playing along, just to hear Ruby's voice because I missed her. I especially loved the last song on the album, "Tainted." Her voice was so angry and her lyrics were so powerful it propped me up a bit. That was the Ruby Sky I worshipped, the Ruby Sky I knew. She was a creature who didn't care what anyone thought, didn't care how boldly she wore her feelings. I wanted to be like that Ruby, the one who shoved it all out there for the world to hear and feel along with her.

I'd always been too careful. It limited my connections with people and with my music. My songs were sad and sometimes hopeful, but definitely not angry, tortured or unshackled. They lacked that recklessness, that range. How was I supposed to be brave in my own voice?

Where did people find courage? Did it come packaged with loss? Did superpowers belong only to those who had sacrificed for them? I'd been sheltered and I was finally beginning to see the extent of it. My thresholds were dangerously shallow in this world of much deeper loss and suffering. There was only one answer. I would have to keep throwing myself into the fire to get the burns, to prove to myself I could handle the pain.

Why had I even come to LA? It wasn't for glamour or money or fame. Being around all that showed me there was no real appeal there. Fame felt like a hollow trick, the emperor's clothes that could be blinked away at any moment. So what was I looking for, underneath it all?

The reason was suddenly so clear to me, as I looked down at the scribbled pages of stronger lyrics than I'd ever written before.

I'd come to rough myself up in the name of art.

Yeah?

I was brewing myself a fresh pot of coffee when the doorbell rang. Stardust stood outside in an orange camouflage dress that perfectly matched her glasses and wristbands. I was so relieved to see her that I threw my arms around her and probably squeezed too hard.

"Hi," she said into my shoulder.

"I'm so glad you're here."

We broke apart and she looked at me.

"You look thin. And a little strung out, to be honest."

"There's no food in this house," I said apologetically. "It's okay, though, there's lots of coffee. Do you want some?"

"I'm fine," she said. "Let's sit outside in the sun."

The sun was blazing high in the sky and the neighborhood was quiet. We sat in dusty chairs on the patio. It was peaceful with the birds chirping and the faint scent of eucalyptus trees.

I wondered why I hadn't sat out in the sun more these past lonesome days, instead of floating around the house like a lost ghost. The fresh air and sunshine made me feel a lot better.

Stardust took her boots off and set her feet up on another chair. Her toenails were painted yellow. I admired her body, which was thin and muscular at the same time. She looked both healthy and cool, which I realized was kind of rare. We sat there for a minute, absorbing the sun. I was unsure of what Stardust knew and didn't know on the subject of Ruby so I started with another subject.

"Robert's been in his room for days. I'm not sure what to do."

Her face creased into a frown. "What do you mean? What's wrong with him?"

I sighed. "We went looking for Ruby that night she didn't show up at rehearsal. We stopped at the Rainbow Bar and while we were there, Linda Crosby showed up with her new boyfriend."

"No." Stardust put her feet on the ground and her eyebrows shot up.

"Yeah. It was really bad. They said horrible things to each other and then Robert punched the guy she was with."

"He didn't."

"He did. He punched him hard, too. The guy was down on the floor, bleeding, and we ran out of the bar and drove off at top speed. He was so upset he went straight into his room and I haven't seen him since. I noticed a mug left out on the counter one morning, so he might be coming out really early to get some coffee or something."

"What is with the planets right now?" Stardust sighed while looking up at the sky. "Mercury must be in retrograde or something. Everything is totally upside down."

I was a little relieved that she seemed to think this was worse than normal. I'd been wondering how weird life could get and still be considered "normal" in this part of the world.

Stardust shook her head. "Someone should have told you that Robert isolates sometimes. It's not a good sign. Have you tried to knock on his door?"

"I've thought about it, but something keeps telling me not to do it. Maybe I'm afraid of pissing him off. He's been mumbling so maybe he's been on the phone. I did leave the house and walk to Ruby's the other day."

She nodded. "I heard."

"So you've talked to her?"

"I was over there earlier today. She told me how you came by and broke into her house. Ballsy move, especially after I told you about the last keyboardist and his boundary issues."

"Is she upset with me?" I asked, though I dreaded the answer.

"She's upset with the world right now."

"Is she going to be okay?"

Stardust ran a hand through her hair and crossed her legs. "So, this is why I came over to talk."

Right there in her tone I knew that everything was about to change.

"She's not herself. I've never seen her like this."

She was quiet for a moment. I grabbed a cigarette. When I lit it, she looked over at me and raised her eyebrows.

"You're a smoker now?"

I was struck by her surprise. I'd thought that was expected. Then I realized I'd never seen Stardust smoke.

"I guess so," I said, feeling lame about it for the first time. "It's been something to do while sitting around, stressing out, you know?"

"It's a gross habit, but listen," Stardust said, moving on. "We're going to her place to take care of her while she does an at-home abortion."

It sounded terrifying. I had no idea what an at-home abortion entailed.

"She doesn't know that I'm bringing you, but we have to do this as a team, whether she likes it or not. I'm not going in there alone."

I nodded, in shock. "She's brave to do it at home."

"Sometimes self-destructiveness gets mistaken for bravery. It's not right for her to handle these things alone. She pushes people away when she needs them the most. That's not bravery to me. That's more of a self-pity move. Everyone needs someone. And band is family. Never forget that."

I had hoped being in a band would give me a sense of family. But the thing was, I didn't have a strong feeling of family in the first place. With no siblings and two very difficult parents, my life had never been a lovely picture-book kind of place. To build an idea of "family" was totally foreign to me. But even in my inexperience, I knew that what it would take was guts, and I had those. Glitter Tears was my family now, and I didn't want to be on my own, so I would do whatever it took to hold on to them—even if I was panic-stricken the entire time.

GET RUGGED

RUBY'S EXPLANATION OF WHAT WAS GOING on sounded like the lyrics for a new Glitter Tears song.

"I took these pills that are gonna blow me up from the inside."

We were sitting in Ruby's living room, waiting it out. I was perched on the antique couch and Ruby was lying on the Persian rug. Stardust was in the kitchen making tea. I was acting like nothing had happened between Ruby and me, and she didn't seem to want to revisit it, either.

"What kind of pills?"

"I don't know. Some ulcer pills that happen to also induce abortions. I didn't ask too many questions." She rubbed small circles in her lower abdomen. "I have to do it this way, so it doesn't really matter."

"Why do you have to do it at home?"

"Kevin said I had to," she said in a monotone. "Word got out last time when I went to the clinic. Our fans are mainly teenagers, and . . . two abortions, you know . . ." A few tears rolled down her cheek. "Let's put it this way: I'm no role model. They should hide me away."

I stared at Ruby, speechless. It seemed crazy that Kevin could make that call. It was Ruby's body, not his, but I didn't want to make matters worse by saying that. Besides, she knew that already. I was the fool who hadn't realized that in showbiz, such personal decisions could be dictated by your management.

"When is it going to happen?" I was hoping to have more time to prepare for the terrifying idea that while we were sitting here, Ruby's body would be going through such insane turmoil, and neither Stardust nor I had the slightest idea what to do for her.

"No idea. I'm waiting, and it's the worst feeling ever. An endless landslide in your head getting bigger and bigger every minute. Seriously, you both should get out of here before this goes down. It's not going to be pretty."

I shook my head.

"We're not going anywhere," Stardust called from the kitchen.

She sucked in a breath and lowered her voice to a whisper. "I'm sorry you have to be here for this. I wish I could always be pretty for you."

"You are," I said. "You always will be."

"Yeah, right." Her un-glittered tattoo tear was wet with real ones. "Look at me, I haven't showered for days. My hair's an oil slick and I'm wearing Brian's old sweatpants and a diaper-sized pad. It's disgusting. I'm disgusting to myself. I'll never be pretty again."

"Impossible," I said, instantly nervous that I was coming on too strong again.

She clutched her stomach suddenly and her face seized in pain.

"Oh, *damn it*," she gasped as she sat straight up. I winced while watching her, imagining all sorts of horrible things going on inside her body that seemed hardly built to carry itself, let alone another being.

A kettle wailed in the kitchen.

"Chamomile or mint?" Stardust called to us as the teapot stopped whistling.

"Mint," Ruby whispered.

"Mint!" I shouted back.

Ruby crawled over to the armchair and grabbed a crocheted blanket off of it, wrapping it around herself. "Brian . . ." she trailed off, a wall of wetness forming over her eyes. "I won't tell him, he can never know." She shook her head. "I can't believe I've even told you. You can't say anything to anyone, okay? Especially not to him. I can't let this get out, I can't face the hate. I'm the type of person people love to hate, you know?"

I nodded, feeling the curling whip of protective anger around my chest. Hate Ruby? What was wrong with people? Condoms break, birth control pills fail, accidents happen, people lie. It was crazy how many huge negatives came along with sex, when it was so overhyped. Suddenly, I felt relief that I didn't have any urge to be with guys: an unexpected breath of fresh air in my dark and lonely closet.

I looked Ruby square in the eyes. "I promise. This is completely between us."

Ruby scratched her scalp, her violet locks so tangled and dirty they were almost dreadlocked.

"There's something else you should know," she said, speaking slowly, yet firmly. "We're obviously not going to be rehearsing for a while, and I'm thinking about canceling the tour."

The sentence hit me like a punch to the gut. A hole ripped through me. Then, waves of overwhelming numbness. I couldn't hear or feel anything. All the noise and scenery around me started to flicker, buzz, and fade away.

"Kyla? *Kyla!*" Stardust was shouting from two inches above my face.

I opened my eyes and sat up. "What happened?"

"Um, you fainted," Stardust said, pressing her hand to my forehead. It felt cool and soft. I was grateful for her anchor-like presence.

"Everything started to fade out like the end of a movie."

"It's not the end of the movie yet," Ruby said sharply, looking especially disgusted with me. "You need to not pass out when I tell you things. You can't be fainting at my abortion. Pull it together."

"Yeah, sorry. Um . . . Can you excuse me for a minute?" My tongue tripped and I swayed for a moment. I didn't understand if she was kidding. Reality was closing in, swallowing what was left of me. I was drowning in the thick air of Ruby's living room. A cold, sweaty film broke out on my face. "I, uh, I need to go to the bathroom."

I got up shakily and shuffled down the hall to her bedroom. I'd barely gotten the door closed before letting out one deep, throaty, gasping sob. I started pulling my arm hairs to calm myself, my latest nervous habit.

What was I supposed to do if the tour was cancelled? Go back home to Massachusetts and beg Holyoke to reconsider? That was impossible, considering I hadn't even graduated high school. Maybe Robert would let me stay with him and I could find another gig or something. I wasn't ready to go home, nor was I welcome there anymore. I had no savings, no security, and no contract; only the small weekly cash stipend I'd gotten since being out there—but that would go away without the tour.

How could Ruby do this to me? How could the whole thing be over before it began? We didn't even really rehearse together yet. My heart sank. My dad was right. I should have gotten something signed upfront. I was so furious I felt pinprick stabs at my temples.

I sat still for a moment, tasting the bitter, vengeful juice of fresh-squeezed anger, quickly followed by a washdown of shame as the sound of Ruby's anguished wail invaded from the front room. How could I even think about myself at a time like this? Was I already some sort of self-centered diva now that I'd been in LA for barely a month? Ruby was in there going through something horribly painful. She needed me. *She. Needed. Me.* And I needed to get it together, get back in there and help her. I needed to find my guts and stick it out. Grabbing a few tissues, I wiped my makeup-streaked face as I looked into the mirror. I willed myself to be stronger and calmer. Right now, Ruby needed to be reminded that everything was going to be okay more than I di—

A piercing cry rang out from the living room, the sound of a cat when you step on its tail. I ran to find Ruby doubled over on the floor, shaking.

"Make it stop, make it stop," she choked. "I need more painkillers."

"Kyla, grab them from the kitchen counter," Stardust commanded.

I stumbled to the kitchen and groped for the pills on the table. There were so many bottles I couldn't tell which of them were right so I scooped them all up in my arms. A couple bottles fell with a booming rattle to the floor. As I bent to scoop them up, more bottles dropped. I grasped around, struggling to fight down the tears.

"*Kyla,* where are those pills?!"

When I finally made it back to the living room, Stardust was kneeling opposite Ruby, who now lay curled up in the fetal position, shaking and gasping.

"I—can't—breathe—it—hurts—so—much—"

"Hydrocodone," Stardust directed as I joined them and released all the pills to the floor with an explosion of jangles. "Find Hydrocodone."

I started frantically looking through them. Ruby grabbed a bottle and whipped it at the fireplace with surprising strength. "Yes, more pills! What do any of these *actually do,* anyway? Look at me, I have all the pills you could ever need, and I'm in great shape—"

She dissolved, hyperventilating and crying at the same time. I searched until I found the bottle marked HYDROCODONE. Ruby snatched it from me and hastily poured a few directly into her mouth. I handed her a glass of water from the table, which she swallowed down in a gulp.

"It's going to kill more than the fetus, I can feel it already," she said with an ominous yelp of laughter. "But what else can be taken? I've already given it all away."

I wasn't sure I'd ever know the exact pain Ruby was going through, but I did feel like I already knew what she meant. I cradled her head until her sobs finally subsided and she drifted off to painkiller paradise.

EXPOSURE IS EVERYTHING

I WASN'T SURE HOW STARDUST CONVINCED me to go to a premiere party with her just two nights after the traumatic scene at Ruby's. I was still in shock about the news of the tour potentially being called off, and the vibe at Robert's had become downright grim. Forget prison, it felt more like a mortuary. Every day that Robert stayed shut inside his bedroom, I grew more desperate. It had been a week since the encounter with his ex now, and being confined and alone for that long could drive anyone insane. Being near his tomb-of-a-room was unsettling. It haunted the entire house. No matter which room I was in, I wasn't safe from the chilly energy that seeped out under his door.

To quench my jitters, I lit a cigarette as I sat on the patio, waiting for Stardust, exhaling the smoke so it seemed to swirl over the moon, which was full and high in the sky. The glittery party dress I wore in honor of Ruby itched and I twisted uncomfortably on the outdoor barstool. The premiere party was for the *Sour Grapes* movie, incidentally titled *Sucker Punch*. I was glad Robert wasn't around so that I didn't have to tell him about it. *Sour Grapes* was a popular cartoon about a dysfunctional family of purple people that lived in a small town and were always happy-drunk on the local intoxi-cating punch.

Stardust told me about all the actors and directors that were going to be there as we crawled down the 405 toward Santa Monica. She could have been speaking Finnish. My thoughts stayed on Ruby, Robert, and the tour possibly being off. Occasionally, she would look over at me to make sure I was okay. I could offer her no reassurance, nor did I want to ask her what she thought about it all for fear she'd lay on some even worse news. She always told it like it was, and I admired her for that. Still, my morale was a popped balloon; shredded, deflated and flat on the floor. It seemed like my only hope was to let go, distract myself and have some fleeting fun.

The party was in a huge tent at the Veteran's Memorial Grounds. Stardust showed her invitation to the guy at the tent door and we walked into a dome of chaos lined with purple & white Christmas lights. Purple and silver balloons floated above us. There were women in wine-colored spandex suits twirling flaming hula-hoops. Men in plum four-piece suits with top hats handed out purple lollipops and lighters. There were banquet tables overflowing with figs, grapes, cheeses, doughnuts and cupcakes with lavender frosting. There was a centerpiece fountain of deep purple "sucker punch"—the first sip proved it a mix of sparkling grape juice and vodka—with orchids and chopped fruit floating in it.

"Wow," I breathed. "Ruby should *so* be here."

"I know."

We passed a booth where they were making peanut butter and grape jelly sandwiches on all kinds of bread. Next to it was a candy bar and corn dog deep frying station. My mouth salivated but I wasn't quite hungry.

Stardust stopped and slowly inhaled. I watched her nostrils expand and contract, curious. "Calorie-free eating," she said when she caught me staring.

I took a deep breath with my eyes closed, concentrating on smelling everything as richly as possible. The scent of fried dough, candied nuts, hot dogs, and melted chocolate filled my nose. It was surprisingly satisfying. I opened my eyes.

"Yummy!"

"I know. At least as good as the real thing. Usually better."

Excitement tugged at my chest. I needed this break from the stress of the last few weeks. Stardust and I began to dance to the band playing onstage, her shiny black pigtails flipping in rhythm with the beat. I threw myself into the music, arms and legs bending along with the pulse of the kick drum, moving with abandon more so than ever before. When girls eyeballed me, I eyeballed them right back. When guys bumped me with their elbows, I bumped them back—even tipping my drink on them to get them to really back off. I was eager to be playful after being serious for so long. I deserved a liftoff from the dark planets of Robert and Ruby, from my own family, from the bad patterns I kept falling into. I was determined to have a good time.

I felt close to Stardust. We danced for the band's entire set. Everything felt bizarre but it was thrilling to not feel other people's pain for a moment. All the guests around me seemed to be important and fabulous, and I could fit in for once, strangely sure of myself as if the party was the final boost I needed.

We continued to sip "sucker punch" and things got blurry. Stardust and I danced with the hula girls by the stage. Some

friendly-looking strangers gave me a "bump" in the bathroom. Time sped up, a bouncy moonwalk of movement. The
band went on break again. Stardust asked me if I felt daring.

"What do you mean?"

"Let's crash the stage."

"Huh?"

"Yeah, get up there and play, *duh*. The sound guy's at the
bar and the band left their instruments on and everything,
look. All we have to do is switch the amps back on. You sing
and play the keys and I'll play drums."

"You play drums?"

Stardust nodded. "I play everything."

I surveyed the stage and the crowd. Normally, I'd be
scared to crash anything. After all, I almost refused to get up
on a table to dance at the club that first night in Hollywood.
But something had shifted in me since then. I felt bold and
reckless in a way I could get used to. Stardust's idea shot me
up with adrenaline, and I wanted more.

"I'm in."

She nodded and we climbed onstage. No one appeared
to notice us. We turned the amp on. The previous keyboardist sang backup vocals so there was a mic already
positioned over the board. I started playing a little carnival-
esque ditty and Stardust launched into a natural backbeat
under it. People turned their heads toward the stage. I felt
overwhelmingly confident (*had I ever liked myself so much?*)
and launched into an improvised song about glamorous
purple people in a tent under the starry sky. Stardust kept
up impressively. How amazing it was to play with instrumen-
talists with such skill. It was freeing. It felt powerful. I was
made for this.

People gathered near the stage, but I didn't quite register the depth of the crowd. When we finished our song there was an enormous response, a thunderous rip-roar of clapping and cheering, stuttering fireworks of camera flashes. Stardust and I went to the front of the stage to take a bow. With a sudden stroke of dumb courage, I stepped up to the microphone.

"Thank you! This is Stardust Wu and I'm Kyla Bell, and we're going to be on tour—ahh—"

Stardust grabbed my arm and dragged me offstage to behind the makeshift back wall.

I rubbed my wrist. "What's wrong?"

"You were mentioning the tour? We don't know if it's still on, yet."

I sighed as I realized how much I was still in denial. "Oops. My fault. I'm a little waste-faced. I was so excited about playing with you on drums."

That made her smile. "You do a crazy vibrato thing with the higher notes. How'd you learn to sing like that?"

I shook my head. "I don't know. I never took formal lessons."

"Far out." It was the first time I'd seen her impressed. I was so flattered I almost forgot what had gone down. Someone coughed right next to us. We turned to find the lead singer of the booked band standing there looking angry.

"How'd our equipment work out for you?"

"Oh, it was, like, just okay," Stardust said, deadpan.

The singer didn't seem amused—probably because our little splash of stage time had gotten a bigger reaction from the crowd than they had. I wondered why the event coordinators had booked his cheesy band for such an outrageous party, anyway.

"You didn't have permission to use our gear," he said, arms crossed.

"Um, are you kidding?" Stardust asked. "Sorry, hall monitor. We won't do it again." She crossed her arms and mimicked him.

"Look, just because you're chicks . . ." His face intensified and his veins seemed to balloon in his neck like my dad's did when he was watching his favorite sports teams lose. Or watching me tell him I was going to drop out of high school to join a rock n' roll band.

I grabbed Stardust's arm. "He's gonna blow! *Run!*"

"Eat my shoes, dude!" Stardust yelled over her shoulder as we tore back through the crowd, people whooping and whistling as we fought our way to the edge of our unauthorized premiere. I stumbled a couple of times on my platforms but Stardust caught me both times and we continued to escape as if the world was after us. We didn't stop running until we got to the parking lot elevator.

It was the most fun I'd had in LA since I arrived.

Back at Robert's, the roar of silence crashed against my ears. All of the joy from the premiere evaporated. I tossed and turned in bed and stared at the moon that hung full outside my curtainless window, an annoying light bulb that wouldn't shut off. I lay under the blankets, shivering in a way that had nothing to do with the temperature. A few chirps rang out. If I could get to sleep before the birds all woke up, I would probably survive. I didn't want to think about anything that flashed in my mind. Everything about my surroundings and situation seemed totally bleak. My life seemed completely out of control.

Then, a realization that was a further-sinking stone: if I'd stayed home, I would still be living according to someone else's plan: my father's. I was so sick of other people's ideas of who I should be. I needed to take as much of my life into my own hands as possible, make a conscious effort to do what I wanted, instead of trying to make things easy on whomever happened to be directing my life at any moment.

The last thought I had before finally falling off was that if Robert didn't emerge from his room tomorrow, I was going in.

MAKE HEADLINES

I woke up mid-afternoon, mouth dry as a sand dune, and headed downstairs for a glass of water. He appeared as an apparition: Robert's slight frame seated at the table, illuminated by the midday sun, bent over an open newspaper, a steaming mug by his side. I slunk into the kitchen, afraid I'd scare him away by making a sound. My spirits lifted higher when I saw he'd brewed a pot. It had been forever since I'd come downstairs to fresh brewed coffee. The mug clinked against the side of the cabinet as I took it out. My hands were kind of shaky. Robert finally looked over.

"Hello," I said.

His voice came out creakier than ever. "You say hello like I might burst into bits at any second."

"I'm sorry. Hey!"

A tired half-smile formed on his face. "That's better. Come have a seat, Trixie. Bring the sugar over with you. Think I need some sweet in my veins."

I grabbed the box of sugar and sat next to him. He smelled of stale cigarettes, coffee, and sour milk. I didn't say anything, only smiled at him in the bright morning sunshine. He looked ragged—drooping bags under his eyes, salt-and-pepper stubble, and as pale as a vampire. Despite it all, I gave him a genuine smile. It was such a relief he was out of his room.

"Missed ya," I said.

"Don't go getting all sentimental on me."

"I'm not. But today, I was planning to go into your room and rescue you."

He squinted down into his coffee mug. "I know you don't understand, but I'm only sparing you."

We sat there for a minute. I watched hummingbirds flit around the hibiscus flower bushes outside. I noticed that Robert's hands were shaking much worse than usual as he flipped the pages of the newspaper. Then he turned to me abruptly and winked.

"Have fun last night?"

I frowned. "What do you mean?"

He pointed down at the newspaper. In the bottom right corner of the front page of the Entertainment section in the *LA Times* was a picture of Stardust and me onstage, "STAGE CRASHERS" under it in bold.

My mouth dropped open as I read: "Glitter Tears bassist Stardust Wu and the new keyboardist Kyla Bell hijacked the stage last night, outshining the hired band, The Stone Collectors, with their one-song set . . ."

Robert leaned back and lit a cigarette. "Impressive. I didn't make the papers for at least six months after I moved here."

"Holy hell. I can't believe it says all that! We were feeling a little crazy."

"I'll say. You two are a couple of head-banging tricksters up there."

I laughed. "No—let me see." I pulled the newspaper closer. There I was, open-mouthed against the mic, fingers poised dramatically across the keys. Stardust was bent over the drums, sticks in the air and pigtails a blur against the backdrop. It was actually pretty funny. We looked like we were rocking out to save our lives.

"Where was Ruby? Why are you two running around without her?"

I shrugged and avoided looking at him.

"Uh-oh. Tell me you found her."

I nodded. "We did. At her house."

"And?"

I grabbed a cigarette from his pack and started tapping it against the table nervously.

"How have you been getting cigarettes?" I asked, trying to deflect the attention back on him. "Have you been leaving the house?"

"Don't worry about me. I have an apocalypse stash in my closet. I'd be fine in there for months."

I shook my head.

"Sometimes we have to shut out the world," he said.

I shrugged. "I guess I get it."

"You really don't, and I hope you never do. So what's up with Ruby?"

I closed my eyes and imagined her—pale face, no makeup, knotted hair, deep in her bed nest. What fragility the headstrong hide. Ruby Sky was both the superstar ice queen and the confused, fallible mortal. I wondered if she'd mind me telling Robert. I hadn't thought about it.

"She's going through . . .women's issues."

He raised his brow. "Regular women's issues or serious women's issues?"

"Serious."

"I see. How serious?"

There wasn't a good way to talk about it. How close Ruby and Robert actually were, I still didn't know. I wasn't sure he knew much about her past.

"She might cancel the tour."

"Shit." He scratched at his neck and I watched his fingernails dig around in his loose, scruffy skin. "Well, where does that leave you?"

"Wicked screwed is where that leaves me."

He smirked. "You're back East already."

"I don't want to go home."

"Then don't."

The way he said it, I suddenly knew I could make something else work in Los Angeles. It was like he'd flipped a little self-esteem switch on inside me. I shot a smile across the table to Robert and lit the cigarette.

"Then maybe I won't," I said.

WHEN THEY SEE YOU SHINE, THEY WANT YOUR TIME

"HELLO?"

"Hey, is this Kyla?"

"Yeah, who's this?"

"Anthony."

It took me a moment. I held the phone from my ear, thinking. Then Ian Somer's long haired, soft-sweatered son popped into focus.

"Oh, *hey*, Anthony!" The surprise was maybe too apparent in my voice.

"I saw you in the paper this morning," he explained. "I didn't recognize you at first, but the pink hair caught my eye and when I read the caption I was like, 'Hey, I totally know that chick!' and I realized I've totally been slacking on calling you up so I asked around for your number. You look pretty hot onstage."

"Oh yeah, funny! Um, thanks," I said, mind racing. Who had he asked for my number? I prayed he hadn't bothered Ruby about it. "I still can't believe they printed that."

"Pretty rad. So listen, what are you doing tonight?"

I was again surprised, but no clear excuse came to mind.

"Um, not sure."

"My friend's doing a release party for his new record. I think you'll have fun, there should be a lot of musicians."

"Um, sure. Sounds good." I sensed impending disaster, but that feeling had followed me around since the minute I first showed up at Robert's. He told me he'd "scoop me up" around eight and to "dress whatever."

When we hung up, I felt weird. He'd sorta asked me out on a date, and I'd sorta said yes. What did that mean? Was I that desperate to get out of the house, or did I have some real attraction to this guy? It was out of character for me to sign up for a potentially romantic guy situation without putting on a show for anyone. Yet there was something about Anthony that made me interested. And it was probably something more shallow than I liked to admit.

The intercom crackled and interrupted my thoughts.

"Drinks in the club room. Get down here."

I practically ran down to join him. Robert had put on some soul tunes and was hitting the pool balls around.

"Any word from Ruby?" he asked as he handed me a fresh cocktail.

I shook my head.

"Who was that on the phone?"

"Anthony," I said. "Ian Somer's son," I added when Robert looked confused.

"Oh? What did he want?"

I tried to play it cool. "He saw me in the paper and was all impressed. It was funny. He asked me to go out with him tonight. Some release party."

Robert bent over to take a shot. The ball tipped into the corner pocket. He turned to face me. "And?"

"And I said okay."

He turned around and started lining up another shot. I stared at his back and wondered why he suddenly seemed mad at me.

"Is that not cool?"

He ignored me and took his shot carefully. The cue ball cut across the table and hit the 8 ball straight into the pocket with a loud crack.

"I'm a bit surprised, is all."

Sparks of defensiveness made me stand up. "Why? Because it's me, little old nobody around here, who suddenly has a date with Anthony Somer? Or because I said yes?"

Robert pursed his lips. "You said yes without asking anyone first."

The words came out in white lightning I never saw coming. "Well, excuse me if I didn't know I had to ask anyone to make a plan when I've been left alone for days and have no schedule at all anymore . . . Ruby won't talk to me, let alone tell me if we're still going on the tour. And we haven't even had one full rehearsal yet! I'm living in some delusional universe, floating around here doing nothing. And Anthony said a lot of music people will be at this thing . . ."

Robert turned sharply. "Ah, so you're networking, trying to make it on your own already. Isn't that a little presumptuous?"

"No," I said hesitantly, unprepared for this counterattack—especially from the person who just told me I could stay in LA with or without Ruby's band. "I wasn't saying that. I just thought it would be cool to meet some more people so I wouldn't be so dep—"

I hardly recognized Robert, he was making such an awful, twisted face as he interrupted, practically spitting the words at me.

"Let me save you the trouble, babe. Nobody's interested in solo acts. You should stick to trying to make the band work out."

He went over to the liquor cabinet and poured himself more vodka while I scowled at his back. "Be careful," he continued. "The ground you're walking on is easy to crumble. An unchecked, overblown ego will trample every blessing in your life. Just because you've been living it up here for a few weeks doesn't mean you're going to make it. Step too far ahead of yourself, you'll trip and fall flat on your face. Or you'll do something that you'll never live down, something that haunts you for the rest of your life."

He finally turned to meet my eyes, his harshness making me flinch and look away. Negativity swirled around him, a dark tornado at the crown of his head. I couldn't look straight at him, didn't want to confirm that he really meant it. Where was this even coming from? I was going out on one date with someone. No big deal in any city, really. No one had said I couldn't, and no one *could* say I couldn't. What was he, jealous? Impossible.

The wound bled out through my sullen mouth. "Well. Thanks for the advice."

"That's what you're here for, right?"

I honestly didn't know anymore.

NEVER STAY IN FOR THE NIGHT

STARDUST CALLED WHILE I WAS GETTING ready for Anthony to pick me up. She had given him my number after Ruby didn't get back to him. Her advice was that if anyone asked what was up with the tour, I should say Ruby went on a retreat to get some time to herself for a little while. I was concerned about her, but at the same time I couldn't help feeling resentful that she'd shut me out after all we'd gone through together. A different sort of uprising was happening to me in the midst of all this distance, a way of being that was entirely my own. It seemed absolutely necessary to get out and forget about everything and everyone for a little while.

I waited for Anthony in the kitchen, pacing in front of the windows so I could run out as soon as I saw headlights. Robert entered with a drink in hand, cigarette between fingers. He examined my outfit—a tight strapless black dress. It fit me better than I'd ever fit in a dress. I felt like a slim slice of prettiness.

He just smoked and stared at me.

The rage was itching right under the skin, now. There was no stopping it. I couldn't take much more of this kind of scrutiny. The words left my mouth with a sour tinge.

"What?! What is your *problem*?"

Robert shook his head and tipped the rest of the contents of the glass down his throat, somehow making me feel like a scrap of a meal that wasn't enough to save.

"This is getting weird," I said through a clenched throat, fighting the words as they made it out anyway. "My own father doesn't even treat me like this."

"Well I'm not your fucking father," he said in such a cold voice that I got chills. "And you're not all that, you know."

That made me even more mad. Was he really going to tell me to stop because I was having one moment of feeling independent and good about myself? It was inexcusable, the nerve. "I don't think I'm all that! Far from it! I'm trying to do something on my own for once out here. I may be inexperienced but I'm not a kid."

"You are in *this* playpen."

"No, I'm not. I can handle myself. I've hardly gone anywhere on my own while you and Ruby have been basically ignoring me. I hate it! It makes me feel pathetic and needy, like a neglected pet or something."

Robert ballooned up, the veins in his neck rippling and straining as if my words had unleashed a dozen snakes inside of him. It was frightening to witness. I almost ran outside, but hesitated. I didn't want to be timid, anymore.

"Well go on, get out of here," he sneered. "And don't come crying to me when your Romeo doesn't want you anymore."

I held my ground and stared right back into Robert's eyes, challenging him to do the thing we both knew he wanted to do, which was kick me out of his place. But would he?

At that moment, the infamous ice-breaker Eduardo flapped into the room, squawking "Bye-bye, bye-bye . . ." I stood there, startled, shaking, angry, and hurt, then turned and bolted outside before things escalated more.

The ground was shifting around me, an earthquake of emotional baggage, things tipping out of control. I heard something shatter in the kitchen but opted not to look in the window to see what happened. I didn't want to witness the after-wrath of Robert. This wasn't church camp with dating rules, a bedtime, or a curfew. It was supposed to be me growing up fast—maybe even too fast—but in the right direction for a future rock star. I should be able to go out with whomever I wanted. What did Robert care, anyhow? There was no way I was going to sit around in that house with him right now. His erratic lifestyle, unpredictable moods, and cutting comments had become incredibly draining. I didn't want to fight with him, but there was a definite wedge of animosity between us that hadn't been before.

Anthony pulled into the driveway at that moment in a cool classic cream convertible. I was excited. An extremely fancy, well-known person was about to take me out. I was eighteen in Los Angeles and finally exploring on my own. I would shake off the drama and rally for the occasion. I promised myself I would not be a drag of a date.

Anthony got out to open the door for me. He'd tied his hair back in a low ponytail and was wearing another thin, soft black cashmere sweater that clung to him in a perfectly sexy way. He winked at me as I got into the car and I gave him a smile that said I was ready for anything.

"So glad you're here," I said. "This place is starting to feel like prison."

We looked at Robert's mansion, shadowy and towering over the bumpy blanket of twinkling Hollywood lights and Anthony smiled.

"I don't think you grasp the concept of prison, darlin'," he said as he shifted into reverse.

The release party was in a warehouse in Santa Monica. We stopped at a liquor store on the way and Anthony spiked a soda bottle with whiskey. When he offered me a sip I took it, enjoying it more than I expected, and by the time we parked behind the warehouse on a side street, I was feeling warm and fuzzy and excited to have my own adventure without the handcuffs of Ruby or Robert.

The door guy wanted to see my ID and I panicked, accustomed to Robert and his friendships with all the doormen in town. I didn't know what to do on my own. Angry that I already needed him, I shuffled my hand around in my purse, stalling while the door guy watched me. Anthony had already gone inside. I was about to shrug and pretend I'd left my wallet at home when some guy stuck his head out the door and said, "Hey, Zed? She's cool. Come on in!" Anthony was waiting right beyond the door, smiling smugly because his friend had gotten me inside. I smiled back, relieved—though he should have told me the plan ahead of time. I'd thought he'd left me hanging.

I surveyed the funky underground club scene. Multi-colored spotlights splashed everything rainbow, a drugged-up kind of Disneyland. People sat on overstuffed couches around candle-lit café tables. House music boomed from speakers in the corners. A disco ball reflected the lights as it swirled around. Gigantic paper flowers hung from the ceiling over the dance floor, leaking dry ice from their centers. LA decorators sure had imagination that I loved—even if the air reeked of spray paint and incense.

Anthony took my hand and we walked through the dance floor to the bar in the back covered with fake spider webs. Plastic bats frozen mid-flight hung on invisible strings above the bartenders' heads. A bartender in a cowboy hat gave us his attention.

"What's the theme of this place supposed to be?" I asked in his ear when he leaned in.

"The theme is that there is no theme," he grinned. "What can I get you, sweetheart?"

I ordered a vodka soda because that's what Robert always ordered and I didn't know what else to get.

Anthony was talking to a group a few steps away. He seemed to know everyone there, but for some reason, I didn't care to meet anyone new at the moment. Maybe I felt every interaction would be fake. Part of me had been jarred by what Robert had said, and it felt sort of traitorous to be out meeting musicians without him or Ruby or anyone from the band. But that wasn't normal, was it? I honestly couldn't tell anymore.

There was a raised private nook across from the dance floor that seemed to be a good place to hide for a moment, so I climbed up a wooden ladder to a platform covered with pillows. A beautiful drunk girl was already there, lying on her back and staring up at the decorative flowers hanging from the ceiling. She had lots of tattoos, long dark hair, boldly-outlined eyes, and as she slurred something about how "all the flowers were spitting rubbish in the air," I noticed a thick British accent.

I laughed and she noticed me for the first time.

"What'a you chucklin' at?"

She had a low-cut stretchy black top and her breasts were half revealed as she rolled over onto her stomach and looked at me. Her arms were covered with tattoos of flowers, feathers, birds and skulls.

"Oh, um, you." I wanted to say something clever, but that's what came out.

"Yeah, I'm a bloody riot." She pushed herself up and sat closer. Her scent hit me, something sugary to it, intoxicating. I suddenly forgot about Anthony's whereabouts.

She reached out and grabbed a section of my hair. "Is this the new strawberry blond?"

I loved the way she said "strawberry" all drawn out. I smiled and nodded, edging nearer to her.

"Well aren't you as cute as it gets," she said, seeing my move and raising me another inch. I finished my drink in a gulp and put it out of the way, all too aware that she wanted to touch me and more than hoping she would.

"My name's Angie," she said into my ear over the bumping club music.

"Kyla," I said.

"What's that?" she said, even closer to my ear.

I was about to repeat myself but she turned her head as I turned mine and suddenly we were locked in the softest, most natural kiss of my life. Our lips were pulsing, velvet pillows and I gave everything up, completely absorbed in the moment. She tasted like donuts and beer, sweet and hoppy. She nibbled my face and bit my earlobe, sending excited chills all the way down to my lower back. We tangled with each other on pillows with tassels, time dissolving into melted pleasure.

I didn't know why she stopped at first. Then I heard her say, "What ya lookin' at, wanker?"

Anthony was standing at the entrance to the nook, staring at us.

"Hi," I said.

"Hey," he said. "You two are, like, majorly hot."

Angie spat out, "Well, it's not a fuckin' peep show, you know."

"It's, um," I fumbled to explain it to her. "I came with him."

Angie made a disdainful face at me. "Really?"

"C'mon, let's hang out. Need another drink?" Anthony held out his hand and I looked regretfully at Angie as I took it. It seemed I always belonged to someone those days, if only for a night.

"Find you later," I said.

"I hope so, kitten." She blew me an air kiss.

We walked over to the bar and Anthony ordered a couple of shots. As he was paying, I felt someone tug my arm and looked to find Angie had followed us. "I have to show you something," she whispered, whisking me off before I could think to let Anthony know.

I eagerly followed Angie down a secret side hallway lined with tall racks of garments. I was still humming from the nook experience and being on the run from my date bumped up the excitement even more.

"What is this, a dressing room?" I asked.

"Shhh . . ." Angie ducked between two racks and pulled me in with her. Suddenly, we were enclosed by bright costumes on hangers and stacks of fabrics. She pressed me up against the piles of clothes, sliding her hands up the bottom of my dress, and I let her. She kneeled and put her face under the fabric, kissing my stomach, hands pressing everywhere, then moved down between my legs, nuzzling the insides of my thighs. I leaned back and felt her take command of my body. A blissful quiet spread across my mind and strokes of pleasure shot up from my hips. Angie gave me a particularly thrilling sensation I'd never experienced before, one that kept building until she was jerking her head back and forth, long hair tickling my thighs. My body shuddered in a tsunami of exhilaration, as I bucked with it and cried out in pleasure. She kept going until I was weak and panting. I almost cried tears of joy. After a moment, she stood up, looking proud of herself.

"What did you do to me," I murmured.

"What, that? That was just a preview of coming attractions," she said, and kissed me.

I felt something I'd never felt so clearly before.

I felt truly set free.

FACE YOUR DARKEST FEARS

THE NEXT DAY, I FELT SPLIT in two. Part of me believed I had betrayed Ruby, and somehow Robert as well, but much less, in a totally different way. The whole night had been a step into another universe that kept coming back in little replays like a vivid dream. The crumpled dress on the floor and my shoes kicked to the side of the bed were the only signs that it had been real. I had vague recollections of escaping Anthony and the whole warehouse scene through a side door and taking a cab home.

When I left my bedroom to search for caffeine, Robert's door was ajar so I peeked through. The room was empty and messier than last time. I continued downstairs, afraid to see him but also kind of hoping that he'd be at the table with coffee and a cigarette and we could pretend that nothing ever happened. The kitchen was vacant, though, an empty coffee pot burning on the warmer. I rinsed it but the dark circle didn't wash away.

I heard the distant ring of the phone and dashed back upstairs to answer it.

"Hello?"

"Hi." There was flatness to the voice that made me wish it wasn't Ruby. I waited for her to say something else, but for a moment no one said anything. I felt the dread rise up and went for something neutral, though false.

"I'm happy to hear your voice."

Another painful moment of silence. Then, "What's Robert up to?"

I shifted the phone to my other ear and looked out the window to the yard and patio. There was no sign of him.

"I don't know," I said. "He doesn't seem to be here."

"I knew it." she said, her voice getting more urgent. "He left a weird message last night when I was asleep. He said, 'The deal's off.' He's not supposed to disappear on you. That was part of our deal, that he couldn't just take off."

I hadn't known about that part of their deal. Maybe that was why he had been so awful about me going out with Anthony. It was suddenly glaringly apparent how little I knew about any of the terms of my situation. I'd been so eager to make it happen I'd glossed over pretty much every detail except getting to join a famous band.

I yanked the phone cord nervously. "We kind of got in a fight last night."

"Oh, no. Tell me everything, immediately."

"Well, um, Stardust gave Anthony my number and he called and asked me out. I said okay because I had nothing else going on, and Robert was mad about it. . . . So, I got defensive and said something dumb."

"Oh my god. What did you say?"

Invisible hands were squeezing my lungs. I didn't want to keep talking but I knew there was no way back, now. She had to know everything. She would hear it all eventually, anyway.

"Well, it sounds ridiculous out of context but . . . I said something about how he wasn't my father . . . and I wasn't a child."

The silence made my feet cold, hands numb, head freeze. My body shut down piece by piece in preparation for what was coming next.

"You *didn't*."

"I know, it sounds immature, but he said some really mean things too and I was cranky and mad, and I didn't know about your agreement," I blurted out. "I didn't understand why he was being like that, it's not like I had plans or anything . . ."

"You've messed up worse than you know," Ruby said. "You don't do that to Robert. He's a raw nerve of a person right now. He made huge sacrifices for you, opening up *his home* to you. And, of course, you can't go doing anything you want. What if something happened to you? He'd feel responsible. I hate to agree with Kevin on this, Kyla, but maybe this was all a bad idea. I *never* thought you'd treat Robert that way. You seemed so easygoing and sensitive, and he doesn't need this turbulence in his life."

Pain and shame raked me from head to toe. I really wasn't used to hurting people. Had I already morphed into a monster, just as Robert had predicted? Was I going to end up homeless because I kept making the wrong choices? How could I fix this?

"I'm so sorry. Honestly, I don't know what's wrong with me! What can I do?"

"We have to find him," she said. "You don't know how he gets when he's upset. I'm still so weak, too. I can hardly get out of bed. Ugh."

That was my chance. "I'll do it," I said. "I'll find him."

"How? You don't even drive."

I swallowed a fear lump as big as a glacier. "I'll drive to find him."

"In what car?"

"I know where he keeps his keys."

"Are you a good driver? You don't even know your way around."

"I can drive," I said, more determinedly. "And he has a *Thomas Guide*."

"Well . . . I guess it's the least you can do. He's probably crouching at a hotel somewhere. Look in small and big places. He has no type. Between the Hilton or the Motor Inn, there's an equal chance of finding him in both."

"What's he doing? How do we know he's not at the store or something?"

"Kyla, as I said, there's a lot you don't know about Robert. He's been on the edge for a while. See if you can track him down. Check for clues around the house. Stay close to Hollywood. He never goes too far. He's stuck on this place. When you find him, call me *immediately*."

"Okay," I said. "I will. I'll find him and apologize."

"It's going to take more than an apology to fix Robert," she said darkly, and hung up.

I wanted to ask her what she meant but now my only mission was to correct my mistakes no matter what; to pull the future back to the place it was headed when I first got here. My dream train was almost derailed and it was up to me and only me to put it back on track.

I went down the hall to Robert's bedroom and stepped inside, immediately feeling the energy vacuum of it. I tugged at my arm hair and hurried over to his desk. There were a few crumpled pieces of paper with lists of song names on them. I found business cards for a restaurant, a recording studio in the valley, and a comedian named Greg Ballsak. I stuffed everything in my pocket then checked the desk drawer to discover a few tiny empty baggies, a lighter, a phone cord, and three pennies. I felt around in the back of the drawer and found an old picture of an extremely good looking guy about my age with his arm around a younger blond kid. I blinked at it, realizing it was Robert, back when he was younger. The flip side had "Riverside, '60" written on it. I studied his face, so boyish and fresh, an unrecognizable innocence in his features. He looked so different, thirty years ago. He looked . . . hopeful.

Unexpected feelings of fondness for Robert coursed through me. Under his jaded exterior he had a good heart. I shoved the picture back into the drawer with a renewed surge of urgency to find him and make sure he was all right.

Down in the foyer there was a bowl on a table by the door to the garage that held a lot of keys. I peeked in and decided I would drive the least expensive-looking car, one that had a little chrome wildcat on the hood and matching icon on the key that was a jumping panther, or something.

But I was having a hard time making my legs work suddenly. They didn't want to walk over and get into the driver's seat. No matter what I did, my body remained frozen by the door. Eduardo flapped into the front hall and perched on the coat rack.

"Bobby beans," he squawked. "Bobby beans the trees."

"What?" I asked him.

"Ladybird, show me your—"

"Shut *up*! Someone should buy you some parrot porn."

That got me annoyed enough to at least propel me into the garage. Maybe Eduardo really did always know the right thing to say.

I unlocked the car and as I climbed in, I immediately plunged into a full-blown panic attack. My eyes snapped shut and my heart pounded fiercely against my chest, trying to eject itself. I'd seen a counselor a couple of times at school after the accident, and she'd said to breathe deeply and let myself feel my way through my thoughts instead of trying to suppress them. She'd said to pay attention to my thoughts. That the only way to heal is to feel.

It had been two years. The blizzard surrounded us. I was driving, my mom was in the passenger seat. We were arguing about how fast I was going as we were going around a turn. I snapped, "I know how to fucking drive," just as we hit the patch of black ice.

I thought I had forgotten the details, but now it all came flooding back into my mind.

The car skidded across the road right in front of an oncoming truck, missing it by fractions of a second before continuing off the road and almost skidding over a cliff. I had to get out as carefully as I could while the car dangled over the edge, ready to tip at any moment. I had to pull my unconscious mother sideways out of the driver's side seat without sending it over as well.

I had never been so scared. I had her by the arms and with my final yank, she came out but I heard something crack in her arm, and then the car went completely over the cliff, smashing on the rocks a hundred feet below.

I held my unconscious, broken mother and waited for the police and rescue to come. I thought my mama was going to die. I wondered if I'd ever have a chance to make up for my nasty last words right before we skidded off the road.

Somehow, she did survive, at least a different version of her did. My reckless driving seemed to have knocked something loose in her brain. And at the age of 16, just a few weeks after getting my license, I never wanted to drive again.

Tragedy seemed to stick around for a while, a haze of unease that coated everything. I wasn't sure if it was ever going to lift. Then Ruby Sky came into my life and there was a sudden unexpected warmth, everything got brighter and the sunshine could cut through again. So I followed the light, and look where it got me: my cockiness had ruined things again. Here I was, right back behind the wheel.

Once again, I was facing the roads, only this time, I was about to drive in an unfamiliar place, by myself, in an unfamiliar car. I was now looking for Robert by myself when I had *just* gone looking for Ruby. Robert was right; I was still a child in a lot of ways, but people much older than me could be even more childish, still running away from their relationships and problems. I didn't want to be like them, either. It was time to prove myself stronger than my age and experience. I had to do this. I would face my past and present. I would find Robert.

NO ONE DOES DRAMA LIKE A ROCK STAR

HOLLYWOOD LOOMED AROUND ME LIKE A fun house, full of secret spots, spooky sounds, distorting mirrors, mirages and dead ends, and plenty of pretty faces at hotel reception desks who shook their heads no at my question of whether a Robert Jeffs had checked in. Then it was back to the car, to conquer another panic attack before I could turn the keys in the ignition and fight through another traffic jam. I did notice that it got a little easier every time. To the annoyance of all the sports car drivers on Sunset Boulevard, I was an absolute grandma on the road. Each time they honked at me, I gave them a big smile and thumbs up, just as Ruby showed me.

I saved the Chateau Marmont on Sunset for last. Robert said it was the prime spot for celebrities to do crooked things behind closed doors. The whole search I had been praying not to have to check there. As I walked up to the receptionist, I conjured up the last shard of hope in my eyes, and she eyed me back like I was going to ask for spare change or something.

"Can I help you?"

"Yes, I'm wondering if a guest named Robert Jeffs has checked in yet."

"Who's asking?"

I'd gotten good at answering that question over the last few hours. With a straight face, looking directly in her eyes, I said, "Kyla Bell from Trace Records. I work with him. He's expecting me."

"Aren't you a little young to work at a label?"

"Yeah. My dad's the CEO."

Yeah right, I freakin' *wish*. But she seemed to buy it enough, raising an eyebrow and typing on the keypad. Time stretched infinitely between when her finger hit the enter button and when she shook her head.

"I'm sorry, we don't have a guest by that name registered here."

Although I should have been used to that response by that point, my spirit somehow found a deeper bottom. I stared at a picture on the wall of a tropical scene. A hammock and palm trees, a parrot perched on a fence. Think, think . . . Don't take no for an answer, again. The two-dimensional parrot stared back at me and suddenly I had an idea.

"How about Bobby Beans? Has he checked in?"

She rapid-tapped the keys again and this time I found myself staring at a nodding face. "Yes, Mr. Beans checked in this afternoon."

"Great, listen. Don't bother to interrupt him with a call. He's expecting me."

She picked up the phone anyway and dialed the room number with a blank face. After a second, she hung up, then went through the same motions again.

"It's busy at the moment, you'll have to wait."

After convincing her that I needed to grab something from him on a tight deadline, she finally rolled her eyes and told me the room number. "Thank you, Eduardo," I whispered as I turned and went to the elevator. When I got to room 211, I stopped outside the door and listened to a TV blaring from inside, and finally got the courage to knock.

"I didn't order anything," I heard a muffled voice say after a minute.

I tried the door and found it unlocked, walking in to find Robert slouched against the wall on the floor next to the TV wearing nothing but a black terry cloth robe. A crumpled cigarette hung from his mouth, unlit. The phone was completely off the hook.

His face fell when he saw me. He looked totally wrecked.

"*You?* How did *you* get in here?"

"The door was unlocked."

There was a funny smell in the room, something chemical combined with the cigarette smoke. I noticed a near-empty bottle of vodka next to Robert and some other things I couldn't make out.

"Thought it locked automatically, damn it," he said, tipping his head back against the wall. "You're not supposed to be here."

"Ruby said you were in trouble," I said gently. "I've been looking all over for you."

He hung his head and didn't say anything. I walked over and perched on the edge of the bed. Only then did I see he had a syringe, a spoon, a thin rubber hose and a baggie of powder strewn around him on the floor. I couldn't hold back my gasp.

Robert raised his head and saw that I'd moved. He closed his robe around his chest and tried to sit up straight, knocking the paraphernalia away from him with an angry brush of his hand. It was an ugly sight. I struggled to remain calm. I'd never been around heroin, only heard the horror stories. I thought of calling Ruby for help as she'd instructed, but I really wanted to handle this on my own to prove my worth.

"You're out of your league here, as usual," he slurred, "but the best part about you is that you do it anyway."

"Robert! What's going on?"

"Why did you come looking for me?"

"Because I care." I wanted to move to the floor but I wasn't sure I should get that close to the snarling, wavering beast that was Robert at the moment. His head kept wobbling like his neck could barely keep it up.

"You don't understand." He dropped his cigarette in the empty glass next to him. "Fuck it. It doesn't matter now, anyway. I wanted to be the guy you wanted me to be. It used to be so easy to impress people. Times have changed. Too many impressive people in the world now. I wanted to show you something special . . . but there's nothing special about me, or my life. I've actually proven dumber than most. Lost or gambled away everything I really had going for me."

He picked up the spoon and tapped it against the side of his head. "Here I am, *trying* to shoot up to finish the great cliché circle of my whole goddamn life, and I can't even do that right. I've tried everything else there is to do out there and this is it, babe. I don't have a lot of first times left, and I still haven't found what I'm looking for."

I considered calling Ruby again, and put the phone carefully back on the receiver.

Robert dropped the spoon, picked up the hypodermic needle, squinted at it, and threw it down again. I kicked it under the bed quickly, hating the sight of it. "Now you burst in . . . Go figure." He chuckled dryly. "Well, you're here to learn, right? Here's a real lesson: go out before you go down. I waited too long. Man, did I wait too long. Look at me. I'm *every single* rock and roll stereotype. I'm the shadow of a has-been who's existed thousands of times before. I should've gone out years ago the way the others do, a syringe in a hotel room when they're twenty-seven and on top of the world. But here I am: an old man who's too pathetic to pull it off."

"No, Robert. You're not a cliché." I said, struggling to find the right words. "You're not like anyone I've met."

"That's because you don't know anyone," he said, laughing bitterly.

He took the vodka bottle and chugged it like water, then wiped his mouth with his wrist. "If you did, you would know better than to take advice from a guy like me. You show up on my doorstep all doe-eyed and I'm supposed to be the good wolf and show you around the woods without eating you. I tried not to bite, I really did. But I'm bad for you, bad for anyone . . . Especially bad for myself. I'm doing us all a favor here."

His face collapsed again and he fumbled with the baggie, cursing loudly when he spilled more powder onto his robe. The rawness of his reality was painful. I had zero experience dealing with people intent on undoing themselves. But I needed to learn everything, even this.

"Robert, please don't," I begged as he tried to dump some of the powder into the spoon. His hands were so shaky he kept spilling powder everywhere.

"Can't you see that I *can't?*" He tried to push some of the powder from his robe back into the spoon, only spilling more, then he got really frustrated and hit his head against the wall behind him with a loud *THUNK*.

"*Stop it!*" I shouted.

His expression softened and he put the spoon down.

"Don't be so melodramatic," he said. "It doesn't suit you. Besides, I'm supplying enough drama for the both of us, don't you think?"

He broke into a sickly smile and I felt nauseous. How could this be a joke to him? Enough was enough. I was officially out of things to say to discourage him.

"I'm going to call Ruby," I said, getting up abruptly.

"Don't," he said firmly.

"Why not? I told her I would as soon as I found you."

"Because it's pointless."

"Why?"

"Because I want to die," he said, utterly defeated. "For a while now. It's all I can think about, all I dream about. It's the only thing left that I really want."

We stared at each other and I slowly sat back down. I had to say something.

"What if I don't care what you want?"

"I love that about you," he said, taking another sip from the vodka bottle. "Always have. You know, even when I pulled out all the tricks, treated you so nice, took you to the hottest spots, brought you into my own little secret society, you still didn't care."

I didn't know what he meant at first. Of course I cared . . . But in what way?

"You're the only woman I've met in a long time who hasn't tried to sleep with me—or at least flirt with me—to get to my money or connections," he continued. "I was trying to tell you that before . . . You showed up at my house and wanted nothing from me but what I chose to share with you, and somehow that showed me how glaringly worthless everything I have is. You never even asked for *anything.* You're so different and all I've done is try to make you more like everyone else."

I was frozen to the edge of the bed. His words were a tape played too many times—stretched out, warbling, familiar in their intent but different in their delivery. He stared up at me with watery, bloodshot eyes and I watched our thoughts slip around in them. I remembered the old picture of him I'd found, the difference so striking between the faces of the same person, one soul split into two by time. The "before" and "after" pictures of our lives could be so devastating. I thought of my mother and wondered what my "after" would look like. The future, my future, was coming to get me, and I had no idea if I should run, how fast, which direction . . .

I breathed in deeply and stared into the spiraling abyss in his face.

"Robert," I said, carefully sliding onto the floor. My heart was practically popping through my chest, thundering for the truth I'd waited so long to say out loud. "You should know that I care a lot about you. Not romantically, though, because . . . Well, because I'm not into guys . . . in that way. I kept waiting to, trying to, but I don't know if I ever will. And, um . . . That's the first time I've ever told someone that. I was trying to tell you that a while ago. I don't know if that means anything to you."

I took his hand. It was cold and rough in mine. It felt like it hadn't been held in a long, long time. I squeezed, trying to shoot my love for him from my fingers.

"Well, you could still break my heart," he said after a moment. "I care a lot for you, too. Even if you're not into men, which I don't blame you for. Men are pigs. We're fucking disgusting. Women are the all-around better choice, so good call, there."

Rough as they were, his words were like a blast of fresh air.

"I won't break your heart if you don't break mine," I said. "Okay? Stick around. Please?"

He continued to look at me for a while. He seemed to be absorbing me like sunshine. I fixed my eyes on him and tried to send him all the warmth and strength I'd held within myself, pulsing strong with relief because he had taken my confession so well, and he'd actually made me feel good about it. In the dim, flickering light of the television, he held out his hand in mock formality.

"Deal."

CHAOS IS CONTINUOUS

IT HAD BEEN SO LONG SINCE I'd seen her that I thought I was hallucinating when Ruby's pink Jeep turned up the driveway. She wore a black sundress with fishnet tights and dark green boots. Her hair was down, shiny purple locks flowing in the sunshine. Her tear tattoo was back in sparkle action. She looked thinner, but her presence felt stronger than ever.

Robert and I stood up from our seats on the patio at the same time, which made all of us laugh. We took turns hugging her and she sat across from us by the outside bar. The sunlight illuminated her pale complexion and set off her sparkles. She noticed me staring and held my eyes. Her emotions were hard to read, but I was pulled in, anyway. No matter how much she put me through, I realized I'd probably always be enchanted by the bright, dark, and tempestuous Ruby Sky.

"So, I've been talking to a psychiatrist," she said after it was clear that none of us knew how to begin.

"Oh, yeah?" Robert smirked. "How's that going?"

"I'm usually skeptical, but this woman's brilliant," she said. "She doesn't just sit there, she actually offers her opinions and gives good advice. She's also hooking me up with some fantastic new meds." Ruby grinned. "I guess they tested well. I'm feeling better every day."

"Great to hear," I said gently. "We missed you."

"I know. Sorry, chickadee. This wasn't how it was supposed to go. But I've been doing a lot of soul searching, and I've decided that even though things have been kind of crazy, the tour must go on. We're going to put together a crammed rehearsal schedule. This spaceship is going to be oiled and ready for launch."

Robert snorted. "Spaceship is right."

She looked at me. "Does that sound good to you, Kyla?"

I nodded enthusiastically. "Yes it does!"

How glorious it was to feel the flash of a green light. It was really happening. Things were back on track. This time, I was not going to blow it.

"Well, this is extraordinary news. I think this calls for an early happy hour," Robert said. "What do you say, ladies?"

"I need to go inside for a second," I said. "Just want to freshen up."

"Hurry up," Robert said. "Don't be a diva about it."

When I got up to my room, the phone was ringing. Everything was so perfect at the moment that I didn't want to answer. The ringing eventually stopped and I breathed relief. Then its shrill cry started again. I lifted the receiver to my ear.

"Hello?"

"Kyla, where the hell have you been? I've been trying you all morning."

"Oh! Um, hi, Dad. Sorry, I've just been . . . in a meeting. What's happening?"

"It's your mother. She's in bad shape. I promised her I would call you and let you know, even though I told her there was nothing you can do about it from three thousand miles away."

"What do you mean? What's wrong?"

"We had to take her to McLean's last night."

The words took a minute to compute. "Wait. The mental hospital? Why? What happened?"

"She saw a picture of you printed in one of the tabloids. There you were, pink haired, kissing that Ruby character. It was quite a blow to your mom. I don't know if you've even thought about your actions having an effect on her."

"She saw my hair?" My voice was so small.

"Yes. And your . . . flamboyance."

The way he said it made me cringe. "I was going to tell you guys . . ."

"Yeah? Well, it's too late. The cat is out of the bag. And you know how your mother feels about homosexuality. That soccer coach of hers really did a number on her back in high school. I don't care, in fact I'm a little relieved not to have to worry about you getting pregnant over there."

I hadn't expected this reaction from him. He was so closed-minded about other things, and I'd certainly felt that he wouldn't approve. I knew all about the shower-spying soccer coach and how uncomfortable my mother was around lesbians. It was part of the reason I'd been so tight-lipped about my situation. But I never thought my pops was open-minded in that department. I almost wanted to thank him, but he didn't wait for me to respond.

"So anyway, after she saw the picture she decided to sneak out at one in the morning and break into the Derrick's garage to steal their lawnmower. She started mowing the side of the street in her robe and almost got hit by a car. The police showed up, she freaked out on them, and I woke up to the cops banging at the door and your mother in the backseat of the squad car in handcuffs."

"Oh no," I breathed. "They arrested her?"

"We worked something out. The Derricks aren't going to press any charges, and neither will the police, as long as she stays at McLean's until we get to the bottom of what's going on with her. I don't know what else to do. I can't stay up all night to watch her, and she apparently needs 24-hour supervision now."

He sounded so weary and defeated. The news spun me out. From the depths of my memories, I tried to recall my mother in her better moments and it was like remembering a dead person. But now—now we had apparently entered a new low. My mother in a mental hospital was a bad mistake. She wasn't *that* crazy, but she was definitely impressionable. If she was stuck in a building surrounded by deeply disturbed people, her mind could wander off somewhere even I couldn't find.

"How long is she going to be in there? What are they going to do to her?"

"We don't know. They're trying to get her stabilized, run some tests, try some new meds, and get her on a regular routine schedule."

The open-endedness of his answer scared me. *Stability* was such an imaginary concept. Life wasn't stable, so why should anyone expect any of us to be?

"How can I talk to her? I need to talk to her."

"Not a good idea right now, Kyla. I'm sure she wants to speak to you, but they've got her on so many meds it wouldn't be a very memorable conversation. I certainly haven't had much luck."

He sighed. I pictured him sitting at our kitchen table in our empty house. The image of him by himself and my mother miles and miles away in a mental hospital broke my heart all over again.

"Dad, are *you* going to be okay? It sounds like everything's falling apart over there."

"Yeah, it's not going well." His voice was hoarse with emotion.

"I wish I was there with you," I said, even though I knew I was opening myself up for harshness.

"I wish you were, too," he said, and made a little gasping noise that I'd only heard him do after each of his parents passed away. It was the noise he made to stifle crying.

"Is it in the papers?"

"Oh, yeah. It made the front page of *Northampton News.* 'Lawnmower Woman Assaults Local Police.'"

I heard Ruby calling me from downstairs. I swallowed and ran my fingers through my hair. "Pops, I really have to go right now, I'm so sorry," I said, hoping to get off the phone with him before Ruby came upstairs. "I'll call you as soon as I get back, okay?"

"Fine," he said curtly, and hung up.

Ruby knocked on my bedroom door.

"You in there, chickadee? We're thirsty out here."

"Be right out," I called after hanging up and grabbing a tissue off of my nightstand. I had to get it together. Someone close to me was wrecked again, but this time I was utterly powerless to help. How had my life taken yet another turn like this? I had emotional whiplash. I wondered when it would be me that was out there, thrashing, drowning, practically dying for help. I wondered who would save me then.

Ruby entered the bedroom. "I can sense sadness," she explained and sat down next to me. "What's wrong?"

I pushed the hair back from my face. I didn't want to bring her into the whole home situation but I also wasn't good at pretending everything was fine.

"It's my mom," I said, finally.

"Oh, no. What's wrong?"

"She's in the hospital."

Ruby's eyes widened. "Oh no! What is it?"

It took a minute to get it out without launching into tears. "She's in the mental hospital."

Ruby's eyes widened. "I'm so sorry. Do you want to talk about it?"

"Nah, let's not right now. Thanks, though."

I sniffled and went into the bathroom to splash some water on my puffy face. A flick of the mascara, a brush through the hair, and I was nearly presentable for the celebration of the tour being back on.

The news of my mother's breakdown set my hopes back to zero. Now that we had long-overdue rehearsals on the schedule, I couldn't possibly go see her, but how would I ever forgive myself for deserting my mom when she needed me most?

Ruby watched me from the doorway of the bathroom. She seemed to be contemplating whether or not to say something.

"We don't have to go," she finally said.

"No. I can't stay here. Let's go."

"Well, let me know if you need to talk, creampuff."

I marveled at how she could go from such a cold, distant person back to this candy-sprinkled charmer. Frightening how stretchy human personalities were. You never knew where you actually stood with people, or even where they were standing at any given time.

YOU CAN'T BE BOTH CLOSE AND DISTANT

ROBERT, RUBY, AND I SAT OUT on the patio at the Belmont, sipping Bloody Marys, each pretending to be fine. I felt a sense of togetherness and alienation at the same time. I noticed Ruby and Robert each masking their own inner sadness, their faces forming expressions of faded grief when they weren't aware of being watched so closely. I'm sure I had the same thing going on, so I tried to stay engaged in the conversation.

I asked how they first connected and they told me the story of their past. Ruby had been romantically involved with Robert's younger brother, Stuart, who was a studio drummer, the blond guy from the picture I'd found. He overdosed years ago while Ruby was with him. She and Robert had been uncannily close ever since. Ruby explained that since Stuart died they'd both suddenly been struck with a sort of sudden emotional telepathic connection; the ability to sense when the other was going through something.

"That's probably why we haven't slept together," Robert said, putting his arm around Ruby and winking at her. "Can you imagine sleeping with someone you're so emotionally connected to? Total disaster."

"We haven't slept together because you're a dirty old man." Ruby playfully punched his shoulder, causing him to knock over the salt and pepper on the table.

"Careful, our sexual tension is making us clumsy," Robert shot back.

"You wish," she responded, flipping her hair.

Regardless of whether the two were actually cheerful or faking it, being with them in a normal public environment helped take my mind off the fact that my mother was now in an asylum.

So Mom had seen *that* picture. I knew it would be trouble from the moment it was taken, but I guess I never wanted to acknowledge how much grief it could cause. It was one of those freeze-frame moments of truth, the snapshot was a song that sang *Here you were before it all went down / Carelessly flashing your queerness around.*

I guess I could have told my mom more. I could have let her in on what was happening . . . "So listen, Mom, I've got pink hair and I'm kissing girls now." Instead, I tried to keep her out of this world for as long as possible. I was sure she sensed that I was withholding a lot from her, which she probably feared ever since I'd told them I was quitting high school and going to LA. She'd felt it and then she'd seen it and then she'd had another breakdown. Could I really be responsible for *both* of her psychotic breaks, though? The thought was too much for me.

"Kyla? Hey! Space cadet!"

"Sorry, what?" I shook my head and reached for my drink.

The two of them studied me. Robert cleared his throat. Ruby looked sympathetic.

"I'm gonna hit the head," Robert said, getting up from the table.

"Are you okay, cherry pie?" Ruby asked, scooting her chair closer to me.

"Trying to be."

She stared at me for a long moment. "I know it's hard to not think about it, but at least we'll be back on schedule soon. We'll be really busy and then we'll all feel a lot better."

I wondered if that really was the only way I was going to feel better: block out my problems with work. It sounded so methodical. And so *typical*. I knew why Ruby was doing it, but my problem back home was a bit different, and only I could fix it. I couldn't just tell my mother that it was all fine over the phone and push this all under the carpet, could I?

I could at least try.

I turned to Ruby. "I need to use the phone real quick."

I found the payphone, dropped quarters in, and dialed the hospital. They put me on hold. My leg bounced up and down, jittering faster and faster in the lobby.

"We have Lillian Bell on the line, about to patch through. All calls will be monitored for the safety of the patients."

There was a little static and then it went quiet.

"Hello? Mom?"

"Kyla." My mom's voice came through as a tiny, wavering sound.

"Mom!" I cried like a choked cat. Now that I had her on the line, I didn't know how to begin. *How are you?* sounded beyond trite.

"So sorry that we haven't talked," I said tearily. "I've been thinking about you all the time."

"Yeah," she said. "I've been worried, you're so different, so far out there. The cloud bears keep telling me you're driving. Are you driving?"

"Maybe," I said breathily, shocked that she somehow knew. "A little bit, just one day." Her imaginary cloud bears were so eerily on-point. I hurried to change the subject, nervous about what else they'd told her. "How is it there?"

"Dreadful," she said, her voice a whisper. "I can't sleep. I can't make sense of this place, these people. They want me to say things I don't want to say."

"I'm sorry," I said. "And I'm sorry for not telling you about my hair and stuff. I don't really know what to say. It's all so new. I'm still figuring it out."

"You're already such a stranger."

I knew this was probably the moment I could tell her about myself, open up a little bit so she didn't feel so estranged from me, but I just couldn't.

"No, I'm still . . . me. And I wish I could be there for you, Mom."

"I know you can't right now, and that should be okay," she said. "That should be okay, but it's not."

It was maybe the worst thing I'd ever heard from my mother. I was quiet out of fear of dissolving deep into my own tears. Then there was a distorted voice in the background, my quarters ran out and the call was disconnected. Phone calls were clearly not going to cut it. I had to see her.

CHASE THOSE SECOND CHANCES

THE THOUGHTS WEREN'T JUST PRESSING. They were relentless. I had to go home.

I felt worthless. I played piano because of my mom—for her, even—but I couldn't even play a solid note if the chords between us were dissonant. When I sat down in the studio to practice, no energy pulsed through my body to my fingertips. My fingers were stiff and clumsy, my voice weak and uncertain. I told Ruby I wanted to go back home for a few days. She said she'd have to think about it.

And then she left me hanging for a while.

I'd managed to grasp one unsettling truth: people in LA said things but didn't necessarily mean them at all. This put me at a disadvantage because I said things I meant, and trusted others to do the same. Back East, people seemed to say the truth even when honesty hurt. But LA people operated on a plane I had no experience with. I'd once believed much of what people said, like that Ruby thought I was the only one meant for the keys in her band. But through her actions, she'd made me all too aware of my replaceability.

I bought my ticket to Boston anyway, before she gave me an answer. It was necessary. How could Ruby not understand that I needed to make things right in person, right away? Was I going to be kicked out of Glitter Tears after dealing with all this turmoil? I knew deep down that I had to put my mom first this time. Especially after all the uncertainty Ruby had already put me through. The band didn't feel like family, but I had one parent that still did. Maybe. If I could see her and convince her that I was all right and she didn't need to worry about me . . .

Part of me wanted to run home to the East Coast and never return, so I could have control over one tiny sliver of my LA story; reject the city and the band before they both officially rejected me. But when I thought about it realistically, I knew I could never be happy with that decision. At least not yet. That ambition that grew in me like a weed was still there—maybe a bit bruised and stepped on, but still alive and reaching for the sun. It seemed there really was no killing it.

Robert had been miraculously busy that week with a new songwriter. When I'd told him that I was going home and that Ruby might kick me out of the band because of it, he'd been relatively unfazed. To my great surprise, he said I wasn't his project anymore, I was family and welcome at his place as long as I liked—no matter what happened with the band. That was all I needed to hear. Robert was my West Coast family, now. He seemed to be genuinely doing better since the night at the hotel room. He'd even gone grocery shopping. I wasn't nervous about leaving, anymore. I was mostly nervous about whether I'd be returning with a clear purpose.

I heard a honk outside. Ruby was sitting in her Jeep checking her makeup in the rearview mirror.

"Hey."

"Hey, c'mon. Let's go for a drive." She finished with the eyeliner, gave me a strange *are-you-game* look as I climbed in and buckled my seatbelt tight, and the Ladybug squealed out of the driveway.

Ruby had endless sides, I thought, as I watched her seem so serene in the driver's seat while driving down the canyon like she had a death wish. One side of her made you believe she would accept anything you said, that she would be open-minded and cool about it, but then there was the sharp-edge side: if you did something she didn't approve of, everything was wrong and intolerable and you were fired.

The wind whipped through our hair as we turned north onto the Pacific Coast Highway. I watched the ocean back-drop: dark craggy rocks and white fuzzy caterpillars of wave crests crawling along the endless sea top. Sights so grand they made our problems seem trivial.

Ruby didn't talk, so I didn't either. Whatever she had to say, she was in no rush to say it. She finally turned off the road and pulled into a place with a sign that said "Lake Shrine."

"Where are we?" It looked like a closed public garden or something.

She shrugged. "I'm a member here."

I had no idea any kind of club existed in a place like this. There were bushes and exotic flowers everywhere. A water-fall tumbled from a mossy cliff above into a pond filled with lily pads. There was an old thatch-roofed windmill across the lake, and next to it drifted an empty party boat. A walking path covered with cedar chips lined the lake. Turtles and ducks dotted the shores. We'd stepped out of Los Angeles into even more of a fairy tale land.

All I could think was that Ruby had brought me to the most beautiful and comforting place to take the edge off of officially dumping me from the band.

We walked the grounds in silence. She led me to a little dock by the boat, grabbing fish food from a bucket and scattering it into the water. A school of koi appeared, calico-spotted blimps flipping their fat tails, sticking their gigantic tube mouths up to suction the pellets off the surface. I wondered how much their huge eyes actually saw. I imagined that they thought they were looking up into an alternate dimension, a land where pink and purple-haired girls tossed delicious flaky substances at the water to watch them eat.

Ruby leaned over the rail, her layered hair dropping over her face so I could only see her nose, lips and chin. She wore dark lip-gloss that made her lips shimmer. Her glitter nail polish caught the light as she clutched the banister. I sighed, suddenly able to fully admit to myself that I was hopelessly, uncontrollably attached to her. She had the power to crush me in more ways than I had ever given anyone. But I didn't remember giving her that power. She must have seized it.

With her sharp looks, sparkles and edges, Ruby was a kaleidoscope that seemed to transcend any norms or labels as soon as you tried to fix one on her. She constantly and effortlessly shifted shape, all the while remaining beautiful. I wanted to be worldly and undefinable, too. I wanted to have unfathomable depths. More than anything, though, I wanted her answer. At the moment, she was drawing out my verdict like a poker pro. I could determine nothing from her actions or expressions. She was putting up a tall, blank wall.

She finally finished with the koi and went to sit down on the bench. After a moment she patted the bench, so I went and sat beside her.

"So, listen," I started, forcing my mouth to speak. I couldn't wait any longer. She shook her head to shush me.

"*We* have to listen," she said, closing her eyes and tipping her head up to the sky. Her glitter tear scattered iridescent reflections in the daylight. She put her hand over mine on the bench, holding me down with her invisible glue. "Just listen."

We sat and listened to the waterfall. At first I was afraid that she was delaying the bad news. Then, after a little, I started to hear. I imagined the water cascading through me, washing all my anxiety away, a rushing, charging channel of fresh energy that uncovered my hope.

"Feel that?"

"*Mmmhmm.*"

"Every time I come here, I feel my clouds disappear for a moment. No matter what's going on, this place makes me calm. That's why I wanted to bring you here. I know it's been a rough ride so far."

I nodded.

"And it's about to get rougher," she continued.

Oh no, I thought. *Here it comes.*

She turned her body toward me and we stared into each other's eyes. I wanted her to just spit it out, but at the same time, I wanted to stretch out the small chance I had that she wasn't going to deliver bad news.

"There's a lot about our situation that you don't know. It's complicated. The band is a machine that took me years to build and I'm very careful when choosing the people to help me run it. When I brought you in, I admit part of me was running on desire. I wanted you to be as perfect as you seemed—so innocent, truly talented, modest and painfully sincere. You were this glowing manifestation of how I wish I could have been at your age. When I was eighteen, I was already so messed up, you know?"

She took a deep breath and stared straight ahead. Was I ever really those things to her? Was I not those things to her anymore? I wondered how I'd managed to pull off such an illusion in the beginning, and how I'd dropped it so fast.

"Part of me selfishly wanted to take you up into the clouds with me," she continued, "Where I am—and always have been—lonely."

I felt myself choke up. She was the most dangerous person in the world to me at that moment.

"And then you got here, and you were here because of me, and I kind of freaked out under that pressure. I wanted you to be able to handle this lifestyle, because I didn't want to think it was that screwed up, you know?"

"Ruby—"

"Let me finish. I went to tell Kevin yesterday that you wouldn't be continuing with us. You've got to go be with your mom, and I don't want to hold you back from doing that. But when I got there I started having doubts."

I still couldn't tell what she was getting at but knew she didn't want me to respond yet, so I shifted around on the cramped edge of total termination.

"What I'm trying to say is I don't want this to be the way it ends. At least not with *you*." She looked at me sternly, not ready for me to feel relief. "This isn't the way things usually work. Normally, if someone can't be where they're told to be, when we want them to be there, we drop them and find someone who will."

"I know. I totally get that. But . . . So you're saying . . .?" I couldn't bring myself to finish the sentence. I needed her to say it.

"I'm saying . . . Are you ready to owe me?" Ruby pinched my cheek and it hurt a little. Still, I nodded eagerly. "Like, big time?"

I could hardly stand the tension. "Yes! I'll do anything, Ruby. I promise. I—"

She held her hand up. "—Enough. Remember that I was so forgiving this time because I was the one who messed up all the work we should have already done together. But there's not going to be a next time."

"I won't let you down," I pleaded. "I'll do everything you want, I promise."

"That's a big promise," she said softly, staring at me in that way that got me excited. Then she laughed and pushed me. "God, you're still so green." She cleared her throat and took my hand again, putting it up against my own chest and holding it there. I hardly breathed. "So, yes. You get your second chance. Also known as your last chance. So be a good girl and don't make your own moves anymore. Go see your mom to show her you're okay and then get the hell back here. Work hard and do everything you're told. Can you do that for me?"

"I can," I swore excitedly.

I was signing an invisible contract, the terms of which weren't exactly clear. Or at all clear. It didn't matter. She was letting me go see my mom *and* letting me stay in the band. I hugged Ruby so hard I thought I might break her shoulders.

She let out a little sigh and then pushed me away, slapping me lightly on my butt.

"Your ass is all mine starting Monday," she said.

My ass is already all yours, I thought.

GO WHERE IT HURTS

I TOOK MY TIME GETTING OFF the plane in Boston, making sure not to be last, though. My dad would know it was on purpose. He was too observant and sensitive. It was frightening to be under his microscope again after weeks of being on my own. I wondered what his first thought would be when he saw me as I filed down the narrow row of strangers, aware of stares that were now becoming normal to me.

I knew I looked different, but never considered how different *he* would look until I met his eyes. Pops stood under the fluorescent lights among the crowd looking thinner than he'd ever looked, wearing his baggy blue jacket with the huge pockets and hood. All the spirit was let out of him.

A little girl pushed past me, saying, "Daddy! Daddy!" A younger man next to my father stooped down to scoop her up. I wished my father's arms were open to me but they remained by his sides. I stopped in front of him and dropped my bag.

"Hey, Pops."

"Kyla," he said. We stared at each other. Something flashed in his red-rimmed eyes and he opened his arms suddenly as if they'd been spring released. I hugged him without hesitation.

My tears merged with the fabric of his jacket, which smelled like exhaust and woodchips. I'd never realized how much comfort I took in that scent. It was a massive relief to be hugging him. Even though we had parted under such terrible circumstances, I forgave him all at once, as it seemed he had also forgiven me, and accepted who I was—all of me—finally. When we pulled apart I gave him a tender smile.

"I love the new hobo look," I said, rubbing his cheek stubble. "Very mountain-man."

"I don't know what you're talking about," he shot back. "I don't take style tips from Californians out of their jurisdiction."

We walked outside and I understood his clothing choices better. It was colder than I'd expected. The air was damp from recent rainfall and squeals of wet tires echoed through the garage. The family station wagon was exactly as I remembered it: My father's driving pipe in the ashtray. The rip in the passenger seat, tan stuffing poking through torn vinyl. The stack of receipts from the dump in the middle console. I sat back in the seat and breathed deeply. It was really happening. I was back.

I could feel my father's eyes on me.

"You've lost a lot of weight," he said accusingly.

"So have you."

"Yeah, well mine's not from a bad Hollywood diet."

He gave me a look that spoke volumes. I swallowed hard. We left the airport as it started to rain again. The windshield wipers squeaked back and forth, counting each painful second we were unable to talk. I sighed at the window. Gray highway and skeletal trees blurred by. I already missed exotic flowers and big, fat palm trees.

He picked his pipe up, tapped it against the side of the door, and steered with his knee as he lit it with a little orange lighter. The smoke came out from his mouth in thick white curls that snaked out the window.

"Will I get time alone with Mom?"

He took another long drag off the pipe, shaking his head slowly as he exhaled. He was so stoic, as if his temper had drained out along with everything else. "You can see her without me there, but it's going to be in a visitors lounge. No one-on-ones for her, yet."

I nodded, miserable. I couldn't have my own mother alone in a room?

"Does she know I'm coming?"

"No. She knows I'm coming. I didn't want to tell her about your visit in case you didn't make it, for one reason or another."

"Oh." I hid a tear by looking out at the budding branches bending in the wind and rain. I wondered how they held on, those delicate little blossoms, through the harshness of the spring storms.

There was a long silence. My mind jumbled with every destructive thought possible: this was a huge mistake. I shouldn't have come. I only made things worse for my mother. This was a pointless mission. This wasn't worth leaving LA for.

Then I remembered I needed my mom. I had come to tell her I loved her, and to hear her say it back. Nothing else mattered.

Belmont was a sleepy town of natural beauty. The hospital looked like an old campus on a rolling, grassy hill. It didn't appear anywhere near as menacing as I'd expected. There were no iron bars or gates. Just large white pillars covered with ivy that seemed to dance in the rain. My father pulled into a parking space and killed the engine, then sighed as he sat back in his seat and stared out at the gloomy sky through the rain-smeared windshield.

"Nicer than I expected," I said, trying for something positive.

"I probably won't be alive long enough to work the bill off."

"Are you coming in with me?"

"Yes. I'll wait in the hall until you're done, then I want to say hello as well."

We sat there for a minute. I understood that he was gathering the strength to go inside. He'd been in there before. I'd never seen him so weak. It was alarming. Even after all the loopy scenes I'd witnessed in Los Angeles, I had a feeling that nothing could prepare me for the one I was about to witness.

The halls were sterile and painted bland shades of mauve and brown. Nurses and patients walked past us as we made our way to the patient quarters. An older lady in a wheelchair pointed at me as she rolled past and said, "Heidi! They're trying to steal his seeds again!" I shook my head regretfully. She dismissed me with a wave as if I were being silly. A tall guy in pajamas by the water fountain watched us silently, itching his head and face, like Slinky on too many drugs. A girl who looked around my age with a shaved head sat on a small couch in the corner of the lounge, chewing the tips of her fingernails. I felt her notice me and gave her a little smile. She froze up and looked away.

The intercom system barked a reverb-y echo of patient names that needed to pick up medications. Certain nurses were to report to certain areas. It all blended and warped, a chilling remix of hospital life. Pops told me he'd be right around the corner if I needed him. That seemed all right, but as soon as he left, I felt totally exposed. People were staring as if I were the new patient, some nodding and waving at me like I was in denial of the present or future of something. Goosebumps popped up all over my body and I shivered.

This dangerous jury knew too much. Too much about unspoken pain and secrets. Too much about realities that shatter necessary illusions. Too much about illusions that shatter necessary realities. My weak grasp on the situation was slipping. How could I face my mother in this place? Why did I even come here thinking that I could somehow help her feel better? Or did I think that it would make me feel better? Was I that selfish or that clueless?

So much of what I already loved about LA came to me all at that moment. The captivating, shifting face of opportunity. The tingling caress of possibility. The never-ordinary life that costs some of your sanity in return. West Coast magnetism had an almost addictive draw when surrounded by these people facing their own grim, fractured realities here in the bleak East Coast suburb behind thick walls. The walls were probably half the treatment. The walls physically separated them from what they feared the most.

My spiraling thoughts dropped off at the sound of her voice.

"Kyla? Is that you?"

My mother—in a pale blue cotton shirt and drawstring pants, hair down and messy around her face. My mother—a different woman every time I saw her, and yet somehow always there, deep inside. I could always find her in her eyes, and I saw it hurt her to see me. I wanted to shrink away but instead I took a deep breath and stood.

"Mom."

I hugged her, even though she was still standing in shock, arms by her side. After a moment she hugged me back. I felt her tremble under her thin hospital clothes.

"Mom, I'm sorry. I'm so, so sorry."

We pulled apart and she touched my hair. She pulled her hand back immediately as if it burned.

"Your hair."

"Yes."

"So skinny, too." She put her hands around her own waist as if to measure against mine. "So skinny." She touched her hair. "The hair . . ."

I nodded guiltily, acknowledging I'd changed parts of myself that had once made her proud. That was when I noticed an attendant standing in the corner behind my mother. He was staring at us and looked like he was formerly in the military or something.

We sat down at a table. She took my hand and looked at me intensely in that way she did, peering straight into my soul. She sighed after a minute. When I glanced back at the attendant, he was still staring at us, a cruel hardness to his gaze.

"This isn't what I expected," my mom said. "But I knew something was going to happen."

"Yeah, you kept telling me to get out of here," I said softly.

"You make me feel better but I could sense the accident, my fall. Remember? You're not supposed to have to take care of me but I can't help it. It's not my fault. Do you believe me? But now everything is wrong. Your hair. Seeing you in that magazine . . . I've lost the best part of my life all of the sudden. I've lost you."

"You haven't lost me. I'm right here. No matter what changes, I'm not going to ever be lost to you. I hope," I took a deep breath, "that you can accept me. All of me."

I met the piercing eyes of the attendant again, feeling a chill run up my spine. People moved around him like he wasn't even there. *Was* he there? Was *I* losing it now?

"I knew you've never had a boyfriend, but I didn't realize you wanted a . . . girlfriend."

There was a long, painful silence. How could my dad be easier to talk to about this? I needed to let my mom into my real life, but maybe now was not the time. "She's not my girlfriend, Mom. That was a dumb publicity stunt. You know, to land us in more papers. But I guess it wasn't dumb, because it worked."

Her forehead raised into its rectangular wrinkle formation. "You mean, you two aren't . . .?"

I shook my head but didn't say anything else. It was still too touchy a subject for the visiting room of a psychiatric hospital. I just wanted to give her relief for now. I hoped she'd be able to come to better terms with her past through the therapy she was getting. Maybe that would be the key. She looked out the window at the rain, which had picked up and was smearing the windows with blurriness. The dark shadow of the attendant stared at me from over her shoulder.

"You didn't look like my daughter. She didn't force you, did she?"

What surprised me about the question was that actually, Ruby *had* kinda forced me, or bamboozled me, rather— though if it hadn't been on a photographer-ridden red carpet I would have eagerly reciprocated.

I tried to play it off. "No. Mom, I'm an adult now, by law, but also a teenage musician. Of course I'm going to make choices you don't agree with, right?"

She shook her head feverishly. "I pushed you to play piano. I dreamed you would play before you were even born. This is all my fault."

Her voice cracked and she started to cry. I stared miserably at her. How could both of us be drawing the same conclusion about each other; that everything was our fault? Maybe blame was something easier turned inward, but who knew what forces were to blame for loving each other imperfectly?

"Mom, I don't think this is . . . an issue of fault."

Had the attendant gotten closer over her shoulder? I couldn't ignore him much longer. It was really freaking me out, the way he was fixated on us, how everyone else seemed invisible to him and he seemed invisible to everyone else. It occurred to me that I might be pre-programmed with whatever my mom was battling.

Next thing I knew, I'd be talking to the cloud bears.

"What is this all really about, Mom? Do you even know?"

My mom grabbed my hand and held tight as she leaned in toward me. She didn't smell like herself, here. She smelled of bar soap and canned vegetables, or something. It unleashed a different type of sadness in me. So much change, so quickly. "I'm . . . It's . . ." She struggled to find words. "My life is a book I've recently reread, and it's so *dull*, Kyla. I can't pretend anymore. I used to want to be someone, you know? Do something, be someone bigger, like you. I used to dress up in my room and give speeches to my cat about all the things I was going to do to change the world. All the way through high school I did that." She sighed, pressing her fingers to her temples. "I know it sounds silly."

"It doesn't sound silly, Mom."

"No?" A thin smile. "It was pretty silly."

I shook my head. "I wish I could have heard what you were saying."

A man at the table next to us started braying like a donkey, breaking the mood. The woman across from him looked around, embarrassed.

"And I wish we could go get some coffee or something, get out of here for a little."

"I'm sorry we can't, but I'm on 'special watch.'"

"What?! What kind of special watch?"

She turned to gesture wildly at the attendant that had been staring us down and inching closer since the start.

"They're making sure I don't hurt myself again."

"Wait, you mean—" It felt like I'd swallowed a coil of thorns and my insides were ripping apart. It was Robert in the hotel room all over again, but even worse. Way worse. Why did the people I loved want to hurt themselves? At what point did life tell them it was never going to get better? "What?" I couldn't hold back the tears. "Mom. What? You can't. No. I'll come home. I promise—just *don't.*"

She shook her head. "Shhh! No, stay away from the fear, Kyla." She started clawing at the air around my head. "Ugh, see it attacking? Fear is the fastest-acting airborne virus. The cloud bears are shooting it down, but it's too strong. You have to help them push it away!"

No. Impossible. No. I couldn't believe it was true that she'd tried to take her own life, that my mother could want to die. I shivered visibly as the attendant seemed to come closer.

"Please. Tell me why?"

"I told you, because it's all a lie! Everything they tell you, from the minute you're born. The cloud bears told me.

Humans aren't natural to this planet, that's why we're so awful to each other, that's why we're messing it up so badly. I can't take it anymore. That's why I told you to leave home, to get out of here before it happened. That's why—I'm serious—I mean this—you should go where you want to go." She reached over and pulled my hand from my face where I was trying to cover my tears. "Do what you want to do." She started waving her arms wildly, and laughed uproariously. It was the creepiest laugh I'd ever heard. "Be who you want to be. Isn't it fantastic to be young and free?"

I felt a rough hand on my shoulder right as the gloomy attendant put one on my mom's. I hadn't noticed him approaching and gasped. My mother didn't seem surprised. I turned to find my dad standing behind me. He nodded at my mom as she stood like a prisoner ready to be taken back to her cell.

"Lillian," my dad said, her name catching in his throat.

"Hello, dear," she sing-songed as she waved at him. "Thanks for coming. Bye-bye, family!"

"I love you, Mom. I'm sorry."

"I love you, my child. None of this is your fault. If anything, it's mine. I'm sorry I inflicted this world on you."

I watched in shock, eyes blurred with tears, as they led my poor, thin mother out of the visiting room. Something broke inside of me, flooded my insides with black water.

"You didn't tell me she's on suicide watch," I blurted out as soon as we got into the car. "I can't believe you didn't tell me."

He sighed heavily. "Yeah. They say she threw herself in front of the car that night. She's made so many contradictory statements these days, I don't know what the hell to believe. But yes. As you saw, they seem to consider her a pretty serious case."

"Why did they drag her off like that? We weren't even done talking."

"How do you think I feel? I didn't even get to talk to her at all. They have to remove patients when they start to get excited, something about chain reactions."

I shook my head and took in a sharp breath. "She's basically in jail, and it's my fault."

"No, Kyla. She's always been out there. I knew she was . . . volatile. When I first met her, I had an idea of what I was getting into but I was in love with her. And she proved to be a great mother, at least, up until the accident. But I've never really considered leaving her, because your mother has a spirit. . . ." He knocked the steering wheel with his knuckles and let out a loud breath. He looked so small in his big blue coat. "A spirit like no other. But when she started breaking laws and endangering her own life and others, she put herself in a new position. She can't make her own choices right now. And that's the simple, sad truth of the matter. It has nothing to do with you."

I appreciated his letting me off the hook, not trying to pin any more guilt on me. But still I felt responsible. "We have to do something, though," I said, weaker this time.

He started the car and we drove away in silence, defeated.

DON'T CARE

I HAD ONE EVENING IN NORTHAMPTON, and I only wanted to do one thing with it: see Jenny. It was nerve-wracking to be facing the aftermath of my recent exposure yet again, with my closest friend in the world. But I needed to talk to her more than ever, so I hoped she'd be cool. I was at least going to give her the chance to be. She was waiting at our favorite picnic bench under a yellow sky in downtown Northampton when my dad dropped me off. I'd asked him if I should stay the night at Jenny's place, but he'd insisted I stay at the house, as a "guest" – whatever that meant. Maybe as long as I wasn't living there, I was welcome there. Who knows. He was never great at apologies, but by this point his life was so hapless I didn't really need one. I just needed him to be okay.

Jenny wore clunky boots and held an umbrella printed with tiny ducks. It was the type of outfit you would never see someone wearing in LA, and I adored it. Rain clouds pressed their cold, clammy hands down on us as we hugged. Believing that everything was going to be fine was a lot easier in a sunny paradise.

I'd missed Jenny so much. Seeing her gave me a rush of homesickness that almost brought back the tears, which I didn't think was possible since I'd pretty much cried the entire two-hour ride from the hospital.

"This 'do, huh?" she said as we broke apart and she fluffed my frizzy hair. Hers was in loose pigtails, always a favorite. "So this is hot right now? I bet it looks a lot better on you in Hollywood. Same goes for the twenty pounds you're missing."

"Thanks. You look like crap, too, but somehow it works in this crappy town."

Her eyes widened and she laughed. "*Ooh!* Watch out, Northampton, she fights back, now. I'm kidding, though. It's awesome to see you."

"I'm kidding, too. I love your outfit."

She shook her head as she ran her eyes over me again.

"They did a fast job on you, huh?"

I nodded, weirdly tongue-tied by the impending amount of catching up we had to do. "It's been . . . a lot."

She nodded along with me, all mock seriousness. "Yes, yes, I do declare. It's. Been. A. Lot."

I shook my head. "You don't even know."

"I know a little," she said, squeezing my shoulder. "I know about your mom."

"*Everyone* must know." I sank down on the bench and looked out across the park. It was unusually empty for a Sunday. The swings rocked back and forth in the wind. A newspaper blew across the playground and wrapped around the pole to the jungle gym, waving in its stuck position. Everything looked as I imagined it would in Northampton right before doomsday.

"How's she doing?"

"Awful," I said, my voice catching. "I don't think I can even talk about it yet. Need a break from crying. How are you doing?"

"Well, I'm doing great. Suddenly the Bells are the most talked about family in town, and you're not even here to witness me getting asked fifty times a day if you're really a lesbian with Ruby Sky now, or if your mom really threw herself in front of a car while mowing the street in the middle of the night, and then tried to punch the cop."

I shook my head. "What do you say?"

She flashed the cocky grin that I loved. "I tell them it's all true, of course! And they all want to be best friends with me because I have inside information on your life. Yeah, the Bells have been really great for my end-of-high-school career, you know. Mickey Schroeder even asked me out."

Yuck. The guy was a big macho football player, a hometown handed-life-on-a-platter hero. One of those guys you can tell is ugly inside despite his chiseled exterior. The idea of Jenny dating him triggered my gag reflex. I couldn't even bring myself to ask if she said yes.

"So, you have a lot of new friends?" I couldn't keep the strain from my voice.

She laughed and kicked my shin lightly.

"Is someone jealous? I always knew you were gay for me."

"Shut up!" I tried to look seriously into her eyes, which was hard when they flickered with laughter. "I'm not . . . all the way gay. But I'm also not sure what I'm not, anymore."

"Well you're definitely *not* making much sense."

I ignored her smirk, fumbling through my awkward confession. "I know this must be strange for you. I'm sorry I didn't tell you sooner. But the weirdest part about all this is how fast everything happened. Like, turbo-morph speed. There's always so much going on. Even when I have a second to myself, my brain barely gets to process what's happened before something else comes up, so I haven't really been able to get a grip. I'm dizzy from the chaos all the time. It's crazy. I'm only now really realizing the realness of everything that's happened."

"'Really realizing the realness?' I don't know, Kyla. Sounds like *really* heavy stuff." She was deadpanning and I was surprised to find myself annoyed. "I can't be sure, but I think you're figuring out some deep stuff in LA."

The annoyance suddenly melted. Jenny was doing what I always counted on her to do: not let me get too heavy with my own thoughts. Not let me spin out to a point I couldn't get back from. She had a way of making everything stressful seem silly. She could flip your problems over, rub their tummies and make them laugh.

"I want to know why you didn't say anything to me," Jenny said, forgoing the humor for a serious question. "I mean, all the talk of crushes and hanging with boys from the coffee shop, tailgating in the woods, hooking up after shows. . . . You weren't into any of it?"

"No," I said, and the simple word made something lift inside. I had waited years to tell Jenny that. "That's why I never did much, why I always ditched them so fast. I didn't want you to feel different around me. I didn't want to feel that different. You know?"

I held my breath, hoping for immediate reassurance. Jenny squinted at the empty tire swing creaking in the wind in front of us.

"Well, I wish you had given me a chance," she said. "A chance to be cool with it. I'm not homophobic and I don't get how you would think that. I applied to Smith, remember?"

"There was that time . . ." I knew she knew what I was talking about. "You know, and you wrinkled your nose and I felt terrible for, like, years."

"Oh my god, Kyla," she said. "I'm sorry, but you're basically my sister, okay? That's why. I couldn't kiss my sister, even if it was 'for practice' as you claimed."

She poked me and I giggled, so deeply relieved. I observed the familiar patterns of the freckles on her face, especially my favorite little triangle constellation under her left ear. I took comfort in those freckles. They were always going to remain the same. Or at least I hoped they would. One spotted point of the triangle seemed to be fading, though, which scared me.

"What?!"

"I was just . . . looking at your freckles."

"And . . .?"

"One of them, one of them is maybe getting smaller."

She stared at me to be certain I was serious. "Well, that's great news. I could stand to lose, I don't know, all of them? Don't you guys have something over there in Hollywood that could erase them or something? I bet there's *some* kind of treatment. Do some research for me, okay?"

"No."

"No?"

"I love your freckles."

She smiled. "Aw. That's cute. You sure you're not all the way gay?"

I leaned back and closed my eyes. "I mean, I'm pretty sure, but who knows. Still figuring it out because there's been some interesting . . . developments."

Jenny hit my shoulder. "*What?* Do tell, Bell. I knew you'd been holding out on me. I mean, I thought the infamous picture in the paper was for shock value. I know all that stuff is staged."

Do tell, Bell. I'd forgotten about that. I nodded. "Yeah, that was staged. But Ruby goes both ways. And maybe so do I, because I did go on a date with Anthony Somer."

"Wait, WHAT?!"

"Yeah, I don't know. I'm kind of attracted to him for some reason—"

"—Maybe because he's freakin' gorgeous!!!—"

"—but then when we were on the date I met this girl at the club, and she stole me away from him and we did stuff, and it was maybe kind of the best stuff."

"Wow. You ditched Anthony Somer for a girl? That must have been a really hot girl. Best stuff, huh?" she said, quieter. "Sounds *juicy*." She laughed and almost wrinkled her nose, but caught herself. I felt a small flash of shame and swallowed it. She was just joking around.

"Nobody over there seems to care. Nothing necessarily means anything, it's all, like, in the moment or something. There aren't any expectations so that makes it a tiny bit easier. I mean, I'm supposed to be there doing music, you know, but I'm dealing with all these other things."

"What kind of things, other than coming to terms with your . . . preferences?"

I shoved her a little harder than I meant to.

"Fine, I'll stop. Sorry. It's funny, I've been telling everyone you couldn't be straighter—"

"Well, whatever! It's no one's business. Why does it matter?"

"Right." She jumped up and turned her cheerleading moves on. "Give me an A! Give me a G! Give me an *Alllll* Gay!"

I laughed it off. I knew she really didn't care but she was being so awkward about it. I guess we all loved each other imperfectly. There was a lot I didn't want to tell Jenny. I knew how everything

would sound—the stuff about Ruby, the stuff about Robert—
and telling her would be facing the truth from outside the
bubble. I didn't want to reveal how unhinged and precarious my
situation in Los Angeles was to outsiders *or* myself.

As if she could read my mind, she said, "You guys at least
sounding good for tour?"

I knew the answer would sound so insane. Swallowing
hard, I shook my head and told the truth. "We actually
haven't even rehearsed, um, yet."

Jenny looked as shocked as I'd ever seen her. "But . . .
wasn't that the whole point of it?"

"I know. Yeah. So, there's been a lot going on."

"What?! So what have you been *doing* over there all
this time?"

I racked my brain for something that wasn't utterly
depressing. "Um, having experiences to write new songs about?"

She laughed. "*Okayyy* . . . I guess that counts for something."

I shook my head. "It's all wrong, isn't it?"

"Hey. Don't think like that. It'll work out."

"It doesn't exactly feel like it."

"Have some faith, Kyla. You should be out there getting
noticed because you're awesome. Screw what anyone says. You
don't have to care about any of the drama. Rockstars don't give
a damn, right? When you stop caring, it makes people care
more. That's, like, the ultimate irony of life, or something."

I laughed, choked up. "Jenny, you're the best stupid friend
anyone could possibly have."

She shrugged and smiled.

"I do all right for a dumb kid."

ROCKSTARS DON'T DO RULES

BEING IN MY BEDROOM WAS MUCH worse than I'd expected. I climbed onto the empty bed of my frighteningly clean room and stared out the window at the tree house. I couldn't think or relax like I used to be able to by looking at it. The space felt too small, encroaching, history-drenched and closet-like. I felt snobby thinking it, but it was true. I'd outgrown my room.

I didn't even want to go down to the basement, close my eyes and play our old piano to the musty smell and dusty photographs. It was late but I had to get out. My pops was already slumped over in the den, snoring softly from the couch. I took his glasses off carefully, the old routine. He twitched his nose and continued to snore. I gave his scruffy cheek a scratch for good luck. My pops really was a good guy, despite his prickly exterior. He was trying to protect the people he loved most. And who could blame him for being tough? The Bells were not especially easy to handle.

The night was chilly for late spring but the air smelled fresh and deliciously earthy. I walked slowly, watching headlights pass on the main road. I wondered what my mom was feeling that moment she threw herself into a car's oncoming beams. I wondered if she wished she'd died the night of the first accident. Our accident. The whole world of my childhood was so warped now. I was in the place I knew best but it had changed. The streets were narrower, the houses smaller, and my mother wasn't up in her bedroom, she was miles away in a locked ward. I found that to be the most unnerving part, like when a tooth falls out and there's a creepy gap that's all you can feel.

I kicked pebbles down the road, looking into all the dark windows on the street. When I passed the Derrick's place I stared at their closed garage. I pictured my mother coming outside in the middle of the night, breaking into the garage, and stealing their mower. My undoubtedly disturbed mother, running wildly toward death in the darkness. My throat closed up. Why did she feel the need to mow things, anyway? What was that really about?

I finally saw the familiar sign of Store 24. There was the old homeless lady, still standing by the side of the building, smoking a cigarette. She smiled at me when I walked by and I returned it. I'd known her for years now, but this time her eyes eerily reminded me of someone.

I scanned the shelves of the convenience store, unsure what I wanted or what I was doing there. It was just comforting to be there. I looked over at the guy behind the counter and he flashed me a grin. He was clearly waiting for me to notice him.

"Hey, dollface," he said. He was tall with greasy skin and a shaggy haircut. I didn't recognize him, but I'd probably gone to school with him. "Hey, you're Kyla Bell, right?"

"Yeah," I said warily.

"I'm Tyler. I go to Northampton High too, junior."

"Oh," I said.

"You live in LA now, right?"

I didn't want to disclose anything about myself, but it was either that or be rude to Tyler in his polyester green Store 24 vest.

"Um, I'm living there right now, yeah."

"Cool, yeah. Heard something about that. I play the drums, you know, so . . ." He leaned across the counter, pulled a couple pieces of beef jerky out of a canister, and started drumming with them. I burst out laughing as a piece of jerky broke off and bounced up into his eye.

"Shit," he said, holding his eye. "That wasn't cool at all, was it?"

"Um, no," I said, "But it was hilarious."

"I'll take hilarious," he said. He had a nice smile, and I felt bad for laughing at him. "So, can I take you out some time while you're home?"

"Oh. Um, I'm leaving tomorrow."

"Okay," he said as he shoved the beef jerky back into the canister. "Okay, yeah. Whatever. All good."

"Thanks, though," I forced another smile and started toward the door. I couldn't be sure, but I thought I heard him mutter "dyke" as the door chimed when I walked out. I looked back and he was giving me the finger. When he saw I caught him, he spun around and started messing with the cigarette packs.

It stung like a baby bee bite. After all I'd been through, I realized that was one silver lining—I definitely had thicker skin now, especially with strangers. I honestly could care less about that dude. The homeless woman was still outside smoking. The wrinkles of her face shifted into a crinkled smile lit by street lamps. Smoke came out from her lips in little bursts. Her hair was silver and short and she wore dirty coveralls and boots. She'd always seemed pretty comfortable to me in her iconic position as the Store 24 lady. I'd always wanted to talk to her, find out her story, but had been too timid.

Leaning against the concrete wall, I sighed and wondered what I should do next. The echo of total dullness rang around me. Nothing exciting happening for miles and miles. I suddenly wanted a cigarette, but realized I couldn't go in there and face the twerp without saying something nasty, and it had been way too much of a long day for any of that.

"Excuse me, um, do you have an extra cigarette?"

"Sure thing, little lady." The homeless lady took out a pack and offered me one. I took it hesitantly, feeling strange about taking something from someone who had so little, less than I'd ever experienced. At the same time, I felt closer to her than ever, especially since I'd been one fight away from homelessness my whole time in Los Angeles. "Not old enough to buy 'em yet, huh?"

I was used to being asked that in a place I wasn't actually from, but the moment had shown that I was a stranger in my hometown already. "I mean, I actually am, I just don't like that guy in there."

She cackled at that. "Yeah, he's an asshole." She took a last drag of her cigarette and stomped it out with boots held together with duct tape. "I don't mind sharing. It's what keeps me alive."

I hadn't expected her to be so talkative. I asked her the scariest question I could think to ask. "Are you an artist?"

"Yeah, I guess. Started out as a pottery artist. A few bad decisions later, I lost my studio and my home. Now I make sculptures out of junk I find down at the overpass. Sometimes I get lucky and sell one. They usually end up getting thrown out by the city, but that's fine. I stopped caring about what happened to the things I make a long time ago."

"You don't do pottery anymore?"

She shook her head. "My fingers retired early." She held out gnarled hands that shook with tremors. "Now, I rely on the kindness of strangers."

"Oh," I said, hastily searching my pockets for change but finding none. "I'm sorry."

"Don't be. Never would have amounted to much, anyway."

Something was deeply bothering me, something my mom had said. I hadn't known she'd had to swallow her creative dreams to start a family, and that she regretted it so much. She had always baked and done arts and crafts, but I hadn't thought she had wanted more to life than what she'd already had.

On impulse, I said, "Hey, can I ask you something?"

"Shoot."

"Do you have any regrets?"

"Well, shit, girlie," she cackled. "No one lives without regrets." She pulled something in a paper bag from her pocket and took a swig. I smelled the prickly-sweet scent of whiskey.

"So did you . . . choose this life?"

"Hell no. I saw where I should've took a turn, and I blew right by it. But my mistakes weren't entirely my fault. No one's are. We're all misled at some point. That's why you can't play by anyone else's rules." She put the brown bag back in her pocket and pulled out another cigarette, lit it and exhaled. "You seem like a girl who's looking for answers in all the wrong places, though. Why don't you stop asking around and start doing what *you* want. You can bet your ass it won't turn out like you think it will, but at least you'll have done things your way."

I agreed, but I also felt overwhelmingly saddened by her words.

On the walk back toward the house that no longer felt like home in any way, I felt invisible in the chilly air: a lonely, pink-haired phantom floating down a street dark enough to hide her tears. Nothing made sense no matter how many people you spoke to from any walk of life. No one was going to make me feel better about my choices and sacrifices but me.

What bothered me most was this: people set their own limits, made their own decisions, yet they never seemed content, even when they achieved what they thought they wanted. The woman outside Store 24 hadn't surrendered to love, ambition, or any type of conformity for that matter— and she wasn't content. Meanwhile, my mother had shared years of love with her husband and daughter, but she was still grossly unsatisfied with her life. And then there was Robert, who took his ambition and ran with it, wrote and produced music that would continue to blaze through the world for decades, *and* he had attempted to love fearlessly, but none of it seemed to have brought him a single slice of satisfaction. Even Ruby, a fiery leader who'd fought her way to the top of her dreams, was all over the place. It was a crazy thing to consider. We could have success and independence, we could have love, a family, and a non-ambitious existence, or we could live on the streets with no one to answer to and nothing to show for ourselves, and none of it would necessarily make us happy.

So where did that leave me, then? All I'd ever known for certain about myself was that I was a musician, someone who lived to play and listen to music. Sure, what seemed like the right choice could ultimately lead to bad places. That was the thing about life, though: there were no guarantees. You had no way of knowing where you were going to end up, even if you risked it all. Doing anything creative took more courage than anyone seemed to acknowledge. Just for fun, I imagined if my dad had heard my choice to drop everything to be in an established band and had patted me on the back, told me he admired my bravery. Had any parent ever done that in the whole history of kids dropping everything to pursue their dreams? Or was trying to go out on a limb always viewed as an unfortunate thing?

So far, the universe had seemed to be encouraging my choices. I'd won a slippery spot in a great band after playing just a few live shows. And, yeah, I might be hopelessly in love with the lead singer, but this was what I wanted to be doing, and that was pretty much the end of it. I was going to ride it out and try to keep my eyes open for the twists and turns. I just hoped it wouldn't cost me all of myself in the process.

Suddenly I itched to be back in the ocean-desert city full of atomic-colored possibilities more than anything. To get back to the potential and away from the past. Get back to the creative chaos, the pains and pleasures of popularity, the electric pulse of the dreamscape. Music might break my heart a million times to come, but it was still my first and only true love, and there was nothing to do but keep putting myself back out there.

THE FEEL EVERYTHING RULE

I ARRIVED AT THE FIRST FULLY-ATTENDED and functional Glitter Tears rehearsal dressed in a mesh camouflage dress and combat boots, ready for anything. The gang looked relieved to see me—well, everyone except Ruby, who was all business.

We launched into the first song without much small talk. There was a lot of ground to cover. My fingers found the right keys and chords easily, locking into place with precision and rhythm. Stardust would occasionally nod at me, and Jeremy would flash me an encouraging grin when I'd look back at him. Even Slinky seemed to be considering me in a new light. I finally felt like it was my place to make music with these radical members of an established band. I deserved it because I loved it *and* had earned it.

I wondered if Ruby could feel it, too. She hadn't looked at me at all while we were deep in song. Maybe I hadn't been doing as well as I'd thought. Maybe my best was never going to be good enough for her. At least I could walk away knowing I'd offered it.

The song ended and I awaited her verdict, trying not to fidget. Ruby adjusted her mic, took a sip of water, and turned to face us.

"That was cool," she finally said. "Let's try it again."

It wasn't electrifying approval or anything, but I could work with that. I was there to grow, not question myself. I had found the guts to hang on, now, because it was clear that being out there risking it all to do what you love made you feel *everything*, and that was pretty much the definition of being alive.

THE END

ACKNOWLEDGEMENTS

PUTTING OUT MY FIRST BOOK WAS an especially long haul. I'm grateful for all the people who helped me carry the weight of the task. From its inception under the mentorship of author Holly Payne in 2009, who had the first encouraging words to say, to its finish in the hands of editors and publishers Kat Georges and Peter Carlaftes, it has been one twisted, crazy, true rock 'n' roll adventure. A hearty forever thanks to Kat for being the editor who knew exactly what to do with this manuscript, and cheers to Three Rooms Press for keeping publishing cool since 1994.

The biggest thanks possible to my parents, Charlie and Allyssa, who eagerly embraced my early identification as a devout bibliophile and writer. They worshiped the written word so much that, to me, there was nothing higher on Earth than books. There was no book my parents wouldn't buy me; there was nothing I could write that would make them upset. They even named me after writer Jessamyn West. Thank you, Mom and Dad, for absolutely everything.

My brother Nick is a real-life hero who has impacted me in so many ways. Thank you for the love and encouragement, and for reminding me when to get out of the way of myself—as a great sibling does, even when it's, ahem, not exactly welcome.

To my grandmother, Mary McCabe, who cherished books and crosswords more than anyone, taught English to high schoolers her whole life, and always believed I could and would do this. I miss you dearly.

To my husband, best friend, and partner, Vince; thank you for the care, nourishment, and gentle love that coaxed me to find the endurance to cross the finish line. There is nothing that can't be overcome by your fearless positivity and no bitterness that can compete with the depth of your sweetness.

Eternal thanks to my lifelong inspiration, the steadfast champion of this book, and my fairy godmother, Alice Hoffman. You are truly the hero of my artist's heart.

Terrific thanks to my sister-by-choice, Tess Hunt, for being supportive of me in so many ways throughout the years that you have actually achieved "angel status" because you are life-changing and luminous and make everything better.

Special thanks to author Tom Comitta, who was a instrumental and ingenious guide in the process of finding this book a home. Mad gratitude to artist John Kutlu who fueled my inspiration by creating brilliant visuals to my work over the years. Real love to Eva Gardner, who has been a dream to collaborate with in so many different ways, and who proofed this book for authenticity as a real '90s Hollywood high school rocker.

Thanks to so many others for their energies and efforts that boosted me so much throughout this winding journey of life as a writer: Luke Carlson. Gayle Cuneo. Sue Standing. Michael Kelley. Peter Banker. Jill McCorkle. Jennifer Egan. Devon Halliday. Gary Johnson. Rami Jaffee. Jessy Greene.

Brett Callwood. Jessie Ann Foley. Maya Miller. Susan Rogers. Tegan Quin. Peyton Bighorse. Jeff Zentner. Jamie Beth Cohen. John Beradino. Kenton DeAngeli. Najva Sol. Curtis Armstrong. John Lasky. Paul Mandelbaum. Karina Gardner. Kelly Ann Jacobson. Rob Senn. Ian Van Zile. The person I started writing these rules with long before I'd joined a band—Samantha Sanchez. My teenage partners-in-crime in countless Northampton adventures—Julia and Brooke Chandler. The seriously talented book cover designer who pulled this one off with such vibrancy—Corina Lupp.

And I must also thank you, reader, for finding and reading this book and for continuing to use your manual imagination in this automatic world. It is our greatest superpower.

ABOUT THE AUTHOR

JESSAMYN VIOLET IS A WRITER AND musician, born and raised in Massachusetts. She received her BFA in Writing, Literature and Publishing from Emerson College, and her MFA in Creative Writing from San Francisco's California College of the Arts. Her poetry has been published in numerous journals and her poetry book, *Organ Thieves*, is out through Gauss PDF. Her feature screenplay, *Exit Strategies*, was a quarterfinalist in Scriptapalooza. Her short stories have been published in assorted journals such as *Ploughshares, Adelaide*, and *3 Elements*. Jessamyn plays drums in the internationally-acclaimed band Movie Club. *Secret Rules to Being a Rockstar* is her debut novel. She currently lives in Venice Beach, California.

RECENT AND FORTHCOMING BOOKS FROM THREE ROOMS PRESS

FICTION

Lucy Jane Bledsoe
No Stopping Us Now

Rishab Borah
The Door to Inferna

Meagan Brothers
Weird Girl and What's His Name

Christopher Chambers
Scavenger
Standalone

Ebele Chizea
Aquarian Dawn

Ron Dakron
Hello Devilfish!

Robert Duncan
Loudmouth

Michael T. Fournier
Hidden Wheel
Swing State

Aaron Hamburger
Nirvana Is Here

William Least Heat-Moon
Celestial Mechanics

Aimee Herman
Everything Grows

Kelly Ann Jacobson
Tink and Wendy
Robin and Her Misfits

Jethro K. Lieberman
Everything Is Jake

Eamon Loingsigh
Light of the Diddicoy
Exile on Bridge Street

John Marshall
The Greenfather

Alvin Orloff
Vulgarian Rhapsody

Aram Saroyan
Still Night in L.A.

Robert Silverberg
The Face of the Waters

Stephen Spotte
Animal Wrongs

Richard Vetere
The Writers Afterlife
Champagne and Cocaine

Jessamyn Violet
Secret Rules to Being a Rockstar

Julia Watts
Quiver
Needlework

Gina Yates
Narcissus Nobody

MEMOIR & BIOGRAPHY

Nassrine Azimi and Michel Wasserman
*Last Boat to Yokohama: The Life and
Legacy of Beate Sirota Gordon*

William S. Burroughs & Allen Ginsberg
*Don't Hide the Madness:
William S. Burroughs in Conversation
with Allen Ginsberg*
edited by Steven Taylor

James Carr
*BAD: The Autobiography of
James Carr*

Judy Gumbo
*Yippie Girl: Exploits in Protest and
Defeating the FBI*

Judith Malina
*Full Moon Stages:
Personal Notes from
50 Years of The Living Theatre*

Phil Marcade
*Punk Avenue: Inside the New York City
Underground, 1972–1982*

Jillian Marshall
*Japanthem: Counter-Cultural
Experiences; Cross-Cultural Remixes*

Alvin Orloff
*Disasterama! Adventures in the Queer
Underground 1977–1997*

Nicca Ray
*Ray by Ray: A Daughter's Take
on the Legend of Nicholas Ray*

Stephen Spotte
*My Watery Self:
Memoirs of a Marine Scientist*

PHOTOGRAPHY-MEMOIR

Mike Watt
On & Off Bass

SHORT STORY ANTHOLOGIES

SINGLE AUTHOR

Alien Archives: Stories
by Robert Silverberg

First-Person Singularities: Stories
by Robert Silverberg
with an introduction by John Scalzi

Tales from the Eternal Café: Stories
by Janet Hamill, with an introduction
by Patti Smith

*Time and Time Again:
Sixteen Trips in Time*
by Robert Silverberg

*The Unvarnished Gary Phillips:
A Mondo Pulp Collection*
by Gary Phillips

*Voyagers:
Twelve Journeys in Space and Time*
by Robert Silverberg

MULTI-AUTHOR

*Crime + Music: Twenty Stories
of Music-Themed Noir*
edited by Jim Fusilli

Dark City Lights: New York Stories
edited by Lawrence Block

*The Faking of the President: Twenty
Stories of White House Noir*
edited by Peter Carlaftes

*Florida Happens:
Bouchercon 2018 Anthology*
edited by Greg Herren

*Have a NYC I, II & III:
New York Short Stories;*
edited by Peter Carlaftes
& Kat Georges

*No Body, No Crime: Twenty-two Tales
of Taylor Swift-Inspired Noir*
edited by Alex Segura & Joe Clifford

*Songs of My Selfie:
An Anthology of Millennial Stories*
edited by Constance Renfrow

*The Obama Inheritance:
15 Stories of Conspiracy Noir*
edited by Gary Phillips

*This Way to the End Times:
Classic and New Stories of
the Apocalypse*
edited by Robert Silverberg

MIXED MEDIA

John S. Paul
Sign Language: A Painter's Notebook
(photography, poetry and prose)

DADA

*Maintenant: A Journal of
Contemporary Dada Writing & Art*
(Annual, since 2008)

HUMOR

Peter Carlaftes
A Year on Facebook

FILM & PLAYS

Israel Horovitz
*My Old Lady: Complete Stage Play and
Screenplay with an Essay on Adaptation*

Peter Carlaftes
Triumph For Rent (3 Plays)
Teatrophy (3 More Plays)

Kat Georges
*Three Somebodies: Plays about Notorious
Dissidents*

TRANSLATIONS

Thomas Bernhard
On Earth and in Hell
(poems of Thomas Bernhard
with English translations by
Peter Waugh)

Patrizia Gattaceca
Isula d'Anima / Soul Island
(poems by the author
in Corsican with English
translations)

César Vallejo | Gerard Malanga
Malanga Chasing Vallejo
(selected poems of César Vallejo
with English translations
and additional notes by
Gerard Malanga)

George Wallace
EOS: Abductor of Men
(selected poems in Greek & English)

ESSAYS

Richard Katrovas
*Raising Girls in Bohemia:
Meditations of an American Father*

Far Away From Close to Home
Vanessa Baden Kelly

*Womentality: Thirteen Empowering Stories
by Everyday Women Who Said Goodbye to
the Workplace and Hello to Their Lives*
edited by Erin Wildermuth

POETRY COLLECTIONS

Hala Alyan
Atrium

Peter Carlaftes
DrunkYard Dog
I Fold with the Hand I Was Dealt

Thomas Fucaloro
It Starts from the Belly and Blooms

Kat Georges
Our Lady of the Hunger

Robert Gibbons
Close to the Tree

Israel Horovitz
Heaven and Other Poems

David Lawton
Sharp Blue Stream

Jane LeCroy
Signature Play

Philip Meersman
This Is Belgian Chocolate

Jane Ormerod
Recreational Vehicles on Fire
Welcome to the Museum of Cattle

Lisa Panepinto
On This Borrowed Bike

George Wallace
Poppin' Johnny

Three Rooms Press | New York, NY | Current Catalog: www.threeroomspress.com

Three Rooms Press books are distributed by Publishers Group West: www.pgw.com

CPSIA information can be obtained
at www.ICGtesting.com
Printed in the USA
JSHW030413220223
38076JS00005B/5